KINDRED SPIRITS

A Selection of recent titles by Jo Bannister

The Gabriel Ash and Hazel Best Mysteries

DEADLY VIRTUES
PERFECT SINS
DESPERATE MEASURES
OTHER COUNTRIES *
KINDRED SPIRITS *

The Brodie Farrell Mysteries

REQUIEM FOR A DEALER
FLAWED
CLOSER STILL
LIARS ALL

* *available from Severn House*

KINDRED SPIRITS

Jo Bannister

This first world edition published 2018
in Great Britain and the USA by
SEVERN HOUSE PUBLISHERS LTD of
Eardley House, 4 Uxbridge Street, London W8 7SY
Trade paperback edition first published
in Great Britain and the USA 2018 by
SEVERN HOUSE PUBLISHERS LTD

British Library Cataloguing in Publication Data
A CIP catalogue record for this title is available from the British Library.

ISBN-13: 978-0-7278-8796-2 (cased)
ISBN-13: 978-1-84751-920-7 (trade paper)
ISBN-13: 978-1-78010-976-3 (e-book)

All Severn House titles are printed on acid-free paper.

Severn House Publishers support the Forest Stewardship Council™ [FSC™],
the leading international forest certification organisation.
All our titles that are printed on FSC certified paper carry the FSC logo.

Typeset by Palimpsest Book Production Ltd.,
Falkirk, Stirlingshire, Scotland.
Printed and bound in Great Britain by
TJ International, Padstow, Cornwall.

ONE

The woman said, 'You know what to do?'

The man said, 'Yes.'

The woman said, 'Don't make any mistakes. You won't get a second chance.'

The man said, 'There won't be any mistakes.'

The woman said, 'You have the photograph?'

The man sighed. 'Yes, I have the photograph. I have made copies of the photograph. Everybody will have one. Anyway . . .' He didn't continue.

The woman raised an eyebrow. 'Anyway what?'

'She shouldn't be difficult to spot. How many Chinese girls do you think will be outside the school at chucking-out time?'

'I don't know,' the woman said pointedly. 'Neither do you. That's what the photograph is for. So you can be sure.'

The man nodded. 'I'll be sure.'

'The hired help. You can count on them?'

'Yes.'

'How much do they know?'

'Almost nothing. Just enough to do the job.'

'Where did you find them?'

'Up north. And they'll be on their way back there as soon as their job is done and they've handed over their . . . consignment.'

'They know not to hurt the children?'

The man bridled. 'Of course they know not to hurt the children.' His head turned and he looked past her. 'Where's the wall-art?'

The woman smiled. A cold, cold smile. 'Where people wandering into my office won't see it, of course. Don't worry, it's safe. Personally, I'd as soon have a nice print of *The Monarch of the Glen*, but perhaps I'm a philistine. The main thing is, it's back where it belongs. No one on this earth has a better right to it.'

'You won't tell' – discretion won – 'anybody?'

Her gaze was withering. 'Who would I tell? Who would I trust with that kind of information? Who *deserves* to know? This is our secret, yours and mine. And I know *I'll* keep it safe, so you'd better be sure you do too.'

He shook his head. 'I have as much to lose as you have.'

'More, in fact.' She looked him up and down, seemed to find him wanting. 'The only thing that ever really mattered to me, I've already lost.'

He had no answer to that. 'This will be over soon. Then . . .' Frowning, he couldn't find a suitable end for the sentence. That painting she saw no merit in, that oblong of ancient paint on ancient canvas, had been valued at millions. To him, and to her, it was just a symbol, but an important symbol. It meant that a quest which had dominated so much of his life was entering the end-game. Right now he couldn't imagine what they'd do with themselves, what they'd talk about, what would occupy their thoughts, when it was finished.

The woman said, 'Just don't make any mistakes. I've waited long enough.'

TWO

Gabriel Ash pivoted on his heel, gazing up at the shelves stacked to the ceiling, and considered the distinct possibility that he'd gone mad. Again.

If there was ever a time in the history of the printed word *not* to be opening a bookshop, surely it was now. Hardly anyone he knew bought books. He didn't know that many people who *read* books, but those who did bought them on-line, and more often than not downloaded them digitally to one of those . . . gadgets. Perhaps he was the last man in England – the last man in the civilised world – to enjoy the sensation, both sensual and intellectual, of paper pages curling away under his fingers. Of words, and the ideas they encoded, waiting for him to find them – and staying close at hand after he'd read them, in case he needed to flick back a page or two to check something. If he was, his venture was doomed before it had even started.

It wasn't as if he had any experience of the book business. He'd never run a bookshop before. He'd never *worked* in a bookshop, or any other kind of shop. He'd taken the gamble for two reasons, and only one of them was good. He had to open his own shop because he didn't think anyone would employ him in theirs, and in that he was probably correct. And he'd chosen to stock it with books for the commercially absurd reason that he didn't think they would attract too many customers. Gabriel Ash had spent too long as a recluse to be comfortable with crowds now.

The one saving grace of the whole enterprise was that he didn't need it to make much money. He'd be satisfied if it broke even in the first three years. He wasn't working because he needed an income, he was doing it because he needed to work. He had two young sons to raise, and it seemed to him that one of the best things he could teach them was that the way to get the life you wanted was to work for it.

Almost as if she'd read his mind, the young woman standing high on the stepladder feeding the last few books into the top shelves turned her head and smiled down at him. 'It's time I went for the boys.'

Ash looked at his new watch. He hadn't worn one for so long that the strap was still irritating his wrist. 'Frankie will meet you at the school gates.' His gaze dipped, embarrassed. 'I wanted her here too. She's part of the family now.'

Hazel Best regarded him fondly. Coming from a man both physically and intellectually substantial, that schoolboy diffidence still had the power to charm her. 'Of course she is. She's the best thing that's happened to you since . . . since . . .'

'Since you,' said Gabriel Ash simply.

Hazel jumped the last three steps to the ground with a grin. 'And don't you forget it. I'll be about fifteen minutes. If you can refrain from reading the merchandise, you'll have the last of the stock on the shelves by the time the mayor arrives to cut the ribbon.'

Ash looked up and down his new shop, daunted by the task he'd taken on. 'I'm still not sure about this cataloguing system.'

'For today,' Hazel said firmly, 'all that matters is emptying the cardboard boxes and filling the shelves. Just do that. From tomorrow you can arrange the books alphabetically, by subject, or even by the colour of the covers, in the gaps between customers.'

Ash suspected he'd be able to write some new books in the gaps between customers. But he said, 'Go get the boys. Patience and I will finish up.'

After she'd gone, he emptied the last box onto the long table running down the centre of the shop, and attempted to find logical places for its contents on the fast-filling shelves.

When it was done, he glanced at his assistant. 'What do you think?'

Patience gave a non-committal shrug with her eyebrows. Not really my field of expertise.

'You think it's mine?'

It's your shop.

Ash sighed. 'Humour me, will you? Just tell me the books look fine, the shop looks fine, everything's going to be OK.'

His assistant gave this some thought. Then: There aren't enough blue ones.

'Blue . . .?' He hadn't even thought of the colours. But she was right, the shelves were heavily weighted towards the red end of the spectrum. Ash fought the urge to pull all the books out and start again. Then he frowned. 'I thought you were colour-blind.'

Believe that, yawned Patience, and you'd believe anything. And that's the mayor's car arriving.

She was never wrong about sounds. Or smells. Ash raked a distracted hand through his thick dark hair and hurried to the door, pinning in place a smile that he hoped looked competent and welcoming, and not harassed and confused which was what he felt. 'Your Worship. Welcome to Rambles With Books. It's very kind of you to perform the official opening.'

Norbold's mayor was a stout, astute man who sold shoes for a living. He'd put on his chain of office but not his robes and certainly not the hat with the plume in it, which he considered ridiculous and donned only for state occasions. 'Funny name,' he remarked, tilting his head back to scrutinise the new signage.

'Still, ours is called Parsons, so who am I to judge?' He extended an arm. 'This is my lady wife, Mrs Parsons.'

In contrast to her husband, the mayoress positively relished a fancy hat. Hers had both plumes and beads on it, and she wore a lighter version of the mayoral chain about her narrower shoulders.

'Madam Mayoress.' Ash hoped that was the correct form of address. 'I'm Gabriel Ash. And this is Patience.'

A mayoress has to attend a lot of events she wouldn't choose to. The ability to look at least mildly interested at a school play, a cattle show or a ball-bearing production line is an important qualification for the job. Audrey Parsons had climbed down from the mayoral Rover with polite interest pinned securely in place, ready to make admiring noises about the town's new bookshop for the twenty minutes this was going to take, for the sake of the love she bore her husband.

But at the sight of Patience, waiting by the door, her expression changed – warmed, softened, became animated. 'What a delightful little doggie!'

Patience rolled her toffee-coloured eyes at Ash, and in the privacy of her head she said, The things I do for you!

Ash ushered them inside, taking them on a brief tour of the shop. Returning to the table where Hazel had laid out his mother's silver tea set, he glanced apologetically at his watch. 'My sons were supposed to be here to show you round.'

Mrs Parsons took the cup he offered. 'How old are they?'

'Seven and nine. My friend Miss Best went for them in her car. Do you know Miss Best?'

The first citizens exchanged a significant glance. Oh yes, they knew Miss Best.

'I expect they'll be here in a minute,' said Ash, a shade desperately as he ran out of small talk. 'Something must have held them up.'

'That must be it,' agreed the mayoress, while the mayor helped himself to the smoked salmon sandwiches.

Hazel pulled up outside the school just as the boys spilled into the playground. She spotted the diminutive, self-assured figure of their nanny Frankie Kelly waiting by the wrought-iron gate then shifted her attention to the parking space that was opening up as a big 4x4 trundled off with its cargo of small children.

So she didn't see the start of the incident. Even the sound of children screaming was not enough to distract her from claiming the space. It was her experience that young children needed very little excuse to scream, and several hundred of them had just been released from classroom confinement with energy to burn. They were running and bumping into one another, and dropping their school bags and yelling and laughing and, yes, screaming, just as they did at this time five days every week.

Then one voice reached her through the general din, and it was a voice she knew. It was only one word – 'Frankie!' – but Hazel knew that shocked tone was no part of playground histrionics. Gilbert Ash, aged nine going on thirty, was not a child for football, or running round with a gang of mates, or shouting mindlessly because other boys were doing it. He was a quiet, stubborn, difficult, intelligent boy, and getting him to ask for help was like pulling teeth. But Hazel knew instantly that he needed help now, and she was shrugging out of her seatbelt, abandoning her car still halfway into the road, before she was aware she'd made the decision to.

Hazel tended to act on instinct. It was a habit that had got her into trouble before now. And also, before now, had saved lives.

What she saw, as she dodged between the cars, was a grey van backed up against the pavement with the rear doors open. One man – average height, average build, nondescript clothing – was bundling a small Asian woman into the back of the van while another was wrestling with two young boys. The boys were Ash's sons, the woman was their nanny.

There must have been forty parents, mostly mothers but some of them fathers, standing within a few metres; and they were decent people who would not have stinted the effort or even the risk involved to prevent a crime. But shock affects most people like a powerful tranquilliser. They freeze. They don't know what to do. They wait for someone who might know what's going on to give them a lead. None of those forty people lifted a hand to help, and it wasn't because they were afraid for themselves or even for their children but because nothing in their lives before had prepared them for a kidnapping in broad daylight outside their local primary school.

What set Hazel Best apart from the other people at the school gates that afternoon was the fact that she was no stranger to criminal activities. That was only partly because she was a police officer. Partly it was because she was a friend of Gabriel Ash.

So instead of freezing, Hazel moved into overdrive. She fixed her eyes on the grey van, and used all the strength she could muster to force her way through the startled, confused, indecisive crowd until she reached the van.

Whoever these men were, whatever their purpose, she didn't think they'd consent to being arrested so she didn't try. She used her momentum to ram shoulder-first into the man holding Frankie Kelly by the arm. As he staggered forward, Hazel bounced off him into the van's back door, slamming it shut. It might only buy a few seconds, but you can't force someone through a closed door. She flung one fist in his face, hoping he'd have ducked before he realised how little he had to fear from her, and grabbed Frankie with her other hand.

By now the crowd was starting to react, to gather around the second man and the boys. A handful of them were moving purposefully towards the van. The man holding Frankie hesitated, then throwing her arm back at her reversed quickly towards the driver's door. Two of the fathers moved to intercept him but he shoved them aside, banging the door shut behind him.

There was a second's pause then, where nobody seemed to know what came next. Hazel looked at the second man, who was holding Gilbert Ash's wrist in one hand and Guy's collar in the other, and he looked back at her with furious dislike. Then Frankie swung her bag – a substantial piece of kit that contained not only personal items but spare hankies, shoelaces and socks for the boys, a simple first-aid kit and a small selection of fruit to last them until dinner – with real venom, and the brass reinforced corner laid his cheek open.

That was the end of it. By now everyone had recovered their wits and the power of movement, and there was no possibility that the two men could finish what they'd begun without producing a sub-machine gun. The one still on the street dropped Guy and slapped a palm to his bloody face; Gilbert writhed determinedly out of his grasp; the man pushed past Hazel and piled into the van beside his colleague, and the vehicle took off at speed, adults and children skipping out of its way.

'Are you all right?' Hazel shook Frankie's arm to get her attention. 'Frankie – are you all right?' The other woman blinked rapidly several times and then nodded. 'Gilbert, Guy – where are you?' Hazel scanned the bank of agitated faces until she found them. 'Are you all right? Are you sure?' But they both nodded, and apart from Gilbert's torn blazer and the tears on Guy's face they seemed unharmed. 'Stay here. Stay right here with me. I'm calling the police, and they'll be here in two minutes.'

She raised her voice. 'I need everybody to stay right here. We're all witnesses to a criminal act, and it's important that we tell the police what we saw while it's still fresh in our minds.' Even as she was speaking she had her phone out, her fingers keying the number automatically.

Before Hazel had finished speaking to Meadowvale Police Station, Elizabeth Lim had raced across the playground to the scene of the drama she'd seen unfolding from the principal's office on the second floor of the secondary school next door. 'Is everyone all right? Miss Kelly? Gilbert, Guy? Miss Best? You're sure? Thank God for that. What *happened*?'

Hazel used her free hand to calm the anxious teacher. 'Everyone's fine. The police are on their way. But I need to call Gabriel. I need to let him know there's been an attempt to kidnap his children. Another one.'

THREE

It was just as well Norbold wasn't full of people itching to get into a bookshop, because even those few who were interested were barely through the doors before they were being turned out again. It was the shortest official opening anyone could remember, and it only lasted as long as it did because Hazel arrived at Rambles With Books in time to pour the mayor a second cup of tea. White-faced, Ash was already heading for his car before it occurred to him to ask where his sons were now.

'Highfield Road,' said Hazel. 'Frankie's with them, so are a couple of coppers. Just in case. Everybody's fine, Gabriel – everybody but you. Don't drive. The area car's right behind me – they'll take you home.'

When she'd seen him safely dispatched, she returned to the shop. The mayor raised an interrogative eyebrow: Hazel replied with a sickly smile. 'You didn't really expect everything to go smoothly, did you?'

Parsons gave a prodigious sniff. 'I remember when Norbold were that quiet you could have a reign of terror with a balloon on a stick. Look at it now. Murders. Abductions. Drug dealers, corruption . . . What's the place coming to?'

Some sort of answer seemed to be required. 'I wasn't here when it was that quiet,' said Hazel politely.

'No,' rumbled the mayor darkly. 'I know you weren't.'

'This was Cathy,' said Ash.

Hazel felt her eyes rounding, her jaw dropping. 'Someone saw her?'

'No. She's too smart to come here in person – she's still too high on Scotland Yard's wanted list. But this is her doing.'

By the time Hazel was able to shut the shop and drive round to the big stone house in Highfield Road, Ash had got over his first, entirely natural reaction which was panic. The boys were indeed fine: Hazel hadn't lied about that. Frankie too was largely intact, although she was going to have bracelets of bruising on both arms where she'd struggled with her assailant.

Ash had tried to make her go to bed for an hour while they waited for Detective Inspector Gorman to arrive, but the tiny Filipino woman, with her sun-touched skin and her glossy black hair, only looked like a delicate doll. In fact she was as tough as a Royal Marine, and she was more concerned with calming her young charges than going to bed with a cup of hot sweet tea. She had lit a small fire in the sitting room – the June day was mild but there was a chill on every heart – and was kneeling in front of it with them, toasting marshmallows and talking quietly about what had happened. Hazel and Ash, and Patience, were in the kitchen.

'I don't see how that's possible,' said Hazel reasonably. 'Cathy must be half a world away by now. She knows she'd be arrested on sight anywhere in Britain.'

'Who else could it be?' Ash was now struggling to contain his second entirely natural reaction, which was fury. 'They're not princes of the blood, or heirs to a great fortune. They're two unremarkable young boys. The only people they have any value for are their father and their mother. We already know what Cathy would do to get them back. She killed one man. She almost killed me.'

It was true. There had been a time when they'd thought Ash's sons had been kidnapped to keep him from exercising his skills as a government security analyst. But that, it turned out, was Cathy too. His wife and sons had been living comfortably in Cambridge for four years while Ash, believing them dead, went mad with grief and guilt.

Hazel sucked in an unsteady breath. 'If it was her, she won't stop because her hired hands got run out of town. You're going to have to look at your security.'

'What do you suggest? Bodyguards?' He meant it as a joke. But before the words were out, Ash knew that was exactly the kind of security he would have to look into. They had been lucky at the school. The next attempt would be made somewhere quieter, with no bystanders to get in the way, when Wonder Woman was busy doing her laundry, when only Ash or Frankie stood between the boys and their mother's twisted love, and it would succeed. Next time the hired hands would be hired guns.

'Yes,' said Hazel simply. 'Gabriel, you need the best protection you can buy. Don't wait until she tries again.'

'I'm not sure how Dave Gorman will feel about that.' Ash was finding it hard not to snarl at her, and that was crazy; he owed his sons' safety to Hazel's quick thinking, and he knew it and was incredibly grateful. But he was so wound up by the episode, so full of anger and adrenalin, that being in the same room with him was like cleaning out a tiger's cage with the tiger still in it.

'He won't like it,' agreed Hazel. 'But it's not his sons who are in danger. I promise you, if it was, he'd want the best too.'

She tried to explain in a way that was fair to Detective Inspector Gorman without misleading her friend. 'He'll tell you that protecting the public is the job of the police. And he's right. He'll do his level best to keep the boys safe. But Norbold CID's best is the area car running up and down the street two or three times a night. We don't have the budget to do anything more. You need someone who has only one job to do, only one task to focus on, and that means a security expert specialising in close protection. I'll make enquiries, if you like – help you find someone suitable.'

It was a big step to take, to entrust the safety of his family to someone working outside law enforcement. It wouldn't gain him any Brownie points at Meadowvale. 'You really think it's necessary?'

Hazel's eyebrows rocketed. 'You don't? Gabriel, if I'd hit traffic lights driving across town, you'd be sleeping in this house alone tonight. They were seconds away from succeeding. Those men would have pushed Frankie out of the van a mile up the road, got onto the motorway, changed cars at the first truck stop and vanished. We've been lucky to get a warning. We won't get a second one.'

The bell jangled at the front door, making both of them jump. DI Gorman wasn't alone: he'd brought two of his DCs. Emma Friend went through into the sitting room to join the marsh-mallow brigade, Mark Lassiter went upstairs and pulled a chair near to Gilbert's bedroom window, watching the street from the shadow of the curtain.

Dave Gorman helped himself to coffee from the pot on the kitchen table. 'Nasty business,' he growled. 'I take it we're all thinking the same thing?'

Ash nodded grimly. 'Cathy.'

'Have you heard from her recently?'

Ash's eyes widened briefly, then narrowed. 'I haven't heard from her at all. I promised to tell you if I did.'

'No offence, Gabriel,' said the detective. 'Only, I know how you felt about this woman.'

'That was before she traded my soul for a nice flat in Cambridge! I haven't seen or heard from her since she left me bleeding on the floor of a houseboat on Ullswater. All right?'

'All right,' agreed Gorman. 'I had to ask.'

'Now you know the answer.'

Gorman nodded. He was a solidly built individual, not so much heavy as square, as if he'd been designed by someone determined to pack as many people as possible into a panel van. Hazel, who had considerable respect and even affection for the DI, nonetheless suspected that when anthropologists found the missing link between man and the apes, it would look very much like Dave Gorman.

He said, 'I need to talk to the boys, and your nanny. Now, while everything's fresh in their minds.'

Ash frowned. 'Frankie's finally calmed them down. I'd rather they didn't get wound up again just before bedtime.'

'Talking about it is better than not talking about it,' offered Hazel. 'They're better getting it out of their systems than trying to pretend it didn't happen.'

Reluctantly, Ash agreed.

Hazel gave her own account first, providing as much detail as she could remember. There wasn't much: the whole episode had lasted no more than a minute, and for most of that time Hazel had been acting rather than looking. She rather felt that a trained police officer should have done better, but Gorman seemed satisfied, even quietly impressed.

He talked to Frankie next, just the two of them in Ash's study. Then he had Ash bring his sons in one at a time, and talked to them. Guy was his usual helpful self, doing his best to answer the questions put to him; but it soon became apparent that the speed of the attack had overwhelmed him. He had nothing useful to contribute. The only description he could give of the two men was, 'Big.' But Guy Ash had just turned seven years old: most people seemed big to him.

Four hours on, Gilbert was beginning to get a perverse pleasure from his close encounter with disaster. He enjoyed being the focus of attention and having his words closely listened to, but so far as his father could judge he was resisting the temptation to exaggerate. His description of the men with the van tallied closely with Hazel's. The one who grabbed him and Guy was the bigger of the two, and also the older – he was going bald. But the other man, the one holding Frankie, seemed to be in charge. He drove the van, and he was the one who'd decided it was time to leave.

Gorman nodded appreciatively. 'That's good observation, Gilbert. That'll help us find them.'

Ash wanted to believe him. He wanted to believe that Gorman would have the men in custody by midnight, and by breakfast tomorrow they'd have led him to Cathy. He desperately wanted to believe that the sudden intrusion of violence into the life he was building for his sons would not be repeated. Realistically, though, the two men could be anywhere by now. If the police found the van, there would be nothing to link it to any identifiable individuals. The only chance to apprehend them had been at the scene, and it had been missed. There would only be another if there was a fresh attempt to abduct the boys.

'Until we do,' continued DI Gorman, 'I'll make sure there's always a police officer close at hand to keep you safe. There'll be someone there when you come out of school, and they'll see you safely home, and then they'll keep an eye on the street.'

'For how long?' asked Ash.

Gorman wasn't going to lie to him. 'For as long as I can.'

'I could hire a specialist.'

The policeman looked straight at him. 'I'd rather you didn't.'

'Because . . .?'

'Because a specialist in close protection will want to carry a gun, and there are very few situations which cannot be made worse by someone carrying a gun. Even specialists make mistakes. It's not always the bad guys who get shot.'

'They're not your sons,' gritted Ash.

'No. Gabriel, I understand how you feel. But the best thing you can do is leave it to us.'

Gilbert was following this exchange as astutely as ever. 'You don't need to worry about me and Guy.'

Ash forced a painful smile. 'Of course I worry ab

you. I've only just got used to having you around – I don't want to have to get used to *not* having you around again!'

The boy grinned at that. 'No, I mean, it's not us you need to worry about. It wasn't *us* they were trying to kidnap.'

Dave Gorman frowned. 'What do you mean?' He switched his gaze to Ash. 'What does he mean?'

Gilbert favoured him with the exasperated look that any parent of a nine-year-old would recognise: the one that says, And there was me thinking you couldn't possibly be as stupid as you look. The one he practised regularly, on his brother, his father, his teachers and just about everyone else he had dealings with.

'I *mean*,' he said distinctly, 'that it wasn't me and Guy they were trying to put in the van. It was Frankie. I tried to help her, but the big one wouldn't let me. That's why he was holding us – so we couldn't help her. It was Frankie they were trying to kidnap.'

FOUR

'Could he be mistaken?'

Ash shrugged helplessly. Frankie was putting the boys to bed so he and Gorman had the study to themselves. 'Of course he could be mistaken. He's nine years old, and this came out of the blue and was over in about a minute. There wasn't enough time to make a reasoned assessment of what was going on – who was being pulled and who was being held. But if you're asking whether I think he *was* mistaken, then the answer is no. My elder son is stubborn, arrogant and often rude, but he is very, very smart. If he thinks it was Frankie those men were interested in, I'd put money on him being right.'

DI Gorman looked bemused. He'd hurried to the house in Highfield Road thinking he knew what he was going to be dealing with. He was familiar with the family's history, and knew that one day Cathy Ash would try to get her sons back. The suggestion that someone had tried to kidnap their nanny had his brain spinning its wheels. It was as if he'd raced to investigate a murder, only to have the corpse sit up and insist it was all a misunderstanding.

'But . . . who the hell kidnaps nannies?' he demanded plaintively.

'I don't know.' A hard edge was creeping into Ash's voice. 'But I know who to ask.'

Employing Frankie Kelly had been one of Gabriel Ash's all-time best decisions. She had moved into a chaotic household where Ash was struggling to apply what he could remember of parenting to two boys who hardly knew him, who had been living almost as outlaws, and one of whom was as clever as he and less scrupulous; and within days – perhaps within hours – she had established rules, boundaries and incentives which not only convinced Social Services that he was a fit person to raise two children but also gave Ash the first heart-swelling hope that he might actually enjoy the process. Before Frankie, he had been so overwhelmed by the granting of his dearest wish that it seemed his sons might complete the job of driving him insane.

But what, in all honesty, did he know about her? She had come from a respectable agency, but he hadn't followed up her references. He hadn't known what questions to ask her, or how to interpret her replies. She had seemed so exactly the answer to his desperate prayers that he had welcomed her into his household, into the lives of his two young sons, with less caution than perhaps he should have done. Apart from the fact that she was born in the Philippines, had two teenage children of her own living in Manila with their grandmother, and had a framed certificate from the college she attended on the chest of drawers in her room, what Ash knew about Frankie Kelly was limited to what she had shown him of herself. That she was good at her job. That she was reliable: when she said she would do something, it would be done. That she had a strong sense of what was appropriate, mitigated by a down-to-earth cheerfulness.

And it wasn't enough. He had trusted her with two living souls he cared about more than anything in the world – for whom he was ready to die. If there was something in her past that made her the target for violent men, it wasn't only Frankie who was at risk, it was also his sons.

She knew from the tone of his voice that something had changed. When he'd reached the house and found his sons safe, he'd been intensely grateful to her for protecting them. She'd explained gently that he was thanking the wrong person, that Hazel alone was responsible for thwarting the kidnappers, that she herself had been helpless to resist and they would all have been in the hold of a banana boat with sacks over their heads if it had been left to her to save them.

But even as she deflected his gratitude, she'd known he wasn't really capable of taking it in. He was so inexpressibly glad that the boys were safe, so shocked at how close he had come to losing them, that he just kept nodding and thanking her.

Somewhere in the last hour, though, there had been developments. When she came downstairs, Ash asked her back into the study because Detective Inspector Gorman had some more questions for her. But he didn't ask her to sit down, and there was a reserve in his manner, a coldness even, that she had not seen before.

Dave Gorman waited for as long as seemed reasonable, but when Ash still said nothing he vented a small sigh and gestured towards a spare chair. 'Do sit down, Miss Kelly. Is that right, or is it Mrs Kelly?'

But Frankie knew she was on trial here, and she gave him a small, polite smile and remained standing. 'Miss Kelly is fine. I am in fact a widow, but I never used my married name professionally.'

That was something else Ash hadn't known about her. There were too many things – things he hadn't known, and hadn't known enough to ask. He'd been desperate, and he'd been new to the business of hiring staff; and if it turned out that his naivety had exposed his children to fresh dangers just when he'd thought the old ones dealt with, he would carry the guilt to his grave.

Gorman nodded and made a note. He didn't return her smile, but he was scrupulously polite. 'Miss Kelly, then. I want you to think about this before you answer. Had you ever seen either of the men before?'

She did as he asked, but it didn't help. 'I hardly saw them

this time. The one who had hold of me grabbed me from behind – I only saw him when Miss Best knocked him sideways, and then he was mostly turned away from me. I don't think I'd recognise him if I saw him again. I can't be sure if I ever saw him before.'

'And the other man?'

She shook her head, blue-black hair brushing her shoulders. 'The same. He was behind me most of the time. The only time I looked at him was when I was hitting him with my handbag. He seemed bigger than the man who was holding me, and I think he was bald. He was white. They both were. No,' she corrected that, 'they were not obviously *not* white. Light skinned, anyway. I'm sorry I can't be more specific.'

'Would you recognise them in an identity parade?'

Again Frankie shook her head. 'Only if the big one still has a cut on his cheek.'

Gorman went on looking at her, still polite, still unsmiling. 'Then, can you think of any reason why anyone would want to kidnap you?'

It is perfectly possible to feign astonishment. For all Ash knew, Frankie Kelly might have been a superb actress, capable of depicting a wide range of emotions at a moment's notice. But her amazement appeared genuine. She blinked, and her lips parted in a puzzled O, and she looked from Gorman to Ash and back, and back again.

Then she frowned. 'But Mr Ash, you must know who was responsible for this. This is what you warned me about when I took this job. And your wife has no reason to kidnap me.'

'What if it wasn't Cathy?' asked Ash in a low voice.

'Who else *could* it have been? No one kidnaps children in a crowded place except their own estranged parents. Or conceivably for ransom, if the family is wealthy enough. I know you're financially secure, Mr Ash, but I don't think you have the kind of conspicuous wealth that attracts people who kidnap as a commercial enterprise.'

'I don't think my sons were being kidnapped for money either. I don't think they were being kidnapped at all.'

So far as he could tell, Frankie Kelly was genuinely confused. 'Then . . . what *do* you think was happening?'

'I think one of the men was keeping the boys out of the way while the other put you into the van.'

She stared at him, her delicately tilted eyes wide. Her voice was restrained, but not soft. Steely. 'That is an absurd suggestion, Mr Ash. I think, when you have recovered a little from the shock of this, you will see what an absurd suggestion it is. I have no enemies, and no jealous lovers. I am of no monetary value to anyone. Only my mother, my children and you would even notice if I disappeared, and you would have found another nanny by Monday.'

They regarded one another from close range, Gabriel Ash seated being approximately the same height as Frankie Kelly standing. Dave Gorman watched them with interest, unsure who would blink first.

After a long moment Ash said, 'Whoever those men were, it was you they were interested in. The man holding the boys wasn't trying to put them into the van – he was trying to hold them back.'

'Who told you this?'

'Gilbert. He tried to come to your rescue. The second man pulled him away. Which makes no sense if the boys were the target.'

It was Frankie who blinked. 'No . . . no, I see that. Yet still it makes no sense. Surely you see, Mr Ash, how very pointless it would be to kidnap a domestic employee whose only family live on the far side of the world and would struggle to raise an airfare, let alone a ransom. Whereas you have made no secret of your fear that your wife will one day attempt to regain custody of your sons. I think Gilbert must have been mistaken.'

'That's possible,' murmured Gorman. 'He's nine years old, and it all happened pretty fast. He may have been confused.' He directed at her a sudden, disconcertingly direct gaze. 'On the other hand, this particular nine-year-old is his father's son. Everybody says so. He notices things, he remembers things. I'm not going to discount him as a witness because he's only nine years old. So give it some thought, Miss Kelly. Who is there, from your past, who might want to hurt you, or frighten you, or for some other reason snatch you off the street in broad daylight? Who feels that strongly about you?'

Perhaps she thought about it, but not for long. She shook her head crisply. 'No one. Inspector, there is no one – not here in England, not at home in the Philippines – who has a reason to do this. I am not kidnap material. I have a mother, and two teenage children, and a brother somewhere, although I haven't heard from him in years. I have been modestly successful in my career, so that my children live more comfortably and receive a better education than if I worked in Manila. But – even in Manila – this is not the kind of lifestyle that attracts envy, or thieves. Except to my family, I am nobody. Nobody knows, or cares, how or where I make my living. Nobody would know how to find me if they wanted to.'

'Your family would,' Gorman pointed out. He didn't go on to add what he was thinking: that they could have been compelled to share the information.

'Why on earth would my family want to kidnap me?' demanded Frankie impatiently. 'If they needed me to return home, I would return home. Truly, you must find some other theory, for this one is a fantasy!'

Ash bridled. 'What happened isn't a fantasy. My sons were put in danger, by men who tried to force you into a van. Even if Gilbert is mistaken, which I don't believe, those are the facts, as reported by you and Hazel and others. You need to give me some explanation for them.'

She did not wilt under his fierce gaze but nor did she meet it. She stood like a soldier, staring at a point a little above his right ear. 'I cannot. I have no explanation.'

Ash rose quickly from his chair, unfolding to tower above the small woman. Gorman wondered if he knew he was actually shaking with anger. 'Frankie, I asked you into my home to look after my sons, not to get them hurt! I don't know what it is that you're hiding, but you're no longer entitled to consider it private. You had no business accepting this job if there was any risk of someone attacking you while you were in charge of two under-tens. Your past is not your own affair if it impacts on my sons' safety.'

After a long moment she cranked her head back and looked him squarely in the eye. 'I see. Well, clearly you wish to terminate my employment. In the circumstances I will not ask for notice as per contract. I'll go to a hotel tonight. I would appreciate it if you would store my belongings for a few days.' She turned precisely on her heel and left the study, closing the door quietly behind her.

Hazel had been reading the bedtime story. She came downstairs as Frankie crossed the hall. It was an old stone house, built to last: she hadn't heard anything of what had been said in Ash's study. 'Are we any closer to understanding what it was all about?' she asked.

Frankie turned on her almost sharply. 'Yes, indeed we are. Before I was a nanny, I was a high-ranking member of the Mafia. Those men were sent by a rival godfather. Mr Ash is a little annoyed that I didn't warn him that this might happen, and would prefer that I seek other employment.'

Hazel stared at her, stunned into silence. Then she managed: 'You're kidding, right?'

'No,' said Frankie levelly, 'I'm reporting the findings of the kangaroo court in there.' She indicated the study door with a crisp nod before proceeding upstairs, leaving Hazel astonished and bewildered.

When the door opened again Ash thought, and to some extent hoped, that it was Frankie coming back. He was angry, he was upset, but he didn't want them to part like this. But it was Hazel, wide-eyed, who looked at Ash, and looked at Gorman, and looked back over her shoulder, although the hall was now empty, before spreading her hands uncomprehendingly. 'Well?'

Gorman gave her an abridged version of what had been said. Short as it was, he had to finish quickly before she hit the roof.

'*You've sacked Frankie?*'

'Pretty much,' gritted Ash. 'I didn't feel I had much choice. She was putting the boys in danger.'

'You think *Frankie* was the target this afternoon?'

'Yes, I do. You said it yourself: she was the one being forced into the van.'

'Why?'

'I asked her that. She claimed not to know.'

'Maybe she *doesn't* know!'

'Of course she knows. You annoy someone enough that they take out a contract on you, you're going to know about it!'

They glared at one another, their breathing heavy with mutual indignation. They put Dave Gorman in mind of a pair of bulls about to go head-to-head.

At the last moment, nose-rings clashing as it were, Hazel took a step back. Remembered how frantic Ash had been. These were his sons, that he'd lost once, that he'd gone through hell to get back. Whether or not they were the target at the school, they had certainly been in danger. It spoke volumes for his progress towards mental and emotional stability that he was able to string coherent sentences together. That he wasn't curled up under his own desk, chewing the carpet.

She made an effort to speak calmly. 'Gabriel, you know Frankie better than I do. You've trusted your family to her for the last eight months. Before today, have you had any reason to doubt what she was telling you?'

He didn't even have to think. 'No.'

'But you think she's lying to you now. About something so serious that it could get her hurt, or the boys, or all three of them.'

The answer came slower this time. 'Yes.'

Hazel shook her head. The unfortunate red dye was a distant memory, but her fair hair had yet to regain its original length. 'I don't. She loves those boys. I don't think she'd do anything to put them in danger.'

If someone had asked him yesterday, Ash would have agreed. Would have been surprised at the question, since he wouldn't have employed her if he'd thought anything else. 'Maybe she didn't expect this to happen. Maybe she really was as shocked as the rest of us. But she must know why. And if she won't tell me what it's about, I can't see any alternative but to let her go.'

'You're sure it wasn't Cathy?'

'If it had been Cathy, the boys would have been thrown into the van and Frankie pushed aside.'

'I agree. I don't agree that necessarily makes Frankie a liar.'

Ash didn't want to believe it either. It didn't fit with what he thought he knew of the woman. But all his protective instincts had been aroused, and he couldn't – he *couldn't* – take chances with his sons' safety. 'I don't know what else to believe. What else to do.'

Hazel thought for a moment. 'Me neither. But maybe there's another explanation – something we haven't thought of yet. Maybe Gilbert's right *and* Frankie's telling the truth. If you sack her, and you find out later that she wasn't to blame, (a) you're going to feel like crap, and (b) you're going to be back where you were a year ago, fending off Social Services because not only are you still a former mental patient trying to raise two young children alone, but now you're trying to run a business at the same time! I don't know what the answer is, Gabriel. But that may be because we're asking the wrong question.'

At least he was able to consider the possibility. 'What do you think I should do?'

'I can't tell you what to do. They're your sons: you must do what you think is best for them. But if they were *my* sons, I'd want to be damn sure there was no choice before I'd part with Frankie Kelly.'

Squirming on the horns of the dilemma, he turned to DI Gorman. 'Does it alter what you propose to do? If it was Frankie or the boys who were the target?'

Gorman shook his head. 'Until we know for sure, probably not. We have to assume there could be another attack, whether Miss Kelly is here or not. That being so, it would be better to have her under the same roof, so we can protect all of you at the same time.'

Ash nodded slowly. 'I can see that. You mean to leave your officers here?'

'Certainly overnight. We'll reassess tomorrow.'

Ash stood up. 'Then I'd better go upstairs and ask Frankie to stay. At least for now; at least until we can figure out what's going on.'

Hazel approved. 'Do you want me to come?'

'No,' he said reluctantly, 'it's my job. If I've misread the situation, I owe her an apology. And if she's going to make me grovel, the fewer witnesses the better.'

FIVE

Ash's apology was less than wholehearted, and it was accepted in much the same manner. Ash still thought Frankie was keeping something from him; and Frankie, who spent her professional life reading the minds of children, was well aware of the fact. They reached a kind of armed neutrality, whereby Ash made it clear he *would* apologise wholeheartedly if it became clear that Frankie was not keeping secrets, and Frankie might well accept *that* apology although she was clearly hurt by his refusal to take her word for it.

One thing they agreed on: though the police wanted her to remain at Highfield Road, her duties should not involve either taking the boys out or staying alone with them. Until the reason for the attack was known, there could be no confidence it would not recur.

'How will you manage?' asked Hazel.

'The way we managed before Frankie came,' said Ash. 'I'll take the boys to school and pick them up. I'll get the groceries.'

Hazel refrained from pointing out that, before Frankie came, much of the job of running the Ash household had fallen to her. 'You have the shop now.'

He shrugged. 'I can shut the door and wait for things to settle down. It's not like books need feeding, or exercise; and most of my stock passed its sell-by date twenty years ago.'

It seemed a shame, when the drama had publicised the opening of Rambles With Books better than a half-page advert in the *Norbold News*. 'I'll help out when I can,' promised Hazel.

Ash smiled. There was a fragility to it that took her back more than a year to when she knew him first: the uncertain smile of a broken human being. He was stronger these days, had become stronger month on month; but this attack, coming out of the blue, had hacked at the foundations of his recovery. His eyes were haunted, deep and dark.

'I hoped you would,' he admitted. 'I'll try not to be a nuisance. Your own work has to come first. Anyway, Frankie will still be here, she's happy to go on taking care of the boys. For as long as Dave Gorman can leave someone with us, there shouldn't be a problem – I can open the shop late, and shut for half an hour while I collect them in the afternoon.'

'If nothing else happens, Dave won't be able to keep someone here for long,' Hazel warned him.

Ash nodded. 'I know. More pressing demands on the budget . . . We'll just have to be really careful about our own security – keeping doors locked, checking in with one another at regular intervals. Patience will tell me if there's anyone hanging about.'

Hazel looked at the pale dog curled up on the kitchen sofa, one ear – the speckled one – over her eye. 'I feel safer just knowing she's here,' she said sardonically.

Just for a second, the speckled ear twitched and the lurcher opened her caramel-coloured eye to give Hazel a cool look.

Hazel blinked and changed the subject. 'I think the mayor was impressed. He reckoned the shop will lift Norbold half a notch on the culture scale. Maybe not Hay-on-Wye yet, but he thinks you could give Brighton's Lanes a run for their money.' She glanced away and cleared her throat. 'He asked me about the name.'

Ash's gaze was inscrutable. 'Did he?'

'Seemed to think it was a weird name for a bookshop.'

'What did you tell him?'

She could have told him it was a sly joke: Ash getting his own back on his detractors. When Hazel first came to Norbold, the general consensus at Meadowvale Police Station was that he was a hopeless idiot. Familiar with the sight of him walking Patience, shuffling along, reclusive behind the turned-up collar of his old coat, they'd called him Rambles With Dogs.

'I said I didn't know,' she confessed.

The weekend brought fresh dilemmas. No school – no need for an anxious running of the school-gate gauntlet, eyes on swivels for the sudden arrival of an unexpected vehicle – but instead the worry of what to do with two young boys who might not be safe even in their own back garden. Frankie kept them busy indoors on Saturday morning while Ash opened his shop, and Hazel and Patience took them to the park in the afternoon.

DC Friend went with them. If Gilbert was right and it was Frankie who was the target, there was no need for a police guard. But Gilbert could have been wrong, and Hazel couldn't refrain from making regular three-sixty turns, scanning everyone in the street, listening for the stand-out roar of a speeding car. At the park she relaxed a little. With no roads running through it, it made a poor venue for a kidnap.

She found Emma Friend watching her with candid interest. Hazel gave a wry little grin. 'Sorry. I'm not trying to do your job for you. It's just, if anything *does* happen to them, it won't be you Gabriel comes after with a flame-thrower, it'll be me.'

The detective chuckled. She was Hazel's age but had been longer in the job. She'd done things like this before. She knew how to observe her surroundings without spinning like a Dervish. 'Have you known him long?'

Hazel squinted at her, pretty sure this was disingenuous. Friend had arrived at Meadowvale within the last six months but she must have heard the stories. The events that had thrown Gabriel Ash and Hazel Best together had also deprived Meadowvale Police Station of its last chief superintendent.

But that was complicated; it was easier just to give the information she'd been asked for. 'A little over a year. And the answer to your *next* question,' she added, just a shade tartly, 'is No, we aren't. We're just friends. He has a wife. And I haven't time for a boyfriend.'

'He owes you a lot.'

'Yes, he does,' agreed Hazel. 'I owe him a fair bit too. We stopped keeping count a while back.'

They walked on. Guy had Hazel push him on the swings. Gilbert found some joggers to sneer at. Patience had brought Spiky Ball, and had each of them in turn throw him for her. Then they walked home, steam duly let off, still unmolested.

Ordinarily, Frankie took Sundays off. She went to church, met up with friends, had lunch out. But DI Gorman thought that this Sunday it would be better for her to risk the wrath of God than the renewed attentions of the men in the van, so she stayed at Highfield Road, reading in her room.

Hazel was working. Ash took the boys to the shop with him, to finish the cataloguing. Mark Lassiter came with them, and so of course did Patience.

Guy was bored within twenty minutes. Ash sat him down at the big central table with a selection of children's books – not comic books, which Ash disapproved of – but Guy wasn't much of a reader. DC Lassiter talked to him about football, which interested him more. What his father knew about football you could put in your eye without blinking.

Gilbert, older by two years and usually harder to entertain, became interested in an atlas he found on a bottom shelf. It was an old atlas, and he was fascinated by the fact that some of the countries in it had since disappeared. 'Where did they go?'

'They didn't go anywhere,' explained Ash patiently. 'Some of them got new names. Tanganyika became Tanzania. Northern Rhodesia became Zambia, Southern Rhodesia became Zimbabwe. Some of them got absorbed into other, bigger countries. Some of them got split up. And sometimes a part of a big country wants to split off and go its own way. India wanted independence from the British Empire. Then Pakistan wanted independence from India, and after that Bangladesh wanted independence from Pakistan.'

'Who gets to say whether they can or not?'

'In an ideal world, the people who live there. That's the democratic way. You put it to a vote, and do what the biggest number of people want. In practice, it can be the people with the most money or the biggest guns.'

The mention of guns may have been unfortunate. Gilbert went quiet. Ash continued working through his stock. At length, his voice gone small, Gilbert said, 'Do you think we'll ever see our mother again?'

Ash's heart wrung within him. The boy didn't know what to call her. When they'd lived with her, they'd called her Mummy. But that no longer felt comfortable, evidence of how much her departure had affected him. Ash thought the boys liked living at Highfield Road, even found him a moderately satisfactory parent. But what they'd lost could never be replaced.

'I don't know,' he said softly. 'I hope so. But . . . she got herself in some trouble. You know that, don't you? She probably went abroad where no one was looking for her. She'll be missing you like crazy, but it could be a while before she finds a way to see you again.'

Unless Frankie was right, he added in the privacy of his own mind, and those men weren't after her at all.

And then it was Monday. Ash took the boys to school on his way to work. He was in the shop, alone except for his dog, when DI Gorman came in. Ash knew what he was going to say before he opened his mouth.

'You're calling off the surveillance.'

'I'm sorry, Gabriel. I can't afford the manpower. We'll keep you high on the drive-by list, but I can't give you twenty-four-hour cover any longer.'

'Those men are still out there.'

'I know they are. You'll need to be careful. If you see anything – *anything* – that concerns you, call me immediately. I'm sorry, I know it's not enough. There's nothing more I can do.'

Troubled as he was, Ash knew there was no point being angry with Gorman. The man worked within constraints – time constraints, money constraints – like everyone else. 'What's your best guess? Was it the boys they were after, or Frankie?'

Gorman considered. 'I'm inclined to trust Gilbert's assessment. I'd know if someone was dragging me towards a van or holding me back, and I think he did. God knows why, but I think they were trying to snatch your nanny.'

'I think so too.' Ash bit his lip. 'Which means it would be safer to have her out of the house.'

'Safer for the boys, yes.'

'But not for Frankie.'

'Probably not. But maybe you can't afford to worry about that.'

After the policeman had gone, Ash made himself a mug of coffee in the tiny kitchen at the back and sat at the long table, sipping it. Patience had set up home under the table with a dog bed she'd had him bring down from the house – a dog bed he'd bought when he was new to the business of dog ownership, and didn't know that she'd actually be sleeping on *his* bed. Now, unseen, she lifted her head and placed it on his knee, and he reached down to stroke her ears.

'I wouldn't do anything – *anything* – to put my sons in danger,' he said quietly. 'But now Frankie is part of our household too. If she leaves Highfield Road and takes a flat somewhere, she'll be much more vulnerable if someone *is* trying to hurt her.'

Yes, said Patience.

Gabriel Ash wasn't sure if his dog actually spoke to him or not. The most rational part of his mind took the view that, since dogs cannot speak, it must be a residual effect from the post-traumatic stress he'd suffered, and what he thought was Patience talking was just another facet of his own brain struggling to be heard. That made a kind of sense to him; but Patience thought it was hogwash.

'If someone – if Cathy – is after the boys, they'll be no safer if I send Frankie away. They would in fact be safer if she stayed to help keep an eye on them.'

Yes, said Patience.

'But if someone is after Frankie, the boys would be safer if she left. As long as the people looking for her knew she'd gone. We'd have to advertise the fact. Then we'd be safe, but she'd be in more danger.'

Yes, said Patience again.

'I owe Frankie Kelly more than she draws in salary every month. She's made it possible for me to keep my children. I could have lost them to Social Services if she hadn't come along when she did. She's been good for the boys, and good for me. She is a good person. Suppose she was the target of this attack – does that suddenly make her a *bad* person? And if it doesn't, how can I even think of turning her out?'

Hazel said . . .

'*Yes*,' exclaimed Ash, remembering. 'She said she could find someone to help. If the police can't give us ongoing protection, we need to find someone who can. I'll call her, see what she suggests.'

SIX

Martha Harris had an unnerving talent for knowing what people wanted as soon as they knocked on her door. Before Hazel was far enough into her office to say, 'Hello,' and remind her that they'd met before, Norbold's only private investigator said, 'Gabriel Ash send you, did he, pet?'

'Er – sort of.' It wasn't often Hazel found herself wrong-footed like this.

'Well, you'd best come in properly and tell us what it is he needs.'

Hazel had done her police studies course in Liverpool before being posted to the Midlands: she was familiar with a range of dialects. But Martha Harris had lived in Norbold for over twenty years, which suggested a certain obstinacy in the way she'd clung onto her *You see a vowel, you bloody well sound it* Geordie accent.

Hazel took the chair she was offered. She also, this time, took the chocolate she was offered. The last time they'd met she'd been on her dignity and declined. If Martha remembered – and Hazel would have put money on her remembering – she didn't hold a grudge. A chocolate wasn't a line in the sand, it was only a chocolate, and there were always chocolates on Martha's desk. They were bad for her waistline but good for her soul.

'I'd better tell you from the start,' said Hazel.

'Aye, pet,' said Martha, settling herself comfortably with a raspberry ripple. 'Tell us everything that happened outside the school on Friday.'

Hazel squinted at her, but Martha kept a straight face so Hazel did as she was bid. Everything she'd seen, surmised and been told from the moment the van arrived at the gates of Norbold Quays School. The first conclusion Ash had jumped to, and the later one. What Dave Gorman had said; what Frankie Kelly had said; what Gilbert had said.

Martha listened in silence – possibly because it was good

professional practice, possibly because the last chocolate in the box was a jaw-breaker toffee. When Hazel had finished, the older woman leaned back – her chair gave a long-suffering groan – and remarked to the ceiling light hanging over her desk, 'So Mr Ash thinks it wasn't his boys the kidnappers was after. He thinks it was their nanny.'

'Yes.'

'But she says there's no reason anyone should want to kidnap her.'

'Yes.'

'Sounds like a police matter to me.' Martha should know: she'd been a CID sergeant until she took an early pension.

Hazel agreed. 'But you remember what it's like. There's only so much manpower to go round. They can't keep a presence at the house for weeks at a time. When nothing more had happened over the weekend, our minders were moved on to more pressing matters.'

'So you came to me?' Martha hooted in amusement. 'What do you think I'm going to do? Patrol Highfield Road with my Yorkshire terrier?'

Hazel grinned. 'Maybe. I've known Yorkshire terriers *I'd* run a mile from. Or maybe you could talk to Frankie and see if you believe her. If you were to call in the morning, while Gabriel's at the shop, it would also mean she wasn't alone in the house – I'm pulling all the night shifts I can, but there are times I can't be there. And if someone is trying to hurt her, the less time she's on her own the better.'

'Aye, I see that.' Martha ruminated. 'It's a wonder, if he thinks his nanny's brought trouble to his door, that Mr Ash hasn't paid her off.'

'He thought about it. He decided he owed her better. That if we were careful, we could protect her without putting the boys at risk.'

'That was nice of him.' She said it as if she knew no higher compliment.

Hazel waited. She presumed that at some point the PI would decide whether or not to take the job. But Martha seemed in no hurry.

'Norbold Quays,' she said thoughtfully. 'Of course, the Ash

boys will be at the primary school. But I'm told the high school next door has a pretty good reputation these days.'

'Really?' With no children of her own, the relative merits of schools held little interest for Hazel.

'Down to that headmistress, I expect. Oh – we don't call them headmistresses any more, do we? We have to call them head teachers. Elizabeth Lim. I mind when she was appointed. Came with all sorts of recommendations. In spite of which she nearly lost out to a bloke who couldn't count past ten without taking his shoes and socks off, but had two grannies in the local churchyard.'

Hazel shrugged. 'That's small-town living for you, I suppose.'

'Funny name, isn't it? Not Elizabeth – the other bit. Not really a local name.'

'Well no. She's Chi . . .'

And there she stopped, struck rigid. It was so obvious, she couldn't believe she hadn't seen it before. But then, that was what being a detective was. Having the ability to look at what everyone could see, and see more.

Martha gave a complacent smile. 'I don't think you need a private investigator, pet. I think you need to pop round to Norbold Quays and talk to Miss Lim. See who might have it in for *her*.'

Hazel was back outside the school as the first children began to emerge. The primary school emptied first, of course, and Elizabeth Lim was principal of the high school. But Hazel had a hunch as to what she would see if she was in position by three fifteen, and she wasn't disappointed. As parents and child-minders began to gather at the gates, a small figure – smaller than many of her senior pupils – appeared in the midst of the running, shrieking exodus and steered a confident course across the playground, exchanging a few words with the waiting adults.

Out of the corner of her eye Hazel saw Ash and his dog turn the corner onto Quay Street.

She shouldered her way through the throng until she was standing in front of the head teacher. Elizabeth Lim looked at her enquiringly.

'Miss Lim, do you know who I am?'

'Of course I do, Miss Best.' The principal gave a tiny, self-contained smile. 'Even without the tights and the big S on your T-shirt.'

If Hazel was right about this, there could be some urgency. 'Then I need you to listen to me carefully. Is this what you do every afternoon at this time? Come outside as the primary schoolchildren leave?'

For a moment Miss Lim considered not answering. But Hazel Best was the reason that the incident outside the school hadn't ended in tragedy; and anyway, she had no reason to deny it. 'Most afternoons. It's a chance to keep in touch with the parents. My pupils are too old to be met from school, but a lot of them have younger siblings, and if I'm around when the parents are meeting them, it's easy for them to raise a matter with me without the formality of making an appointment. Also, the primary children will be at the high school in a year or two. It's a good idea for us to get to know one another before then.'

'But you weren't here on Friday afternoon.'

'No, I had a meeting with one of my governors. Miss Best, why are you interested in this?'

'I will explain,' promised Hazel. 'But right now – *right* now – I need you to come inside. We'll talk in your office. You're not safe out here.'

'*I'm* not?' But even as she protested, Hazel saw something flit across the woman's expression that was not amazement or disbelief but almost recognition. At that point, Hazel knew Martha Harris had been right.

All her life Elizabeth Lim had been likened to porcelain. Her ivory-tinted skin, her glossy black hair, even her delicate diminutive stature, made the comparison irresistible. But porcelain isn't weak. It's vulnerable to shocks, but handled considerately it is strong enough that every day people with no wish to injure themselves pour scalding liquids into porcelain cups so thin that the light shines through, and hold them over their laps.

In fact, Elizabeth Lim was even less fragile than porcelain, because she dealt with shocks on a weekly basis and hadn't broken yet.

She took Hazel to her office, and closed the door, and indicated the chair in front of her desk while she herself slid into the one behind it. 'Is this about the attempt to kidnap the Ash boys?'

'Yes,' said Hazel, 'and no. I don't think the boys were the object of the attack. I don't even think Frankie Kelly was, although it was her those men were trying to force into their van. I think they came for you.'

There was a significant silence. Hazel was determined to say nothing more until Miss Lim offered something in return. And Miss Lim seemed more inclined to think than to talk. She stood up again, and turned away from Hazel to look out of her window. Already the playground was emptying, the children being claimed and removed by parents and carers. Another twenty minutes and it would fill again with a fresh discharge of older children.

Finally she turned back. 'I don't see how that can be,' she said distantly. 'There must be some mistake.'

'There *was* a mistake,' agreed Hazel. 'Those men were sent to the gates of Norbold Quays School at chucking-out time, and told to grab the Asian woman they'd find there. That's what they did. The mistake was, it didn't occur to them they were grabbing the wrong Asian woman. You'd been detained in your office, but Frankie Kelly *was* there. They thought she was you.'

'No.' The principal spoke firmly rather than loudly, but with the clear expectation that with one word she could end the discussion.

But Hazel wasn't one of her pupils. More than that, she too had been a teacher: she knew some of the tricks. She sighed. 'Miss Lim, you can ignore the evidence until you're blue in the face, but this is the only thing that makes sense. Those men intended to abduct you. They're still out there, and you're still in danger. You don't have to tell me who's looking for you and why, but you ought to tell Detective Inspector Gorman. He'll help you.'

'He can't . . .'

'He'll do his level best,' said Hazel stoutly. 'If you level with him.'

'No . . . I mean, there's nothing he needs to do. I'm in no danger. How could I be? Who could possibly want to kidnap me?'

'You'd know more about that than I would. And maybe you've got good reasons for not wanting to talk about it. But ignoring this is not going to make it go away. Those men will have realised their mistake by now. They might wait a few days for the dust to settle, but then they'll be back, and next time they'll make a better job of it. You were lucky on Friday. Circumstances were against them. Next time they may be against you.'

Elizabeth Lim's smile was like the tiny red bow painted dead centre on a geisha's lips. There was no humour in it at all. 'Miss Best, there is nothing for you to concern yourself about. There will be no repetition. As you say, those men will have realised their mistake by now. They will not return. There is no reason for them to come to this school again.'

'I wish I had your confidence,' muttered Hazel; but she knew Miss Lim would say nothing more. She stood up. 'And I really wish you'd talk to DI Gorman.'

'There is nothing to say,' said Elizabeth Lim.

Hazel reported the conversation to Ash. She'd hoped to be able to tell him the whole story, the reason someone would want to kidnap a school principal and accidentally snatch his nanny instead; but if that wasn't an option, at least she wanted to share with him the conclusions she'd come to. It was of course possible that she was mistaken – this happened more often than she liked to admit – but she'd seen that look of comprehension on Elizabeth Lim's face in the split second before she guarded it. Hazel still had no idea who had sent the grey van, or why, but she was pretty sure Ash had some fences to mend with his nanny.

Ash heard her out without interruption, stroking Patience's ears as the lurcher lay on the kitchen sofa beside him. Some people drum their fingernails as an aid to thought, some whistle or stare into the middle distance. Ash's displacement activity was to stroke his dog's ears.

'Do you think she will talk to Dave Gorman?' he asked when Hazel had finished.

She shook her head. 'She insists there's nothing to talk about. That it was a mistake, and they won't come back. It *was* a mistake, but they will come back and next time they'll finish what they were paid to do.'

'Which is?'

'*I* don't know! Maybe just put the frighteners on her. Maybe escort her to a meeting she wouldn't go to by choice. Or maybe someone wants her dead. Right now, there's no way of knowing.'

'Will *you* talk to Dave?'

Hazel nodded. 'I think I have to. Though I don't know what he can do when the potential victim denies there's a problem.'

'I think you should too, if only to cover your own back. If something *does* happen to Miss Lim, he won't be happy that there was a moment when you could have given him the heads-up and didn't.'

'I'm on duty tonight. I'll catch him in the morning as he comes on shift. And you . . .'

'What?'

'Should talk to Frankie.'

SEVEN

Ash didn't wait until morning. As soon as he'd read the boys their requisite chapter of *Treasure Island*, and fielded with his usual response Gilbert's habitual protest that he shouldn't have to go to bed at the same time as his younger brother, he tapped on Frankie's door and asked if he could have a word with her downstairs.

Usually they dealt with the business of the household in Ash's study. This time that didn't seem appropriate. Ash would not have been comfortable sitting behind his desk while the woman he'd wronged stood in front of it. It wasn't going to be a comfortable interview anyway, but at least they could conduct it in the neutral surroundings of the kitchen.

Ash set out his mother's china – its second outing in a week – and poured the coffee as he heard Frankie on the stairs.

She accepted the leather chair which, a little formally, he offered. But she remained perched dead central, her elbows never touching the arms; self-contained, ready to deal with whatever was coming, but not willing to accept responsibility for something that was not her fault. She thought he was going to pay her in lieu of notice and ask her to pack.

She would be sorry to leave this odd, damaged, still somehow admirable household, partly because she would miss the Ashes and partly because she thought they would miss her. But if her employer had lost his trust in her, there was nothing to be gained by delaying her departure. She was confident of finding another position, possibly within days. She had skills that made her eminently employable. She wouldn't look for a flat until she knew whether she would be living in with her next family; until then, a spell in a hotel would be a pleasant change.

She stopped the train of thought right there. There was nothing pleasant in any of this. She had been accused of unprofessional conduct by someone whose opinion she valued, and as a consequence she was going to have to say goodbye to two children of whom, despite their manifest shortcomings, she had become fond. There wasn't an up-side.

She took the coffee but then put it aside untasted. 'Have you decided what you want to do, Mr Ash?'

He lowered himself carefully onto the sofa opposite, Patience moving up obligingly to make room, and nodded. 'Yes. I want us both to forget that, on very little evidence, I blamed you for what happened at the school and accused you of lying to me when you denied it. Since that seems rather a lot to ask, I'm going to hope you'll accept my apology and consider forgiving me.'

If he thought she'd jump at the chance, he was disappointed. She considered for a moment. 'Have you learned something more about the incident?'

'I think so, yes. At least, Hazel has a theory that fits the known facts. If she's right, it wasn't the boys that those men were after, and it wasn't you either. It was Elizabeth Lim.'

That wasn't what Frankie was expecting. 'The principal at the high school? Why on earth . . .?' Then she understood. 'Ah. Yes, I see. We all look alike to you.'

Ash squirmed. It was a low blow – if someone had been guilty of seeing no further than a skin-tone, it wasn't Ash; and accusing kidnappers of parochialism was like claiming that Hitler had been unkind to his mother: even if true, it was a bit of an also-ran on the scale of vices. But he was in no position to protest. He might not have done Frankie that particular wrong, but he had done her others.

'I'm sorry I jumped to conclusions, and I'm sorry I didn't give you a fair hearing.' His voice was low. 'I know I'm neurotic when it comes to the boys: you know why. It's not much of an excuse, but perhaps it's an explanation. I thought I was in danger of losing them again, and I over-reacted. I really am sorry, Frankie. I'm sure that was hurtful, and I wish I'd handled the whole thing better.'

Frankie regarded him levelly. 'Are you saying you'd like me to stay?'

'Yes,' said Ash quickly. 'Of course I want you to stay. I'd be devastated to lose you over a misunderstanding that was entirely my fault. I wouldn't be surprised if you felt it was the last straw, that you don't need the complications that come with working for my family, but I very much hope you'll give us another chance.'

Still she delayed answering him. 'Tell me this, Mr Ash. If the same thing happened again, would you handle it differently?'

It was a reasonable question, and he gave it the thought it warranted. He bit his lip. 'Frankie, in all honesty, I'm not sure I would. I'd still be terrified to think that my children had been in danger, and I'm horribly afraid I'd still strike out at the nearest target, however unfairly.'

Finally Frankie smiled. 'Mr Ash, that is indeed an honest answer, and I thank you for it. Of course you were afraid; of course you wanted to take whatever steps you could to safeguard your sons. Nothing you did was unreasonable.'

'I didn't trust you.'

'Until you had an alternative explanation, how could you? To trust me blindly, uncritically, might have left your sons open to another attack. I would never expect you, or any parent, to do that. Your children have to come first. I wouldn't believe you if you said otherwise. I wouldn't respect you if you did otherwise.'

Ash felt a flicker of hope under his breastbone. 'Do you mean you'll stay?'

'Yes, Mr Ash. If that is what you want, I should be very happy to stay.'

Hazel's interview with DI Gorman was less of a minefield, though she was conscious that the friendly relations between Meadowvale's senior detective and one of its newer PCs was starting to raise eyebrows, not so much in the corridors of power as in the canteen. Colleagues who had only just forgiven her for being right about Chief Superintendent Fountain were starting to look at her askance again. They seemed to think she was a drama looking for somewhere to happen.

Hazel didn't know how to persuade them otherwise, and wasn't sure she cared enough to try. She had less and less patience with their hard feelings and petty jealousies. She did her job, and did it well; being liked was an optional extra. It wasn't something that she'd ever struggled with before, but if it came to a choice between being popular and doing what she believed to be right, she had broad shoulders. She also had options. She hadn't forgotten she'd been invited to apply for a CID posting in Cambridgeshire. There had been reasons for not following up the invitation immediately, but it was a door she'd left carefully ajar.

One reason she hadn't jumped at the chance was DI Gorman. He wasn't an outstanding policeman, not impressive in the way that Chief Superintendent Fountain had been; in any discussion of the great detectives, his was not a name that would have come up. It was likely that he would complete his career without once drawing himself to the attention of the public, the press or the chief constable. But in those years he would put in a lot of hours and do a lot of solid work, and never let anyone down through laziness or inattention to duty, and have his share of good days at the office. A lot of bad people would be brought to book thanks to his efforts, and a lot of vulnerable people would be safer because of him.

Hazel had great respect for an ordinary decent man doing the best he could with the tools and talents he'd been given. If she was going into CID, she would like to work for Dave Gorman.

He heard her account without interrupting, partly out of the same kind of respect that she had for him, and partly because experience had taught him that Hazel Best could be wrong about all kinds of details and still right about the big picture. When she'd finished he reached for his phone. 'I'll talk to Miss Lim. See if she's a bit more forthcoming when we make this official.'

But Hazel quickly realised, even from the one-sided conversation she heard, that there was a problem. After a minute Gorman put the phone down and leaned back in his chair. 'She isn't there.'

Hazel checked her watch. It was now five to nine. 'She should be. Assembly's at nine.'

'She's not coming in. She left a message on the answering machine. She said that a family crisis had forced her into resigning, effective immediately, and she was sorry for the inconvenience but the deputy principal could run the school pending a new appointment. Her secretary called her home but there was no reply, and she isn't answering her mobile.'

Hazel frowned. 'Elizabeth Lim never struck me as the sort of woman to leave loose ends behind.'

'The people at the school are astonished,' nodded Gorman. 'She doesn't take a day off without planning a month in advance. She doesn't take a sick day unless it's something life-threatening. This is not someone who takes her responsibilities lightly.'

'What I told her – that those men were looking for her – that meant something to her. I saw it in her face. She denied it, but I didn't imagine it. She wasn't surprised.'

'And now she's gone to ground. You should have said something to me before you said something to her.'

Hazel gave an apologetic shrug. 'It seemed more important to warn her to stay out of the playground. I told her to come and talk to you.'

Gorman scowled at his big hands folded on the desk in front of him. 'Why would she? Nobody else does.' He made an effort to collect his thoughts. 'On the bright side, she's doing the right things – staying away from places people would look for her, her home and her work. On the *not* so bright side, we won't know if something *has* happened to her.'

'Someone should check her home. She could still be there even if she isn't answering the phone.'

There are few things so irksome as being reminded to do something you had every intention of doing anyway. 'Gee,' he growled, 'I never would have thought of that. We'll look for any signs of friends or family she might turn to in a crisis, too.' The DI pushed himself away from the desk and stood up. 'Are you coming?'

Hazel could have said, 'I've just come off the night-shift, I'm going home to bed.' She could have said, 'I'm not a member of CID.' She could even have said, 'Should you clear it with Superintendent Maybourne first?'

What she actually said was, 'Is the pope a Catholic?'

Elizabeth Lim had a service flat in a mansion block overlooking the park, and that made it easier. Advised that one of his residents might be in trouble, the manager conducted the police officers upstairs. He rang Miss Lim's bell, rapped with his knuckles and called her name. Still receiving no answer, he opened the door.

Hazel hadn't been quite sure what to expect. Signs of a struggle in the hallway, a corpse in the kitchen, bullet holes in the bed? At the very least, indications that Miss Lim had left hurriedly. But no. The flat was as neat and composed as its occupant.

A quick initial search established that she'd taken her handbag and possibly two suitcases – the smallest of what was probably a set of three sat forlorn and alone in the bottom of a wardrobe. She had taken toothbrush and cosmetics from the bathroom.

Since Gorman had never heard of a kidnapper waiting while his victim filled a wash-bag, he was now confident that she had left to avoid a pursuer rather than in the grip of one. He stood in the living room, his gaze circulating like the beam of a lighthouse. 'So where has she gone? Who does she think can protect her?'

'She has friends in Norbold,' said Hazel. 'But she won't have gone to any of them. If she thought she was in so much danger she had to leave her home and her job, she'll have left town altogether. Too easy for her to be found in Norbold; too easy to bring trouble to someone's door.'

'The same applies to whatever family she has. Unless they're in China.'

'Was she born in China?'

Gorman didn't know. 'I'll find out. You look for any papers – old letters, address book, anything like that. Even if she hasn't gone to family members, she may be in contact with them.'

There was a red lacquered bureau beside the living-room window. Hazel made a methodical search of the three drawers and multiple small pigeonholes. She found nothing helpful, and very little that was personal. After several minutes, looking round in exasperation she realised why. Though the rest of the flat was spotless, the grate was full of ashes. Miss Lim had spent time she could ill afford burning papers. It took no leap of imagination to suppose they included anything that might indicate where she had gone.

Hazel broke the news to DI Gorman. He nodded grimly and put his phone back in his pocket. 'That fits.'

Hazel frowned. 'With what?'

'That was Presley on the phone.' Presley was his detective sergeant. 'He's been trying to get some background on Lim – where she was born, where she went to school, who and where her family are.'

'And she doesn't have any family?'

'It's better than that. She doesn't exist at all, and never has. I don't know who's been running Norbold Quays High School for the last five years, but it wasn't the person on the paperwork she provided to the school governors.'

Hazel stared at him, dumbfounded. It wasn't so much that the answer was unexpected, more that it was the answer to a question she had never thought to ask. She'd assumed the problem was going to be identifying the men in the van, not the woman they'd meant to abduct.

Finally she found her voice. 'You mean she's a phony? She isn't really a teacher?'

'Oh, she's a teacher all right. She attended university and qualified twelve years ago, and she has an unbroken and unblemished record of employment since then. But there's no paper trail for her before university. No evidence of Elizabeth Lim being at school; no evidence of Elizabeth Lim being born, even.'

'Maybe she was an overseas student,' hazarded Hazel. 'Maybe the paperwork got lost.'

They eyed one another in silence. At length Hazel sighed. 'No, I don't believe it either. What then? She changed her name?'

'You can call yourself anything you want, but there are various points in your life when you have to prove who you are. Going to university is one. Getting a job as a head teacher is another. You can't just cut yourself adrift from your history. At least, if you don't want it catching up with you, you're going to need help. Lim had papers that stood up to official scrutiny. She didn't draw them up on a home computer – they were a professional job.'

Hazel was counting backwards. 'So, around sixteen years ago, someone with specialist skills created a new identity for her and provided her with documents that would get her into university, get her on the electoral roll, get her a passport. Who? And why?'

EIGHT

'Witness protection programme,' said Gabriel Ash.

Watching him as he tidied the long table, returning books to their shelves before he shut the shop, Hazel's expression was scathing. 'That was the first thing we thought of. Dave Gorman put through a request for confirmation. It came back negative.'

'The National Crime Agency has been known to lie.'

'What would be the point? If Protected Persons have disappeared a witness, they might lie to protect her cover. But once her cover's blown, they need us to know. The blue touch-paper's already alight, and we're the nearest fire-fighters.'

Ash conceded the logic of that. 'Perhaps she disappeared herself.'

Hazel was unconvinced. 'It was a damn good cover story. The school governors looked into her background before offering her Norbold Quays. Her paperwork wasn't put together by an amateur, not even one who was really keen to get the job.'

'What's the alternative?'

'That it was your people. And that, for reasons best known to themselves, they kept the NCA in the dark.'

For a long moment Ash didn't answer. He adjusted some spines that didn't need adjusting and blew the dust off a leather binding that wasn't dusty. Then he turned slowly and met her gaze. 'You mean national security.'

Hazel nodded.

'They aren't my people.'

'They used to be your people.'

'That's a long time ago. And it wasn't what you think. I worked in an office. I read reports. I was . . . a clerk.'

That was disingenuous, and they both knew it. Hazel let the arch of her eyebrow mark the fact. 'You still have contacts there. Philip . . . Thing.'

Philip Welbeck had headed the department in the anonymous offices behind Whitehall when Ash went there ten years ago, and when he was invalided out five years ago, and he still did.

'You want me to make enquiries?'

Again, Hazel nodded.

Ash bit his lip. 'No. I'm sorry, but no. I don't want to keep reminding Philip that I'm still around. I owe him a lot of favours, and I really don't want to have to repay them.'

He might have added, And I don't want to remind him that *you're* still around either; but he didn't. He didn't think it would have occurred to Hazel that Philip Welbeck might have an interest in her. But he'd known Welbeck for ten years, and he was pretty sure that if it hadn't occurred to him yet that Hazel Best would be an excellent recruit, sooner or later it would.

'Elizabeth Lim is in trouble,' Hazel said reproachfully. 'Someone tried to kidnap her. All right, they blew it, but whatever made them try once will make them try again. She knows that. It's why she packed what she could carry and walked out on a job she loved in a town where she was respected.

'But just because we don't know where she is, doesn't mean *they* don't know. If you can make a phone-call and get her some help, and you won't because now you don't need his help any more you don't want Philip Thing taking up your precious time . . . well, I thought better of you.'

Her assessment may not have been entirely fair, but it stung as if it was. 'Hazel, I can't carry the world's problems on my shoulders! I've only just figured out how to carry my own. I'm sorry if Miss Lim is in trouble, but she has the same recourse as everyone else – the police on the end of a phone-line. There's no reason to suppose there's a security dimension. It could be anything from a gambling debt to a spurned lover looking for her. I'm not going cap-in-hand to Philip Welbeck *again* because a woman I hardly know has decided to drop off the radar for a while. Whatever he owed me, he has already paid.'

'He owed you four years!'

'He helped me get my children back.'

Hazel went on staring hotly at him. But she had no answer to that. She knew that the most important things in Gabriel Ash's life were his sons, and at least in part it was thanks to his old boss that he was raising them instead of mourning them.

If she was ruthlessly honest with herself – and Hazel tried to be honest with everyone – she harboured just a little resentment that the lonely, broken man she'd adopted as an act of charity had now so much going on in his life that there was less time for the kind of things they'd done together. They'd helped people who needed help, and obtained justice for some who were beyond it. And those were things that were important to Hazel, both as a human being and a police officer. Now Ash was so busy being . . . normal . . . she felt obscurely abandoned.

Which is perhaps what made her say, in a piqued tone, 'If you don't want to call him, maybe I should.'

Ash's deep dark eyes flared with alarm. 'Hazel, don't go anywhere near those people. You don't want to get involved with them.'

Taken aback by his insistence, she only protested mildly: 'Gabriel – *you're* one of those people.'

'Not any more. Not for a long time, and never again. You

know what it cost me. It cost me my marriage, and four years of my sons' childhood, and it damn near cost me my sanity. No one who walks into that place walks out unscathed. It . . . taints people. I don't want it tainting you.'

She gave a dismissive little snort; but in fact she was touched by his concern. She had never been entirely sure what to call the connection between her and Ash – friendship didn't quite seem to cover it, yet there wasn't a word that got closer – but it was reassuring to know that he felt it too, that he put as much value on it as she did, and that he wanted to protect her even from things she needed no protection from. 'All right,' she said meekly.

'You'll let it drop?'

'I'll let it drop.' Hazel Best wasn't someone who went back on her word lightly. When she gave it, she had every intention of keeping it.

Still, the next morning, which was a Thursday, she made a point of hovering in the corridor where CID had their offices, just in case DI Gorman came looking for her. He didn't. Twice she glimpsed his back before his door closed, and once she saw him thumping the coffee machine at the top of the stairs. But by the time she got there he'd given up trying to get sense, or indeed coffee, out of it and hurried on with his day.

So when she came off shift she went and knocked on his door. As a CID officer, he was unaccustomed to people hunting for him – it was usually the other way round – and he called, 'Come in,' when he probably should have asked, 'Who is it?'

Hazel gave him a friendly smile. 'Are you trying to avoid me?'

Gorman decided that honesty was the best policy. 'Yes.'

'Why?'

'Because you're going to ask me about Elizabeth Lim, and I can't tell you anything.'

She thought he was frustrated with his own lack of progress. 'The answers will come when you find the right questions to ask and the right people to ask them of.'

The DI scowled. 'I'm not asking any questions.'

That was surprising. 'Why not?'

'Because Sir told me not to.'

Meadowvale Police Station warranted a detective superintendent. But after the unfortunate business with Chief Superintendent Fountain, appointing his replacement took priority, so Dave Gorman – with the comparatively modest rank of detective inspector – was the de facto head of CID in Norbold. Superintendent Maybourne was his superior, but to be outranked by a detective he had to look further afield.

'Division have been in touch?'

Gorman shook his head, looking guilty. 'Headquarters. Sir of Sirs.'

'ACC-Crime?' Hazel was astonished. '*Why?*'

'He thinks I should have more important things to do. If I haven't, he reckons he can find me some.'

'More important than looking for a woman who's vanished following a kidnap attempt?' Hazel's voice soared in disbelief.

'Sir pointed out that it was Frankie Kelly, not Elizabeth Lim, who was nearly kidnapped. He takes the view that Lim was free to leave her job if she chose to – she's a competent adult, and she hasn't reported a crime or asked us for help. He doesn't want to hear any more about it.'

'But that's crazy!' cried Hazel in exasperation. 'He can't really believe it was a coincidence that she disappeared only hours after I warned her she was in danger.' Too late she remembered that wasn't something to boast about: she hurried on, hoping he hadn't noticed. 'And what about her fake ID? Dave, there's obviously something going on, and it's Lim at the heart of it, not Frankie. You can't just shut the file on it.'

'I can if I'm ordered to. Unless something else happens,' he added gruffly, 'in which case I'll do what needs doing and ACC-Crime can shout at me later. But nothing else is going to happen – not here, not now Lim has gone.'

A sly look slid sideways into Hazel's usually open expression. 'He told *you* not to spend any more time on it. I don't expect he said anything about me.'

'As a matter of fact he did,' growled Gorman. 'He said not even to *think* of involving you. He said letting you get involved was like taking out a front-page advert in the *Birmingham Post*. He said if he heard you'd been sniffing around, I'd be directing traffic and you'd be looking for lost dogs.'

Hazel shook her head, bemused. It was slightly alarming to think that ACC-Crime even knew the name of one of his newest constables in dusty Norbold, about as far from headquarters as it was possible to get. Of course, her name would have crossed his desk before this.

She frowned. 'Why should he care?'

The DI had been too busy dodging flak to ask himself that. 'Because he's this force's senior detective?'

'That's a good reason for us to avoid annoying him,' conceded Hazel. 'But why would he be annoyed? You're just doing your job.'

'He thinks it's a waste of time.' But now Gorman was wondering why, too.

Hazel shrugged. 'A lot of the things we do *are* a waste of time. That's not a good enough reason for giving up before we even start. Why does ACC-Crime want to stop you investigating a serious incident outside Norbold Quays?'

'He doesn't believe the two are connected – the kidnap attempt and Elizabeth Lim going off-grid.'

'Yeah, right,' said Hazel, heavily ironic. 'A coincidence? Like the way Christmas always falls in December?' She paused to consider. 'So what are you going to do? Pretend it never happened? Roll over and play dead?'

Gorman bristled. As a single man, he wasn't accustomed to being spoken to like this. He made allowances for Hazel only because of their history: of those lonely weeks when she'd stood out for the integrity of Meadowvale Police Station and he'd been one of the few colleagues who hadn't pilloried her for it. If she'd been left with a mistrust of senior officers, it was no wonder. 'That's right. My boss told me to drop the bone, and I'm going to drop it before he smacks me on the nose with a rolled-up newspaper.'

Though she was disappointed, Hazel understood that DI Gorman wasn't a free agent. His orders came down the chain of command. If the Assistant Chief Constable (Crime) wanted him to abandon an investigation, he had to assume there was a good reason. Already she was regretting her intemperance. 'You can't really butt heads with ACC-Crime.'

'No.' Gorman was waiting for the other shoe to drop.

'Maybe some day we'll hear what it was all about.'

'Maybe.' One heavy eyebrow lowered even further, making him look like a quizzical bull. 'So you're going to roll over too? I'm impressed. I didn't expect you to be this . . . reasonable.'

Hazel gave an impatient shake of the head. Her fair hair was down to her shoulders. 'And here we go again with the stereotyping! It's not my fault every time something weird happens in Norbold. I do not go around looking for trouble!'

He nodded. She nodded. She headed for the door; and as she closed it behind her, the DI heard her add softly: 'Trouble comes looking for me.'

NINE

Rambles With Books was never going to be a runaway success. People don't fight over an anthology of nineteenth-century poems in the way that they do over the last fifty-inch television in the January sales. It was never difficult to find Ash alone in his shop.

But Hazel's heart sank at the dearth of customers. Not so much for Ash's sake – he didn't seem to mind whether he sold many books, could afford to run the place more as a hobby than a commercial venture, and would have been appalled to find himself overrun with shoppers – as her own. If he'd been busy, if there had been anyone else there, she could have made coffee in the little kitchen, and stroked Patience, and gone home with a clear conscience. But he was alone, and he looked up with a smile when he felt her watching him, and Hazel knew that when you have something difficult to do, it's better to do it sooner rather than later.

She made the coffee anyway. But then she said, in a low voice, looking anywhere but at him, 'I made you a promise, Gabriel. And I'm going to have to break it.'

He frowned. 'What promise?' But before the words were entirely out, recollection struck him. 'Ah Hazel . . .'

She hated the disappointment in his voice. 'I'm sorry. But that woman's in trouble, and HQ are keeping Dave Gorman from doing anything to help her. They're hoping that if we all pretend there isn't a problem, the problem will go away. Well, maybe it will – in the back of a van. If Miss Lim turns up dead in a ditch somewhere, the fact that she never asked us for help won't be much comfort.'

Ash considered for a moment. 'What did Dave ask you to do?'

'He asked me to stay out of it.'

'What's he going to do?'

'The same. No less a personage than ACC-Crime warned him off.'

'What are *you* going to do?'

When she was thinking, Hazel's eyebrows pinched the top of her nose. 'We know where and when Lim went to university, and we know there's no record of her under that name before 2001. I'm going to look for some reason an intelligent, ambitious Chinese sixth-former would go to university as someone else.'

For his part, Ash was less surprised by this turn of events than he should have been, and less worried than he might have been. Nothing she might learn about events at the school, not even the possibility that she might raise hackles at police headquarters again, troubled him as much as the possibility that Philip Welbeck might make her an offer Hazel wouldn't want to refuse. As long as Welbeck was in London, and Hazel was following her hunches in Norbold, she was probably safe from him.

Which didn't make what she was proposing to do a good idea. 'And if ACC-Crime gets wind of it?'

She shrugged. 'HQ hate me already. They think they can't trust me to be sensible and just do my job and go home at the end of my shift, and keep my nose out of the kind of things that are too difficult to sort out. The kind of things that, even if you find the answers, no one's going to be grateful.'

'Well – they're right, aren't they? They can't trust you to do that.'

Hazel glared at him. 'But I don't work for HQ. Yes, they

hired me, and they pay my salary every month, but the people I work for are the people of Norbold. They're the ones who're entitled to my loyalty. Chief Superintendent Fountain forgot who it is that pays the piper, and half the time HQ forget it as well. And I don't want to forget.

'Them' – she waved a hand towards the street beyond the shop door – 'the people out there, they're why I do the job. To keep them safe, so they can get on with their lives without having to worry who's lurking round the corner. To make sure the little guy's protected from the big guns. When senior police officers start thinking some crimes aren't worth investigating, the one who suffers is the little guy. That's not good enough. If the little guy's always going to get dumped on, what's the point of living in a democracy? What's the point of an independent police service? If Elizabeth Lim's problems aren't worth my time, I don't know what the point of being a police officer *is*.'

'It's possible,' suggested Ash, 'that those senior police officers know more about all this than you realise. That if you had the same information, you'd understand why they're declining to get involved. They may know there's no need to.'

'Then why don't they say that? Let us know what's going on?'

'Because if they've decided that the best course of action is no action, they won't want to say so officially. That's just how it works, Hazel. Sometimes, anything you do is going to cause more harm than good. Sometimes, nothing is the least worst option. It's called using your discretion. But it's hard to do if you have to justify the decision publicly. I think you have to just hope that everyone's acting for the best. That Elizabeth Lim knew what she was doing when she packed her bags and left town, and headquarters know what they're doing by taking no further action.'

'You mean, I should let them muzzle me too?'

Ash chuckled fondly. 'Hazel, no one who knows you thinks you'll consent to being muzzled if something needs talking about. I just want you to consider the possibility that this is something that doesn't.'

'Kidnapping is a serious crime!'

'Of course it is. But maybe the situation has already been

resolved. For all we know, Miss Lim may have known exactly where to go to get help. Steps may already have been taken to ensure that she won't be troubled any more.'

'Then why did she leave town?'

'That may have been the price she had to pay.'

'You really think so?' Hazel sounded deeply unconvinced. 'That I should forget all about it?'

Ash nodded solemnly. 'Yes. You haven't enough information to work with anyway. But just trying, when Dave Gorman has been told to drop it, will be noticed, and not in a good way. You don't need to be making enemies at headquarters.'

'More enemies,' Hazel corrected him absently. 'I suppose you're right. We can't solve every mystery we come across.'

'No.'

She gave in with a bad grace. 'Oh, all right. I'll be good.'

'Good.'

It's no wonder that primitive civilisations believed gods were playing games with their lives. That gods on Olympus or other mountaintops – almost the only thing that believers ever agreed on was that gods were *up there* rather than *down there*, as if a head for heights was an essential attribute in a deity – got their kicks from manoeuvring humans into tricky situations and running a book on how, or if, they'd extricate themselves. Sometimes it's the only way to explain how events conspire to send us cannoning off in improbable directions.

So perhaps it was a quiet day on Olympus, and Hermes had no messages to run and Aphrodite's mirror was in for re-silvering, and one of them, yawning, glanced down on Norbold and drawled, 'I suppose we could always have a bit of fun with *that* one again . . .'

Otherwise we're left to think it was nothing more than coincidence that soon after Hazel clocked on at Meadowvale a report came in of a stray child, too young and distraught to be making sense, at the railway station, and Hazel as the closest WPC was despatched to deal with it.

She arrived about thirty seconds after the child's mother, who had made the fundamental error of believing that a four-year-old would stay with the bags while she went for a trolley just because he said he would. By then the little boy was calming down, his mother was sufficiently recovered to be furious with him, and Hazel was surplus to requirements. Walking back to Meadowvale took her past the little office over the paper shop that was Martha Harris's.

Martha was just parking her car. 'Come up for a coffee.'

Hazel hesitated. It wasn't a strictly legitimate use of police time, although good relations between the police and any private investigators on their manor were in the best interests of both. 'They're expecting me back at Meadowvale.'

'Come up for a coffee, and an informal chinwag you might find mildly interesting.'

Hazel was intrigued. 'An informal chinwag about what?'

'A certain missing person.'

Hazel hesitated no longer.

She was a lot younger than Martha, and a lot fitter, and she waited impatiently as the PI laboured up the stairs. Even then Martha wasn't ready to talk until she was seated at her desk with her shoes kicked off, and a steaming mug and the chocolate-box open in front of her.

Then she said, 'Does the name Jerome Harbinger mean anything to you?'

It did, although for a moment Hazel couldn't think why. 'I've seen it on the side of lorries. Those maroon ones with the gold lettering.'

'You have, pet. He's a big road transport man. I say *is*, though he's retired now. He was a real self-made man – born with nothing, worth millions by the time he was forty.'

'Heart attack at forty-five?' Hazel had no idea where this was going.

'No. It's true to say he wasn't the man at fifty-four that he had been at forty-four, but it wasn't his health that broke him.'

Even if she didn't yet know how, Hazel was willing to bet there was a point to this. 'What then?'

But instead of answering, Martha took a metaphorical step back. 'You mind I worked at Meadowvale for twelve years? I was there before Chief Superintendent Fountain. I know he went a bit rogue towards the end' – she was too tactful to mention what had brought about his end – 'but he didn't have it easy. Norbold was a bit of a one-horse town in those days. And Meadowvale was a lot like the Hole in the Wall Gang.

'Maybe that's not entirely fair,' she reflected. 'It wasn't corruption that was the problem, it was defeatism. Everybody thought it was impossible to do a proper job here so nobody tried. The general feeling was, once you'd issued a crime reference number so the victim could claim on his insurance, there wasn't much more to be done.'

'That must have been . . . discouraging.'

'It was, pet. I was already in me mid-thirties: Norbold was me one chance to get into CID. I'd done the detectives' course, but nobody seemed to have an opening for a fat, opinionated Geordie woman.' She sipped her coffee thoughtfully. 'Can't imagine why not. Except at Meadowvale, where they were hiring anyone who was willing to come. I arrived all fired up with enthusiasm, a DC at last, and I thought I'd landed in some kind of black comedy cop-show. I didn't know what to do about it. I didn't want to cut and run, turn me back on me last chance. But if I stayed, I knew I'd end up like the rest of them: putting in time till me pension arrived. I'll tell you this: when Johnny Fountain started knocking the place into shape, I thought the sun shone out of his left ear-'ole.'

'What had gone wrong?'

Martha pushed the chocolates across her desk: Hazel took a Strawberry Surprise. 'What had gone wrong was, anyone worth a damn at Meadowvale couldn't wait to go off somewhere else. There were promotions. There were sideways promotions. There were early retirements. Nobody stayed longer than it took them to find something better. The upshot was that there was a bloody great vacuum where the leadership at Meadowvale Police Station should have been coming from.'

Hazel wasn't sure why Martha thought this was something she ought to hear. But she didn't think the PI had asked her in simply to reminisce. 'Are we still talking about Elizabeth Lim? Or Jerome Harbinger?'

'Both, pet. Maybe I'm not telling the story very well. Thing is, you're used to working in a well-run police station. Superintendent Maybourne does a good job. Johnny Fountain, for all his faults, mostly did a good job. When I was first there,

Meadowvale was a disaster waiting to happen. And it happened seventeen years ago.'

'Seventeen years?' Hazel stared at her. 'Elizabeth Lim would have been a teenager then. I don't see how . . .'

'Don't rush me,' said Martha heavily, 'I'm getting old. And me memory isn't what it was, which is why I didn't think of this sooner. Of course, a lot of Scotch-and-water passes under the bridgework in seventeen years. But I was thinking about it last night – about Elizabeth Lim, professional woman and pillar of the community, suddenly doing a runner – and damn me but I think I know who she might be.'

Finally. 'Who? And why would someone want to kidnap her?'

Martha went for a nougat log next. 'I'm not a police officer any more. I haven't been one for eight years. And I'm not telling you anything that wasn't common knowledge in the police canteen. All the same, don't be telling anyone I've been running me mouth off. I'll not only deny it, I'll swear blind we've never met.'

'All right.' Hazel took another chocolate. In fact, she took several before the story was told.

Jerome Harbinger lived in the pretty Warwickshire village of Spell, in a five-hundred-year-old farmhouse with room round the back for a couple of lorries. He was in the business of road transport, and from modest beginnings had built up a fleet serving customers across Britain. He had amassed significant wealth, acquired an intelligent and sophisticated wife, and with her had begun an art collection, which had grown until it was regularly lending pieces for exhibition in London, Paris and Berlin.

Possibly the only drawback to that kind of success is that it attracts attention, not only from the European art establishment. One winter's night in 2001, while the Harbingers were attending a Christmas ball in London and their daughter was appearing in a college revue, the house was broken into. Paintings insured for fifteen million pounds were stolen, and the thieves beat up the family's housekeeper.

The drawback with art theft is that anything worth stealing

is probably too identifiable to sell on. This doesn't matter if the original owner, or their insurers, can be persuaded to buy it back. Underwriters facing a £15 million bill will happily sanction a substantial finder's fee. It makes for a tricky negotiation, but the fact that all the parties want the same thing is helpful.

Jerome Harbinger's insurers agreed to pay £1.5 million for information leading to the recovery of the stolen items, and privately considered they had got away lightly.

It was a condition of the deal that the police would not be involved; and again, this suited the insurers as well as it suited the thieves. It's not illegal to pay for the return of one's own goods but it is frowned upon by the authorities, who liken it to rewarding criminals for a job well done. If word of the agreement had reached them, the police would have wanted to arrest the thieves, and art works worth £15 million could have been lost or damaged beyond repair.

More concerned with the prospect of being caught, the thieves specified that the exchange be carried out by Mrs Jennifer Harbinger, driven to their chosen venue – a supermarket car park on the outskirts of Norbold, with immediate access to four major thoroughfares – at three o'clock in the morning by the family's chauffeur. Neither her husband nor anyone else was to accompany them.

'But where does Elizabeth Lim come in?' demanded Hazel. 'She'd still have been at school. You're not telling me she masterminded a major art theft?'

'Patience,' said Martha equably, 'is a virtue, even – or perhaps especially – among police officers. Let me finish the story. I'll take questions, if you still have them, then.'

Martha couldn't say exactly what went wrong. All sorts of rumours had abounded, many of them started by people trying to demonstrate that it wasn't their fault. People had taken decisions above their pay scale. People *hadn't* taken decisions when they needed to, and Division had had to step in. The whole debacle was caused by a beat copper trying to arrest someone he'd seen in a mug-shot.

The official line was that no one, either at Meadowvale or at Division, had done anything wrong. That what happened was the regrettable consequence of an insurance company conspiring with thieves to deceive the police.

Jennifer Harbinger arrived at the rendezvous with a suitcase full of unmarked banknotes. The insurers' negotiator assured her husband that the police knew nothing, and there would be no attempt at a grand slam – recovering the paintings, retaining the money and rounding up the thieves in one fell swoop. Harbinger didn't want to risk either his wife or his collection. This was, after all, the eventuality for which he had paid his insurance premiums.

Martha never heard where the tip-off came from. But at the moment of maximum exposure, with Mrs Harbinger and her chauffeur holding the art – two briefcases and a sports bag contained the lot: £15 million had never looked so unimpressive – and two of the thieves holding sawn-off shotguns while a third counted the money, suddenly squad cars were squealing round every corner, policemen in bullet-proof vests were tumbling out and firearms officers were taking up strategic positions covering every exit.

When the gunfire finally stopped, four people were dead: Mrs Harbinger, her chauffeur, one of the thieves and one member of the Armed Response Unit. Another of the thieves and two more officers were in ambulances ignoring speed limits; and the third thief had made good his escape, unscathed so far as anyone knew, with one of the briefcases tucked under his arm.

The next sound anyone heard was the shrill clamour of people trying to pass the buck.

TEN

It was gone five o'clock before DI Gorman got back to his office, and he hadn't eaten since breakfast. He'd picked up a heart attack with all the trimmings from a local burger bar, and he'd been looking forward to pigging out in privacy. But when Hazel knocked on his door, he made himself do the decent thing and broke it in half.

'Nice bit of minced withers?' Then, seeing the barely repressed excitement in her eyes, he said, 'What's happened?'

'I know who Elizabeth Lim is.'

He stared at her. 'How? Who?' He considered for a moment. 'Both. Who is she, and how do you know?'

Martha had made it clear she wasn't to be involved. 'I know because I've talked to someone who was in Norbold seventeen years ago, when this all started. I can't tell you who, but I can vouch for their reliability. There's no suggestion of criminality on their part, and now I know all that they know.'

Dave Gorman's eyebrows lowered threateningly, but then he nodded. He could go along with that, for the moment.

'Most of what I'm going to tell you came from that source. Then I cross-checked it with newspaper archives of the period, and talked – off the record – to a guy I trained with, who now helps run the Police National Computer. As far as I can make out, this is the real deal.'

'Tell me.'

She told him everything she had learned. There was nothing in the account to identify its source, so she gave him all the details she'd been given or managed to amass, starting with Martha's story.

When she paused for breath, Gorman interjected. 'I still don't understand what any of this has to do with Elizabeth Lim.'

'The Harbingers' insurance company employed a security firm to handle the negotiations. The name of the negotiator,' said Hazel, 'was Edward Cho.'

She heard the cogs of Gorman's brain engage and begin to turn. 'And Edward Cho had a teenage daughter?'

'He had a teenage daughter, and a wife, and a son.'

'So Harbinger blamed Cho for Jennifer's death,' said Gorman slowly. 'Because an ARU turned up when Cho had promised to keep the police out of the picture. Did he threaten Cho? Did he threaten Cho's *family*?'

Hazel nodded. 'He did. Oh, he was entitled to be angry. Cho hadn't enough experience to handle such a tricky negotiation. He was an accountant. I don't know why his employers thought this was a good case for him to cut his teeth on, but they dropped it in Cho's lap and he called the play. Maybe he did the best he could, but still Jennifer Harbinger died. Cho promised she'd be safe, but she died in a shoot-out between the thieves and the police. Harbinger was beside himself with grief and fury. Cho had given his word the police wouldn't be informed until the exchange was completed and his wife was safe. Harbinger swore he wouldn't rest until there was nothing left bearing the name of Cho except gravestones.'

Gorman shook his head dismissively. 'It was the grief talking. He'd just lost his wife. It's not uncommon for the bereaved to threaten those they blame. Most of them calm down pretty quickly. And the ones who don't mostly don't have the means to carry out their threats.'

'That's what everyone assumed,' agreed Hazel. 'Mr Cho expressed his deepest regrets to Mr Harbinger, and undertook to co-operate fully with the police inquiry.'

Gorman sensed a *but*. 'And did he?'

'He didn't get the chance. He met with an unfortunate accident on an icy country road a couple of weeks later. His car went into a reservoir while he was taking the scenic route home to Coventry. Cho drowned behind the wheel.'

Gorman was watching her closely. 'Any signs of foul play?'

'No. No damage to the car that falling into a reservoir wouldn't account for. Ditto Mr Cho.'

'The scenic road from where?'

'That is a really good question,' nodded Hazel. 'And I'm not sure anybody knows the answer to it, possibly because nobody tried very hard to find out. But a glance at a road-map suggests he might have been somewhere near the Harbingers' home in Spell.'

'What did Harbinger say?'

'He said he knew nothing about it. He said what you said: he'd been in a state of emotional turmoil when he made the threat, never had any intention of carrying it out. His housekeeper confirmed he had been at home the evening Cho died. Both of them said Cho hadn't been to the house.'

The DI gave an ambivalent grunt. 'But Mrs Cho still had her

doubts? She thought she and the kids would be safer if they left Coventry and changed their name to Lim?'

'In fact, no,' said Hazel, expressionless. 'Mary Cho was so overcome with grief that, a month after her husband died, she drowned herself in her bath.'

That offended Gorman's professional instincts. 'Nobody drowns themselves in their own bath! They drown themselves in rivers; or they cut their wrists and bleed to death in the bath. You can't just decide to inhale your bath water. Your body won't let you.'

'The autopsy showed she'd taken a heavy dose of sleeping tablets. In the absence of any conflicting evidence, the investigating officer took the view that it was suicide, and the coroner agreed.'

'Regardless of the fact that Harbinger had threatened the lives of both the deceased?' When he scowled like that, Dave Gorman looked more simian than ever. 'It doesn't sound like a very thorough investigation.'

Hazel said carefully, 'I'm not sure a thorough investigation was top of anyone's wish-list just then. A certain amount of pressure may have been brought to bear on the SIO. If neither Meadowvale nor Division wanted their part in the tragedy to be scrutinised too closely, he may have welcomed a plausible explanation that didn't involve the man whose wife was killed murdering the man who tipped us off and *his* wife. Everyone here, everyone at Division and everyone at headquarters would have been happy to go along with it.'

'Keeping the top brass happy is not the function of a senior investigating officer!' snarled Gorman. 'I don't care how embarrassing it was going to be. We are a public service. If we've cocked up, we admit it. We work out what went wrong and try to make sure it doesn't happen again.'

'I'm not sure anyone at Meadowvale *did* cock up,' ventured Hazel. 'Once we found out about the exchange, weren't we bound to try to apprehend the criminals?'

'And that's what they should have said. Dear God, what's wrong with us? When did it stop being enough just to do the job we're paid for to the best of our ability? We're so scared of having to justify good decisions in public that we'd rather make bad ones in private. Like, turning a blind eye to two murders because we don't want to be seen persecuting a man who wouldn't be a widower if it wasn't for us!

'So who was the SIO?' he demanded. 'What shining example of police probity do we have to thank for the mess *we're* having to deal with?'

Hazel shrugged awkwardly. She'd expected Gorman to be angry about what she'd found out: she hadn't expected him to take it so personally. 'I don't know. It'll be a matter of record, if you want to risk Sir's wrath by pulling the file. Dave, I know it sounds bad, but it's easy to have twenty-twenty vision with hindsight. On the information available to him at that time, it was entirely possible that neither of the Chos was murdered. That Edward Cho's death really was an accident – a steep road, an icy evening – and his distraught wife didn't want to go on without him.'

'Of course it was. And a proper investigation would have established the facts, one way or the other. But if there was nothing to cover up, why is someone *still* trying to get at Edward Cho's daughter? Maybe it's Jerome Harbinger, maybe it isn't. But right now I can't think of anyone with a better motive.'

Neither could Hazel. 'Left on their own, the Chos' kids sold the family home and changed their names. She became Elizabeth Lim, and no one she met after starting university knew she was ever anyone else. I don't know what name the son took. They were smart enough not to use the same one. All I know is that they both disappear from the public record immediately after their mother's funeral.'

Gorman was getting a grip on the anger that had made it hard for him to think clearly. 'If they were safe for seventeen years, what's changed?'

'We don't actually know that the brother *is* safe. He could have had an unfortunate accident too, for all we know. Maybe all that's changed recently is that Harbinger finally discovered who Edward Cho's daughter became.'

The DI sucked in a deep breath and let it rattle out. He looked years older. 'OK. Well, I'll have to talk to Harbinger. Today.' He glanced at his watch. 'Well – maybe tomorrow.'

'Will Sir let you?'

'Sir will only be able to stop me,' Gorman said fiercely, 'with a direct order backed up by a flame-thrower. And I doubt he'll go as far even as the direct order. Not now the can's open and the worms are on the floor. Someone decided that lives were a price worth paying to avoid official embarrassment. I'm not having that. It's time to shake the files marked Secret out of an upstairs window and let everyone see what's in them. Once this goes public, I don't think Sir or anyone else will dare obstruct a proper investigation.'

Hazel squinted at him. 'Won't that depend on who threw the Chos to the wolves and what he's doing now? Seventeen years is long enough for a middle-ranking policeman to rise to a position of real power. Blocking your investigation may be his best chance of protecting his pension. And whether or not they approve of what he did, the rest of the top brass will close ranks. "There but for the grace of God" and all that. If that happens, you'll be the one left out in the cold.' Hazel knew what she was talking about.

But Gorman was again fighting a rising tide of fury. He was not easily moved to anger, but once begun, the process gathered momentum like an avalanche. 'Hazel, I don't think I care. If that's their priority – looking out for each other, wall-papering over one another's cracks – I don't *want* to go on working for them. I've always been proud of what I do. I may not be brilliant at it, but on the whole I've made my community safer and cleaner. I've made mistakes – we all make mistakes – but I've owned up to them, tried to put them right, and learned from them. I thought that was what we were supposed to do.

'Now you're telling me that, in order to duck the blame for Jennifer Harbinger's death, senior officers of this Division allowed a bitter man to crucify the family of the man he held responsible. That's not OK. That is *so* not OK that I have to do something about it. If it means going head-to-head with people further up the pay-scale, fine. They can sack me if they want to. But if it's the last thing I do as a policeman, I will see Elizabeth Lim safe, and I will find out which of my superiors thought their reputations more important than her life.

'And before you even ask,' he added testily, 'I have no idea how I will do these things, except that I will.'

'I believe you,' said Hazel softly.

ELEVEN

About the time Dave Gorman was working up a head of steam over at Meadowvale, Ash was closing his shop. He was replacing the last few books when a low growl warned him of a last-minute visitor. This surprised him on two counts. Patience knew better than to discourage a customer, and people didn't usually come in at five to six. Book-buying is a leisure occupation: most of his regulars – and he was beginning to build up a small phalanx of regulars – arrived mid-morning or mid-afternoon, often armed with biscuits, and browsed the shelves while Ash put the kettle on. Rambles With Books was almost as much a social club as it was a bookshop.

He looked round amiably. 'We usually close at six. But if you want fifteen minutes, I can do the accounts first.'

Philip Welbeck said, 'Not a massive task, then, doing your accounts?'

Welbeck had been Ash's boss for five years, and a good friend for another five; but right now he was an unwelcome reminder of the past. 'Philip,' he managed after a pause too long to be taken as a compliment, 'whatever are you doing in Norbold?'

'Just passing through, dear boy,' Welbeck said airily. 'Nice doggy.' He leaned down to pat Patience on the head.

He just patted me on the head, said Patience.

Ash ignored her. 'On the way to where?' Norbold was one of the few places in England where the Romans hadn't bothered to drive a road.

'Now, now.' Welbeck smiled impishly. 'Don't let's be indiscreet.' He was a smaller man than Ash, dapper in a 1950s sort of way, the thin dark hair Brylcreemed back, the tie silk, the cufflinks gold. He told friends he was something in the City; more casual acquaintances took him for a second-hand car dealer.

Ash knew him as a clever man, a good man, a brave man; and a dangerous man to cross.

My *head*, said Patience with renewed emphasis. He patted me on my *head*. He called me a *nice doggy*!

As time went on, Ash was making a better job of seeming normal. He almost never held conversations with his dog now unless they were alone. He cleared his throat. 'To answer your question, no, I don't need the services of a tax-avoidance specialist yet. But we're doing all right. There's more coming in than going out.'

'Delighted to hear it. Seriously, Gabriel – I'm glad you've found something to channel your energies. This' – he gazed around him, not exactly critically but then again, not exactly not – 'may not be the optimum use of your talents, but it's more than I'd have expected two years ago. You're looking well. You're looking better than I've seen you since . . . well, you know.'

'Since my wife conspired with an arms smuggler to drive me mad,' stated Ash.

'The very words I was looking for,' said Welbeck smoothly. 'And the boys? Well, I trust?' Ash nodded cautiously. 'And your little friend Miss Best. I was half expecting to see her here.'

'She's working.' In fact, Ash wasn't sure what shifts she was pulling at the moment. What he did know was that he didn't want Hazel and Philip Welbeck to get better acquainted. 'I'll tell her you dropped by. In passing.'

The intelligence sector is like policing, in that the people you most want to talk to are seldom keen on talking to you. Welbeck had been shown so many different doors in so many different ways that he hadn't taken it personally for years. But nor did he take a hint, even one as unsubtle as this. His smile broadened. 'Gabriel! Are you trying to get rid of me?'

Ash sighed. 'Would it do any good if I was?'

'Probably not, dear boy,' chuckled Welbeck. 'Probably not.'

It was becoming obvious to Ash that he wasn't going to get away from this encounter unscathed. He finished closing the shop, drew the blinds, then plugged the kettle back in and spooned coffee into two of the half-dozen mugs he'd amassed. He proffered the one inscribed 'Friends are God's apology for your family'. It seemed more appropriate than 'Etonians do it up against the wall', the only other clean one, which he kept for himself.

He sat down at the table. 'Out with it, Philip. What is it you want?'

'Your little friend . . .' began Welbeck.

'We're not talking about her,' Ash said firmly.

'How shall I put this politely?' mused Welbeck, blowing the steam off his coffee. 'We'll talk about what I want to talk about. Gabriel, you know the problems I have recruiting suitable personnel. You know the difficulties I have holding onto them. Someone like your little friend . . .'

'Stop calling her that.'

'Like Miss Hazel Best,' continued Welbeck seamlessly, 'might fit into our office nicely. Daughter of a career soldier, high-level computer skills, experience in the police. Oh yes, and not afraid to shoot somebody if the need arises.'

The blood in Ash's veins turned to ice. He knew how much he owed to Philip Welbeck. He also knew that, when Welbeck wanted something, he didn't worry too much about whether he was owed it or not. He did a difficult and important job well, and it was necessary for the good of the nation that he enjoyed a certain amount of latitude. Ash had worked in Welbeck's office for five years and knew that intelligence gathering was by no means as glamorous and exciting as the film industry suggested – that it was mostly done at desks and computers, studying financial records and airline schedules. That was what he had done, what he had been good at. He wasn't a spy, he was a security analyst.

The other thing he knew was that he would do everything in his power to keep Hazel Best from straying into that world. If she did, he was by no means convinced she would settle for working behind a desk.

'You don't need Hazel,' he said in a low voice. 'She's too honest for your purposes.'

Welbeck gave a light tenor laugh. 'You're becoming a cynic in your old age! I'm just saying, it's hard not to be impressed by what she's achieved in the time that you've known her. If she *were* to be interested . . .'

'No.'

'Perhaps we should ask her.'

'*No*, Philip.'

'You're afraid she'd say yes.'

'She's twenty-seven years old! Of course she'd say yes.'

'So what's the problem?'

Gabriel Ash was not a violent man. He was a big man, but he had rarely been tempted to resolve his difficulties with his fists. But once, striking out in the throes of mental anguish about his lost family, he had knocked Philip Welbeck down in Parliament Street. Welbeck had had him taken away in a white van; and he had been right to do so. Ash had been out of control. It was a tribute to both men that neither bore a grudge about the episode.

That didn't mean that either of them had forgotten it.

'You don't really want me to answer that?' said Ash quietly.

Welbeck blinked first. He gave a negligent little shrug. 'You keep drawing that on me like a revolver,' he drawled. 'Gabriel, I was not responsible for what happened to you. Your wife was responsible for what happened to you.'

'It wouldn't have happened if I'd stuck with insurance investigation.'

'Perhaps not. But you wanted the job I offered. Nobody twisted your arm.'

'So why are you twisting it now?'

Welbeck looked away. 'We weren't talking about you.'

One reason Gabriel Ash had succeeded as an insurance investigator, the reason he was recruited for national security work, was his ability to see things that hadn't been written down, to hear things that hadn't been said. This wasn't about his old boss looking him up for old times' sake. He didn't think it was entirely about Hazel Best either.

'No,' he said.

Welbeck raised a shapely eyebrow. 'No what?'

'No, I'm not coming back to work for you.'

Welbeck smiled again. The last time Ash saw a smile like that, it was preceded by ominous music and a triangular fin cutting through the waves. Ash was glad he knew that Philip Welbeck was a good man. If he hadn't, he might have thought he was a very bad man indeed. 'Oh good lord, Gabriel, I'm not *that* desperate! I know we're a broad church, but we do tend to prefer our employees sane. At least most of the time.'

When Ash was genuinely struggling with madness, a remark like that would have been hurtful. Now, his equilibrium largely restored, he found it oddly reassuring. 'So I don't want to work for you again, and you don't want me to work for you. So . . . what are you doing here?'

'I told you. I was in the district, and I wanted to see what you were doing with yourself.' He looked around the shop. 'Well, it's not exactly Foyles, but I suppose it's early days.'

'Yes.'

'Not really a full-time occupation yet.'

'Yes, it is.'

Again Welbeck seemed to change the subject without actually doing anything of the kind. 'The thing is, with all this financial constraint we're labouring under, it's hard to get the work done sometimes. Sometimes it would be splendid to be able to pick up the phone and rope someone in for a day or two. A week at the most. A consultant. Someone with the right set of talents to deal with a particular situation.'

'No,' Ash said again.

'Oh, not *now*,' Welbeck assured him. 'Not when you're so' – another glance around the empty shop – 'busy. But occasionally. Once a year. Maybe twice.'

'*No*,' said Ash again, more forcefully.

Welbeck did the smile again, and went to stand up. 'Well, perhaps it's a little too soon. We'll keep in touch, Gabriel. I'll let you know if anything comes up you might be interested in. In the meantime, give it a little thought. It would solve my problem, you see. If I could call you in, just occasionally, when I really needed to, I mightn't need to look round for new staff. Oh . . .!' As he'd reached to replace his mug on the table, the white lurcher at his feet had stood up, jogging his hand and spilling the remains of his tea down his trousers.

Ash was still absorbing the implications of what he'd just heard. But after a moment he apologised, insincerely, and fetched a cloth. 'I expect she wanted you to pat her head again.'

Ash's instincts had been good even when his mental processes were unreliable. Now they were warning him that telling Hazel about Welbeck's visit would be akin to lighting a big fat cigar in a fireworks factory.

You have to tell her, said Patience.

'That Philip's using her to blackmail me?'

That she's drawing attention to herself in the places where these things are discussed.

The dog – or just possibly that part of Ash's brain which thought clearly even when his mind was in turmoil – had cut straight to the chase. 'You don't think Philip was just passing, then.'

Of course he wasn't just passing. Someone has been talking to him. Someone who's so anxious about what Hazel's got involved in that it seemed necessary to organise a distraction.

Ash stared at the lurcher in admiration. 'You're getting good at this.'

Don't mention it, said Patience modestly.

'The business at the school. Elizabeth Lim's disappearance. Hazel said she'd drop it . . .'

You've known her as long as I have. You didn't really expect her to decide it was none of her business?

When it was put to him like that, Ash had to concede that he hadn't. 'All right. So Hazel's rattling cages again. But who at Meadowvale, or even at Division, would know to talk to Philip Welbeck about it?'

It's amazing what strings people will find to pull if they're worried enough.

Ash nodded slowly. 'If Elizabeth Lim *was* part of a witness protection programme, that will be being managed by the National Crime Agency. Where people may well be acquainted with Philip and his happy band, and would know he had the means to distract Hazel from her latest crusade.'

By threatening you.

Ash rocked a hand. 'He didn't threaten me exactly.'

Do you want to start working for him again?

'Of course not!' He sounded appalled by the idea.

Then it was a threat.

But it had been cleverer than that. 'If I tell Hazel what he said, it won't sound like a threat to her. It'll sound like an opportunity.'

You're afraid she might take that opportunity?

'I'm afraid she'd jump at it.'

And it's not what you want for her.

'I don't think it would make her happy. It's important work, but it's also tricksy and full of compromise. It's about tap-dancing around an open sewer. Hazel is a pretty simple person. I don't mean that as an insult: it's one of the things I like about her. She knows the difference between right and wrong, and she's always ready to back her beliefs with action. By the time she'd realised Philip's world isn't about right and wrong so much as the lesser of multiple evils, she'd be in too deep to just walk away. Trying to do the right thing in those circumstances would break her.'

You could talk to her – warn her of the dangers.

Ash winced. 'Warning Hazel about danger is like issuing her with a gilt-edged invitation.'

You need to tell her *something*. She needs to know that she's under observation.

Ash nodded glumly. 'I suppose you're right. I'll talk to her tonight.'

What will you say?

'I haven't the faintest idea.'

TWELVE

He meant to go round to her house that evening, as soon as he'd put the boys to bed. But she beat him to it, arriving at his door with fish and chips wrapped, as connoisseurs know they should be, in newsprint. 'You haven't eaten already?'

'Er . . . no. Well, the boys have, but that won't stop them eating again.'

'Put some plates to warm.'

Ash did as he was told. He could hardly do otherwise; but he would have preferred to hold the coming conversation in Hazel's kitchen. However angry people become with what you have to say, they very rarely storm out of their own houses.

In one way he was lucky. There was something on the television the boys wanted to watch: Gilbert nudged Guy, and Guy – too sweet-natured to realise he was being used – asked if they could take their chips up to the playroom. Usually Ash would have objected; tonight he was happy to consent.

Sometimes Frankie ate with the boys and left Ash's meal in the oven, sometimes she waited and ate with him, sometimes she had something on a tray in her room. Tonight she realised, from Ash's preoccupied manner, that this would be a good time to take a tray upstairs. 'There's a concert on the radio I'd like to listen to.'

'Of course,' said Ash quickly. 'Why don't you call it a night? I'll settle the boys down in an hour or so.'

When they were alone, except for Patience watching expectantly from the kitchen sofa, Hazel said, 'I'm glad I've got you to myself. I wanted to bring you up to date.' She told him about her conversations with Martha Harris and Dave Gorman.

But halfway through her account, she knew she didn't have his full attention. She didn't understand his reluctance to get involved. They'd always helped one another before: sometimes as a sounding board for ideas, sometimes in ways that were perilously practical. She was annoyed that he had lost interest in the incident at the school as soon as he realised his children were not the target.

She broke off with a frown. 'Stop me if I'm boring you.'

'It's not that,' Ash demurred. 'I'm . . . worried.'

'What about?'

'You, of course. You're doing it again – dashing out onto the frozen pond to rescue somebody's puppy without knowing how thin the ice is.'

Hazel grinned at that. 'Well . . . it's kind of what we do, isn't it? How much choice is there when you know the puppy's in trouble? And maybe the ice isn't as thin as all that.'

'It's pretty thin,' said Ash.

Hazel's eyes narrowed. 'You know that, do you?' He nodded. '*How* do you know that?'

'I can't tell you.'

Her frown deepened. 'You need to find a way of telling me.'

Ash shook his head. 'I can't.'

There was a lengthy pause, during which Hazel studied his face more closely than was comfortable. Finally she said, 'Are we talking national security here? The Official Secrets Act?'

'We *could* be talking national security,' said Ash carefully. It wasn't a lie: anything that involved Philip Welbeck might have security implications.

'Someone's put the frighteners on you!'

'No,' said Ash, 'it was more subtle than that. Elizabeth Lim's name was never mentioned. But it was a friendly warning, and I think you should heed it before it becomes more of a warning and less friendly.'

'How did they *know*?' wondered Hazel. 'That I'd found out about the Harbingers?'

'You've been talking to someone at the PNC.'

'Unofficially! He was a friend . . .'

'Nothing's *that* unofficial when it involves matters the upper echelons thought were safely buried.'

Hazel was a realist. The young man she'd done police studies with at Liverpool wasn't *that* good a friend. 'I suppose. But then, why didn't they put the frighteners on *me*? Why send a message via you?'

Ash gave an uncomfortable shrug. 'I'm already in their pocket. I'm still on the pay-roll – at least, the "discharged disabled" bit of it. Even if I wasn't taking their money, I've asked for their help too often to pretend they have no claim on me. They want you to leave this alone, and they think you're more likely to co-operate if I ask than if they do. So I have to ask. If for no better reason than friendship.'

She didn't storm out. She didn't argue. She smiled, and leaned forward across the remains of their supper, and said, 'There is no better reason.'

Ash blinked. He hadn't expected this to be so easy. 'You'll let it go? You won't ask any more questions about Elizabeth Lim and Jerome Harbinger and the men in the van?'

'I won't ask the PNC any more questions about anything, including the time of day, the weather forecast and who's going to be the next manager of Manchester United.'

Ah. So it wasn't going to be that easy. 'This is serious, Hazel. You're being watched. You can't afford to play games with these people. They're always going to win.'

'You know what you're asking?' she said after a moment. 'That I back off and let Harbinger go after Elizabeth Lim. That I leave Dave Gorman to stand up to the big guns at headquarters alone. Because he wants to get to the bottom of this as much as I do, and I don't think he'll stop if I tell him I've got cold feet.'

'Then the people who leaned on me will lean on him.'

'He may not be willing to bend. He may break first.'

Ash sighed wearily. 'Hazel, I can't keep the whole world safe. I can try to keep you safe. Please do as I ask. Talk to Dave, tell him to let this one go. Tell him the powers-that-be are aware of what's happened. If Elizabeth Lim needs help, they'll help her.'

Hazel regarded him levelly. 'Do you actually believe that?'

'Yes,' Ash said firmly.

'Jerome Harbinger probably murdered both her parents. While we're talking, he may be closing in on her and her brother. And people high up in the police service are pretending to know nothing about it because they don't want to see the bones of a seventeen-year-old disaster dug up and picked over again. Doesn't that bother you?'

'Of course it bothers me!' he exclaimed. 'Hazel, I'm not stupid. I know you want to help the Chos. Regardless of what their father did, they are innocent victims. For seventeen years they've lived with the threat that the man who murdered their parents would kill them too if he found them. Now it seems there's a real possibility that he has. You're right: someone should be helping them.

'But why does it have to be you? Why does it always have to be you? Dave Gorman knows everything you know, and he's in a better position to do something about it. Will you just for the love of God sit this one out?'

Her eyes were troubled. There was no mistaking Ash's distress, and Hazel cared about him enough to regret being its cause. But she had other obligations. One was to protect innocent members of the public from violent madmen. Another was to hold her profession to account when the evidence of wrong-doing became inescapable. Gabriel Ash was a friend for whom she would have done almost anything. But not this.

'I can't,' she said quietly. 'I'm sorry, Gabriel, but I can't.'

The first thing Hazel did the next day was to arrange to take the leave she was owed. She would have been reluctant to ask at such short notice, except a colleague whose holiday plans had fallen through welcomed the chance to swap and get away later.

The second thing she did, as soon as her final shift of the week was over, was change out of uniform and go upstairs to knock on DI Gorman's door. 'I'm yours for a fortnight. How do we do this?'

He stared at her. 'Do what?'

She wouldn't dignify that with a response, just ducked her chin to look down her nose at him.

Gorman leaned back in his chair, perplexity writ large on his frankly ugly face. 'I'm not involving you in this.'

'No,' she said calmly. 'I'm involving myself.'

He sighed. 'Hazel, be reasonable. You're not even on my team.'

'Right now I'm not on anyone's team. I'm on holiday. And if you use your team for this, they'll be back on traffic duty by Monday. You've only got two choices: do this alone, or let me help.'

'I appreciate the offer,' he said slowly. 'But I'm about to disobey a direct order from my Assistant Chief Constable. If I can't prove that he'd no business giving that order, *I'm* going to be directing traffic. Don't hitch your star to me: it's too likely to crash and burn.'

'We can do this, Dave,' Hazel promised. 'Help the Chos and get justice for their parents. And when we do, you'll be a detective superintendent. Damn sure I'm going to hitch my star to that!'

The flare of Gorman's eyes showed what he thought of his chances. 'There's no way it's going to end *that* well. If there's an explanation that means headquarters aren't playing Russian roulette with Elizabeth Lim's life, they'll never forgive us for coming up with *this* one. And if there isn't – if that really is what's going on – they'll never, ever forgive us for finding out.'

'Welcome to my world,' Hazel said bleakly.

'I can probably take the flak,' growled Gorman. 'They can't actually sack me for being right, and if I spend the rest of my career as a DI, well, I was probably going to anyway. But you're at the start of your career – it'll be easier for them to get rid of you.'

Hazel disagreed. 'If it was that easy, they'd have done it last time I embarrassed them. There seems to be a sort of critical mass with embarrassment. Once you reach it – once you're a sufficiently well-known trouble-maker – the consequences of getting rid of you start looking worse than the cost of keeping you around. I suspect I'm pretty fireproof now.'

There might have been some truth in that. It didn't matter. Nothing she said would alter the fact that she was a new constable on her first posting, that she'd already faced enough danger and taken enough knocks to see her through a twenty-year career, and that Gorman could not share the burden of responsibility with her and still sleep at nights.

'No,' he said shortly. 'If I'm going down, I'm not taking you with me. It's not just ACC-Crime – he can only shout at me. If we're right about this, Jerome Harbinger is a dangerous man. I'm not having you dodging bullets again.'

'But I've already swapped my holidays!'

'Swap them back. I mean it, Hazel – I'm doing this alone. At least until I have enough evidence to make it official. When I have, I'll ask Maybourne if I can borrow you. Until then, stay out of it. Go to visit your dad. Or help Gabriel in the shop. But stay away from the Harbingers. They're mine.'

THIRTEEN

The large oak door of the stone-built farmhouse in the Warwickshire village of Spell was answered by an attractive woman in her late thirties, with auburn hair and – Gorman didn't usually notice such things – eyes the colour of ice on emeralds. When he produced his warrant card, she identified herself as Jocelyn Harbinger.

'May I ask what you want to see my father about, Detective Inspector?'

Gorman fell back on the answer policemen always give in these circumstances. 'Just routine inquiries, miss. Would you tell him I'm here and ask for a few minutes of his time?'

She invited him in but didn't immediately do as he requested. 'Is this about my mother?'

There's a stock wooden expression which comes with the stock answer. Gorman levered it into place now. 'I just need to speak to your father, miss. If he has no problems about you being present, I don't either.'

'All right.' Jocelyn Harbinger led him up a stone stairway. 'Perhaps I should warn you, my father isn't well. You'll need to be patient.'

As they reached the landing, one of the doors opened and an older woman stepped out. She looked enquiringly at Jocelyn Harbinger and critically at Gorman. 'I'm sorry, Miss Harbinger, I didn't hear the door.'

'I was right there,' smiled Jocelyn. 'Detective Inspector Gorman, this is Mrs Fisher, our housekeeper. And my father's favourite chess opponent. I play too, but I can't give him much of a game. I'm *not* very patient.'

There had been a game in progress when Gorman arrived. The board was set up on a low table between two high-backed chairs. So far as Gorman could judge – like Jocelyn, he could play chess but not with any great skill – black was winning in terms of pieces but not necessarily of position.

Mrs Fisher leaned over the nearer of the chairs, the one with its back to the door. 'A gentleman to see you, Mr Harbinger. A *police* gentleman.'

A voice, at once gruff and querulous, growled, 'Send him away.'

'You can't just send them away, Father,' Jocelyn said briskly, 'they only come back when it's even less convenient.' She ushered Gorman forward.

Gorman knew that Jerome Harbinger was sixty-eight. If he hadn't known, he'd have thought he was ten years older than that. His craggy face was savaged by deep lines that had nothing to do with laughter and everything to do with bitter unhappiness. His skin was pale and papery, as if he didn't go outside any more. His hair, which had once been the same colour as his daughter's, retained some of the red amid the grey, and it stood up spikily, reminding Gorman of a fox with its hackles raised.

'Who are you? What are you doing here? Have you found my painting?'

Gorman said his name again, more slowly. 'I'm from Norbold CID. There may have been developments in your case – we're not sure yet. Tell me about your painting.'

Harbinger half-turned his head, giving Gorman his craggy profile. 'Caravaggio,' he snapped.

Dave Gorman had reached the age of thirty-eight without learning anything at all about art. He didn't even know what he liked, except that he quite liked the matchstick-men and the cheerful fat ladies. He thought he'd heard of Caravaggio before, couldn't remember the context. 'Is that somewhere in Italy?'

The old man in the chair began to laugh. It had the strained, rusty sound of something he hadn't done for a while, like the creaking of an ancient hinge when someone opens a forgotten door. 'Could be,' he agreed. The rusty laughter broke up in coughing. 'Could be anywhere.'

Gorman looked to the daughter for an explanation.

'Caravaggio was the artist,' murmured Jocelyn Harbinger. 'He's . . . really quite famous. An Old Master. His works are worth millions.'

'And this was one of the items stolen when your house was burgled?'

'It was the only one not recovered. It's called *Anime Gemelle* – Kindred Spirits. It's a portrait of a girl with a songbird. Not one of his most famous works, but still irreplaceable.'

'How come you don't know all this?' demanded Harbinger. 'Read the file, why don't you? Call yourself a detective!'

'Art theft is a pretty specialised field,' Gorman protested mildly.

'Too bloody specialised for the British bloody police!' snarled Harbinger. 'As true today as it was seventeen years ago. I knew it, my insurers knew it, the goddamn thieves knew it. The only ones who didn't know it were the bloody plods!'

'A bit before my time, sir,' said Gorman, expressionless.

'Well – *have* you found it?'

'The painting? Not yet.'

Harbinger gave a disgusted grunt and turned back to his chessboard. 'Then why are you wasting my time?'

Gorman was accustomed to hostility. Every police officer is. He got it from victims and he got it from perpetrators. He even got it from witnesses occasionally. If it stopped short of violence, he barely noticed it. But Harbinger's hostility was making it difficult to get the answers he'd come here for.

Jocelyn Harbinger caught his eye. 'I do wonder, Detective Inspector, if it might be better to leave my father to his game now. I'll try to answer any questions you still have.'

She took him into the garden. If Gorman had known any more about gardening than he did about art, he might have recognised that the knot design dated back to the same period as the house, that the roses peeking over the knee-high box hedges were only the latest in a family line going back to the time of Shakespeare. But he only recognised two kinds of flowers: one was daffodils, and the other wasn't.

'How mobile is your father?' he asked.

If she thought it a curious question, Jocelyn Harbinger gave no indication. 'Not very. He can walk short distances, but he uses a wheelchair even in the house if he's going from one room to another.'

'Arthritis?'

'In part, the last few years. But mainly a broken heart. Losing my mother destroyed him. Before that he was like a lion.' Her voice was full of admiration, which is possibly easier to sustain than love when people we once cared about stop being very lovable. 'Nothing frightened him, nothing stood in his way. He was a superb businessman. People thought he was successful because he was willing to take risks, but that wasn't it. He was incredibly good at calculating percentages. He *knew* how competitors, how customers, how the market, would react in any given circumstance.

'He sent me to business school. They sent me back. I kept

telling them, "That isn't what my father would do." Naturally enough, the tutors found this irritating. But when they put it to the test with a series of fantasy stock-market games, I beat them.' She glanced at Gorman sharply. 'I'm not boasting. I just want you to understand that my father was the best at what he did. But for what happened, he still would be. Locked away inside that broken man is a business titan.'

'Does he still run Harbingers?'

'Only on paper. He's the majority shareholder and managing director, and if he chose to shut up shop tomorrow, or put a match to it, he could. But – like the art collection, and indeed life – he lost interest when my mother died. I take the day-to-day decisions. Actually, I take the big ones too.'

'You must have been very young to take on that much responsibility,' observed Gorman.

'I was twenty. And you're right' – she cast him an impish smile – 'I wasn't ready for it. Fantasy stock market is one thing: keeping real lorries on the road earning real money, keeping real drivers in real work, is both harder and scarier. But you do what you have to do. My father helped with the transition of power. At first it was a distraction from the grief and the terrible anger. He taught me how to run his company although he wouldn't have bothered keeping it running for himself. By degrees he handed over control. Now he plays chess with Mrs Fisher, and rails against the world, and wishes he'd died seventeen years ago.'

'Mrs Fisher,' echoed Gorman. 'Was she your housekeeper when the house was raided? The one who was injured.'

Jocelyn nodded. 'She had quite a bad concussion. She tried to keep them out. Three men armed with shotguns, and she tried to fight them off alone. Mrs Fisher and my father have – or at least *had* – a lot in common.'

Before Gorman could respond to that, Miss Harbinger raised her head and called across the knee-high hedges, 'The roses are putting on a good show this year, John.'

The gardener looked round with a grin. Green twine, knives and secateurs overflowed every pocket of his waistcoat. 'It's that load of farmyard manure I dumped on them in the winter.'

'As I keep telling people,' said Jocelyn, 'everything has its uses. Even bull-shit.'

They walked on. A piece of statuary marked the end of the path and they turned left, along the back of the house. Jocelyn gave Gorman a sideways look and said, 'Are you going to tell me what this is about, Inspector? What it is you suspect my father of having done, except that now you're not sure he's physically fit enough to have done it?'

The DI debated with himself but not for long. He could try again to interview Harbinger, but he wasn't sure how hard he could press him or how much weight he could put on anything he said. Or he could try to find out how much Jocelyn knew, and how much of that she was prepared to tell him. If he came back another time she would be ready for him, would have decided how much information she was willing to share. This was not a woman it would be easy to take off-guard, but his best chance was right now.

He said, 'Are you aware that your father threatened the family of the man he blamed for your mother's death? The insurance company's negotiator?'

'Edward Cho? Yes, Inspector, I was there when he did it.' She stopped and turned to face him, her eyes unapologetic. 'His wife had just been gunned down in a confrontation he'd been promised wouldn't happen. Mr Cho made him that promise. Then car-loads of policemen came streaming round the corner like a Wild West show, and one of them shot her. Did *you* know that?' She saw in his face that he hadn't, and her voice softened a little. 'No. It makes his anger a little more understandable, doesn't it?'

'I had no idea . . .' stumbled Gorman. 'Shit.'

Jocelyn raised one cool eyebrow. 'I would have thought it was a matter of record.'

'It will be,' he managed; and managed not to add, Unless someone's erased it. 'I haven't seen all the records yet. It's an old case.' He winced. That was less than tactful.

Jocelyn thought so too. Her tone grew frosty. 'I know. My father could tell you how old, in years, months, weeks and days.'

And this, thought Gorman despairingly to himself, is what happens when you go into an investigation half-prepared. When you ask questions without knowing what the answers ought to be. When the interviewee knows more about your case than you do.

He pushed his hands deep into his pockets and raised his shoulders ruefully. She must think this is Amateur Night, he thought despairingly to himself. Aloud he said, 'I'm sorry, Miss Harbinger. I didn't know your father was disabled. I didn't know your mother was killed by a police firearm.'

'It was an accident, of course,' conceded Jocelyn. 'He'd been shot himself – his gun went off as he fell. He wasn't to blame. Whoever sent him was to blame.'

Gorman sidestepped that. 'What I do know is that Mr Harbinger threatened the entire Cho family, and that Edward Cho was dead within a fortnight and his wife a few weeks later. And a week ago there was an attempt to abduct their daughter. I suppose what I'm asking is if your father's still strong enough and still angry enough to be responsible for that.'

Jocelyn went on regarding him steadily, her expression unchanging. She said nothing for so long that Gorman thought she was refusing to answer. Then she drew a deep breath and said, 'My father *did* threaten the Chos. Mr Cho came to our house three days after my mother's funeral, to express his regrets. I hope he wasn't expecting absolution, because he was never going to get it. Not from my father, and not from me.

'When someone you love dies, Inspector – even in normal circumstances, even when it wasn't violent and unnecessary – the full impact of it doesn't hit you right away. Shock cushions you at first. Then, as the shock starts to recede, there are things to do – people to notify, arrangements to make, decisions to be made. So many things. They add up to a kind of tide that sweeps you along, so you're doing what needs doing but it doesn't feel like *you* doing it. You're not really *feeling* anything much at all.

'Once all the things that need doing have been done, and there's time to stop and think, *that's* when you start feeling it. When you really start to understand what's happened, what you've lost. When all the people who came round with food and sympathy have left and you're alone, and the house is quiet and grey and so empty you don't think you can bear it.

'And that, Inspector,' she went on, still holding his eye with the icy emeralds that were hers, 'is when Mr Cho arrived at the front door. I'm sure he didn't mean to make things worse. I'm sure he thought he was just leaving a decent interval, and then doing what he believed he ought to do. I don't think he was a monster. I think he was a decent man who wasn't up to a difficult job, and he made a mistake. Talked to someone he shouldn't have done about something he should have kept quiet about. Maybe that's why he came here, to explain what went wrong. I don't know. My father wouldn't hear him out.'

She turned away then and resumed walking slowly, Gorman at her side. 'That's when he threatened Mr Cho and his family. It's perfectly true: that's what he did. There was nothing ambiguous about it. Mr Cho said he knew what we were going through. My father said he didn't, not yet, but he was going to.

'You see, all those early days when there was so much to arrange, he'd managed to hold himself together. Rigidly. He was like a man made of ice: cold and clear and brittle, and I was terrified – *terrified* – that the next thing that touched him would break him in a million pieces.

'And then Mr Cho tried to apologise. He'd promised to keep my mother safe, and she was dead, and Edward Cho stood in our hallway and tried to *apologise*!' She vented an unsteady sigh. 'And my father lost control. All the pain, all the rage, all the bitterness, rose up like one of those great geysers and shot out, boiling and steaming, and Mr Cho was the one standing too close.

'So yes, he did threaten Cho's family. He said anything and everything he could think of to hurt and frighten the man. It wasn't nice. It wasn't edifying. But, Inspector, apart from the minute or two it took to spew out, it wasn't *meant*. My father was a businessman, he ran a trucking company – there was never any prospect that he'd take out a contract on someone. Even someone he was so angry with. He was never going to have anyone killed! Only, for a few minutes, while the grief was bubbling over, it gave him some comfort to say that he was. To strike fear into the heart of the man responsible for my mother's death.'

Dave Gorman knew perfectly well that most threats are not to be taken seriously, that they perform the same function as a pressure-valve. 'And yet,' he said quietly, 'Edward Cho *is* dead.

His wife is dead. And now their daughter has been the subject of an attack.'

Jocelyn Harbinger tossed her head dismissively. 'Edward Cho died in a car accident on a notoriously icy road on a winter's evening. His wife committed suicide. As for their daughter, I know nothing about her. I do know that my father is no longer capable of pursuing a vendetta even if he wanted to.'

The problem was, Gorman thought she was right. Jerome Harbinger was a shadow of the man he must once have been. The wheelchair wouldn't keep him from taking a murderous revenge: a man with financial resources can buy whatever help he requires, even that kind of help. But men with a purpose, even a twisted purpose, don't look as Harbinger looked now. They remain focused, braced by the hunger and the single-minded determination to feed it. It was Gorman's instinct that, if Jerome Harbinger had been behind the attack on Elizabeth Lim, he wouldn't have looked so very diminished now. That a cause this important to him would have kept him from crumbling into peevish, fractious old age.

He couldn't afford to trust his instinct; and he couldn't afford to ignore it. Harbinger was a chess-player – a *good* chess-player. It was conceivable that his broken titan act was exactly that: a performance, designed to throw investigators off the scent. Or that while the manifestations of age and deteriorating faculty were indeed genuine, the hatred still burned brightly enough within him to keep his vicious dream alive. No one was suggesting he was one of the men in the van. To finish what he'd started seventeen years earlier, all he had to do was use a telephone and make a bank transfer. Someone determined enough could do it from an iron lung, let alone a wheelchair.

'The night that he died,' he said, 'had Edward Cho been to this house?'

'Certainly not,' said Jocelyn shortly. 'Don't you think he knew by then that he wasn't welcome here?'

'He might have come anyway, if your father had asked him to.'

'Why would we have wanted to see Cho again? The man was nothing but bad memories to us.' She considered for a moment. 'Why are you asking?'

'Because that road up the Clover Hill isn't one he would

have had much occasion to use. It would take him home to Coventry, but not from anywhere that we know he had a reason to be. His office was in Birmingham. He visited clients in various places, but the only house we *know* he visited in this area is this one.'

'And look how well that turned out,' said Jocelyn Harbinger sourly.

Either there was nothing more she could contribute, or nothing more she would. 'I will need to speak to your father again,' Gorman said.

Jocelyn Harbinger's jaw came up. Her green eyes sparkled, as if the ice was reflecting firelight. 'As you wish. But not now. I shall require his solicitor and his doctor to be present. You can make an appointment, if you like.' A kind of terse humour crept into her voice, making it a challenge. 'Or you could arrest him, and I'll bring them down to your police station. Norbold, did you say? Well, that'll give the *Norbold News* something a bit punchier for its front page than the usual dog and pony show. *Geriatric cripple accused of murder: DI helps defendant up police station steps.*'

Gorman chewed his lip reflectively. He wasn't afraid of anything she could do to him. He wasn't afraid of looking like an idiot: it wouldn't be the first time, it wouldn't be the last. He wasn't even afraid of being wrong. But he didn't want to find himself doing something inappropriate just because she'd told him he couldn't.

'I can come back tomorrow,' he said calmly. 'Or if that doesn't suit, I can come back the next day.'

'Fine,' she said.

Gorman became aware of a presence at his back. The gardener had found a reason to push a barrow-load of clippings up behind them, although there wasn't a compost heap in sight. 'Everything all right, Joss?'

'Hm?' She looked past Gorman's elbow in surprise, as if momentarily she'd forgotten she employed a gardener. 'Oh . . . yes. Yes, of course, John. Are we in your way? I think we're about finished, aren't we, Inspector?'

Gorman smiled politely. 'Until tomorrow.'

FOURTEEN

Hazel did as she'd been told: she went to help Ash in his shop. Perhaps because it was Saturday morning, this was one of those rare occasions when there were customers – customers plural; two women who arrived together and a young man who came in on his own – so she put the kettle on then drifted over to the long table to see what he'd laid out by way of temptation today.

'Dickens,' said the young man who'd quietly drifted over to join her. 'And some poetry.'

'Never saw the point of Dickens,' sniffed Hazel. 'Jeffrey Archer with warmer vests.'

The young man looked taken aback. 'Er . . . well. It's a point of view, I suppose. How do you feel about the First World War poets?'

She shrugged. 'How many rhymes are there for "mud"?'

Gabriel Ash was in many ways a terrible businessman. He didn't know anything about running a shop, he didn't need the income and he didn't like having too many customers. But he had a keen instinct for when Hazel was burning on a short fuse. He left the women perusing a collection of the Brontës, put a friendly arm around Hazel's shoulders and steered her firmly towards the kitchen at the back.

Patience, who was lying under the long table with Spiky Ball between her paws, watched them go with placid, toffee-coloured eyes.

When Hazel was perched on the counter with a steaming mug in her hands, Ash asked, 'What's happened?'

She told him everything. Ash heard her out in silence, giving nothing away. Hazel finished sourly, 'And Dave Gorman won't let me help, even though he'd know nothing about any of it if it wasn't for me!'

'But now he does, it's his job to investigate. It says so on his door: Criminal Investigation Department. You're paid to maintain law and order.'

'Not today. I'm on holiday.'

If Ash felt his heart sink, he managed to keep it off his face. 'Good. What are you going to do?'

'I *was* going to help Dave Gorman. He said I should come and help you.'

Gee, thanks, thought Ash. Aloud he said, 'Then stop upsetting my customers. I don't get so many I can afford to have them frightened off.'

'Then what *am* I supposed to do?'

She sounded like a child on the second week of the summer holidays, and Ash almost answered in the same vein: 'Have you cleaned your room? The dog needs brushing. When did you last write to your pen-friend?' It was curious, and just a little sad, how the return of his children had altered the relationship between him and Hazel. Sometimes he almost forgot she was a woman and a friend, and thought of her a little like a third son. Older and more responsible than Gilbert and Guy, but still not entirely mature. A moody teenager, now generous, now in rebellion.

But it wasn't Hazel who had changed, it was him. When they'd first met she had made time to help him, although her days were already full and he had nothing but time. Now he was busy with his children and his shop, and Hazel would have been less than human if she hadn't noticed that their friendship was having to take a back seat. Ash regretted that, but didn't know an answer to it that didn't involve inserting another three hours into every day.

He couldn't say any of this to her. He focused on the question she'd asked. 'How much background does Dave have to the Harbinger case?'

'All of it,' said Hazel, puzzled. 'In the files.'

'Perhaps he doesn't want to call up the files. If he's been told to leave the matter alone, and then he puts in a request for the Harbinger file . . .'

Hazel caught the direction of his thinking like a hound winding a fox. Her head came up and her eyes widened. 'Yes. If ACC-Crime wants the lid kept on this, he'll have put a note on the file so he'll be informed if anyone asks for it. Rather than risk that, Dave's probably working in the dark.'

'You can't pull that file either. But you could get together as much information as was made public at the time. Harbinger was a rich man and his wife died in a shoot-out: the newspapers must have been full of it. And IT is your thing, isn't it? You could probably put together a file every bit as good as the one Dave would ask for if he dared.'

Hazel brightened at the thought of useful activity. 'Of course I can. Like you say, the Harbingers were important people – reporters on all the nationals must have spent hours dredging up facts about the art theft, the police raid and the aftermath. There'll have been inquests on Edward and Mary Cho, too. Whatever's in the public domain, I'll find it.'

'Excellent,' said Ash, satisfied. Nothing could have pleased him more than the thought of her sitting safe at a computer screen for the next few days.

Not for the first time in these last months, Hazel wished her friend Saturday was here. She no longer thought of him with the sharp pain of grief and guilt that had been enough to make her catch her breath; but the missing him hadn't gone away. She still sometimes heard the narrow stairs of her little house in Railway Street creak, and took it for his footsteps. She still occasionally found herself making late-night cocoa for two.

By any objective measure, he had been a terrible lodger. On what he earned, his contribution to the household had been minimal – leaving school at fourteen to live off his wits on the streets of Norbold hadn't qualified him for anything better than the late-night shift at a service station – and the trouble he'd brought to her door should have outweighed any pleasure she'd found in helping him. Additionally, he left a tide-mark round the bath and could never be induced to put used pots into the dishwasher; and on top of *that*, he put her to the expense of a new hall carpet by braining someone with a cricket bat on the stairs. Yet she missed him. Never a day passed but that she thought about him, and wondered where he was and what he was doing, and even if he was still alive.

Today she had a particular reason for missing him. Hazel

knew computers inside out. She'd taught IT before going into the police. She could do with them just about everything that could legally be done. But somehow Saturday, despite living for years in squats with no broadband and often no electricity, had acquired computer skills that left her gasping. He could do all the things that *couldn't* be done legally.

But though liquor is quicker, candy is still dandy. Time and again in training, she'd been reminded that getting the answer right was more important than getting the answer fast. That used to mean struggling through piles of paperwork, and asking for documents that were being held elsewhere, and being sent the wrong ones, and sending them back and waiting for the right ones, and hoping to God that no one had spilled coffee on a vital page. Electronic data retrieval did away with all that. It was still grunt work, but it was now possible to achieve in hours what used to take days or even weeks. Hazel tried to remember how lucky she was as her eyes started to burn and go red, and then to cross at all the print dancing across her screen.

But she *was* getting a lot of material, and she was fairly sure that the solid core of it was going to be valuable. There were newspaper reports on the robbery and, three months later, the death of Mrs Harbinger. There were reports of the death, two weeks after that, of Edward Cho. She found no suggestion of foul play – he was driving home up a notoriously treacherous hill on a frosty winter's evening – but she did discover where the funeral was held, and that led her to the Parish Church of Saints Philip & James in the leafy suburbs of Coventry.

Further surfing established that the current vicar was too recent an arrival to have conducted the service, but that the incumbent seventeen years ago was Reverend Martin Wade, now serving time as a prison chaplain in Birmingham. She found a contact number for him and tried it, without success. She left a message, and fifteen minutes later he got back to her.

It might have occurred to her at that point that, while trawling the Internet could hardly be described as interfering in a CID investigation, interviewing a potential witness certainly could. In fact, she entirely failed to notice the line she was blithely stepping over. She was just gathering information; the Chos' family priest might be able to add to that fund; if he was happy to talk to her, she saw no reason not to talk to him.

She offered to meet him at the prison. He suggested the more congenial surroundings of a tea-room near the Bull Ring, and he was waiting when she arrived, a younger man than she was expecting with a beard and an almost piratical expression to go with it.

He spotted her before she spotted him, and only partly because the other customers were women doing their weekend shopping, encumbered with carrier bags and small children. 'I saw your picture in the paper.'

'Oh God,' she groaned; and then, apologetically, 'Oh . . . sorry.'

Martin Wade grinned. 'Better to take the Lord's name in vain than forget it altogether.'

'That must have been on one of the tablets that got broken.'

He liked that. He laughed, showing strong, perfect teeth. 'What can I do for you, Constable Best?'

Given his willingness to co-operate, she felt obliged to be honest. 'Call me Hazel. I'm not sure the "constable" bit is appropriate, just at the moment.'

'They've sacked you again?' Clearly, Hazel wasn't the only one who could do a bit of research on the Internet.

'They never sacked me before!' she retorted indignantly. Several of the shopping ladies looked up from their toasted tea-cakes. 'They suspended me from duty, but they never sacked me. They still haven't. It's just, this isn't entirely official. I don't have the authority to demand answers from you if you want to stand on your rights.'

The chaplain squinted at her, looking more like a pirate than ever. 'Why don't you ask the questions, and we'll see if I have any problems with the answers?'

Hazel was happy with that. 'I told you on the phone I needed some information about your time at Saints Philip & James.'

Wade nodded. 'Good old Pip & Jim. It's ten years since I left there.'

'How long were you there?'

'Also about ten years. It was my first parish.'

'I thought you must have been pretty young. Oh, sorry,' she

said again, blushing, 'that's rude. Only I was expecting someone on a Zimmer frame.'

He smiled, soft-eyed with reminiscence. 'I was young. About your age. So' – he spread his hands as if in benediction – 'what is it you want to know?'

'There was a Chinese family in your congregation. Father, mother, son, daughter. You conducted a funeral for the father, seventeen years ago. Edward Cho.'

'Yes.' Wade remembered clearly. 'In fact they were an Anglo-Chinese family – Mary was English. Edward was born here too, although his parents came from Hong Kong.'

'How much did you know about the circumstances of his death?'

Wade shrugged. 'What I was told; what the papers said. There was no evidence that it wasn't an accident, but there was that lingering suspicion. You know about the Harbinger affair – about Jerome Harbinger threatening him?' Hazel nodded. 'The family didn't believe it was an accident. But then, it can be hard to accept something as random as dumb chance. People look for a reason.'

'Do you remember who was at the funeral?'

'Mary, of course, and their children, James and Felicity.' It was the first time Hazel had heard Elizabeth Lim's real name. 'There were people from Edward's firm there, and what you might call the old retainers – members of the congregation who turn out for just about anything in the church. The verger, the organist, the parish secretary.'

'Any close friends of the Chos?'

Wade's face twisted with the effort to remember. 'I'm sure there were. They were regular church-goers – not just hatches, matches and despatches, not even just Christmas and Easter. Mary was in the Mothers' Union, Edward used to help with the grounds maintenance. Everyone liked them. If there was any racial prejudice against them, I wasn't aware of it. But they were a quiet family. Polite but self-contained. I don't remember anyone being particularly close to them – seeing them outside of church, for meals or holidays or . . .'

The sentence died away. He looked at Hazel with a new sharpness in his eye. 'So maybe there *was* some prejudice, and I just missed it. Maybe they were aware of it.'

Hazel was disappointed. She'd hoped there might have been someone Lim would have risked keeping in touch with. A godparent, a neighbour or a school-friend she was unwilling to part from even though she knew the risks. But anyone that close would have been there to support her at the funeral.

If Wade couldn't help her, she'd be reduced to trying house-to-house enquiries in the street where the Chos had lived, and a visit to Felicity's school. But it was all seventeen years ago: young people move, old people die; elderly people forget.

And maybe there was nothing to find. They were a self-contained family with no close friends. They were polite, and people were polite back, but no one wanted to know them better. Maybe it had been easier for Edward Cho's children to turn their backs on the home of their youth than Hazel had imagined.

'You haven't asked about Mary's funeral,' Wade said suddenly.

'I wasn't sure if you conducted that or not.'

The chaplain pursed his lips. 'On the whole, I prefer "officiated". "Conducted" sounds like waving a stick to keep the pall-bearers in step.'

Hazel smiled dutifully. 'So she was buried from the church?'

'Ah.' Again that sharp look. 'You mean, although she committed suicide.'

'That's what the police thought. What the coroner believed.'

'There was no evidence of foul play. But absence of evidence is not—'

'—Evidence of absence,' Hazel finished. 'You must know my first sergeant. No, I'm not sure I believe it, either.'

'It's one hell of a coincidence that Edward drove off an icy road *and* Mary drowned herself before the earth had settled on Jennifer Harbinger's grave.'

That took Hazel by surprise. She was a police officer – a nasty suspicious mind came with the truncheon and the sensible shoes. She hadn't expected a man of the cloth to share the same jaundiced view of his fellow men.

Wade read her mind and flicked a tiny smile. 'I don't know if Edward's death was an accident. I don't know if Mary intended to die in her bath, if she fell asleep or if someone killed her. I hoped the police would establish the truth, but the investigation seemed to peter out. I thought at the time there was a certain lack of effort, but perhaps there was nothing to find.'

He seemed then to change the subject. 'Do you know how many suicides I've buried, Constable . . . Hazel?' She shook her head. 'Absolutely none. I don't believe in suicide as a concept. I think that people who end their own lives have been driven to it – by circumstances, by illness, by mental frailty. If even the law doesn't pillory people for things they do under duress, why should the Church? Why would a loving God?'

But Hazel had seen too many things to believe in a God who saw the fall of every sparrow. 'If one or both of the Chos *were* murdered, it's possible their children are now in danger.' She summed up in a few sentences the incident at Norbold Quays and the subsequent disappearance of the high school principal. 'We want to be sure that they're safe. But we don't know where to find either of them. Do you remember where they went to school? It's a long shot, but they may have stayed in touch with old school-friends.'

Wade hardly had to think. 'Borough High, a few hundred yards from the church. Penelope Reid, our organist, was the music teacher there until she retired. She was always proud of how well Felicity had done for herself.'

'Would it be worth me talking to her?'

'I wish you could.' Wade gave a gentle smile. 'I buried her last spring.'

Hazel looked up sharply. 'Anything odd about that?'

He stared at her. 'Good grief, no. The woman was eighty, she broke her hip falling off a chair while she was cleaning her windows, and succumbed to pneumonia.'

So anything the organist had known had died with her; and probably there had been nothing. The Cho children had done the sensible thing, the thing that people in their position are always advised to do and always find so hard: they had severed all contact with their previous lives.

Except . . .

'She knew Felicity was a teacher, then.'

'It gave her real pleasure. It's human nature, isn't it? – we like to see people we care about following in our footsteps. Penelope steered Felicity towards teaching because she thought she'd be successful. But principal in her early thirties – that was more than even Penny had expected.'

'How did she know?'

Wade raised a grizzled eyebrow. 'Hm?'

'Mr Wade, Felicity Cho disappears from the record at the age of sixteen. Elizabeth Lim goes to university, becomes a teacher, becomes principal at Norbold Quays. How did your organist know it was the same girl?'

Wade's mouth opened and shut a couple of times but no answer was forthcoming. He knew he'd dug himself into a hole.

Hazel said softly, 'You've been in touch with Elizabeth Lim, haven't you? You knew at least something of her new life – the one that was created to keep her safe, the one she wasn't supposed to share with anyone from before. You knew, and you told Penelope Reid – or maybe the other way round. But you knew.'

FIFTEEN

The chaplain spent what seemed a long time considering his options. But actually there were only two: to persist in what was plainly a lie, or to tell the truth. 'You're right. I have heard from her. Not regularly – three or four times a year. And about as often from James. They leave messages with me for one another. They didn't want to risk having each other's phone numbers or addresses, so they leave messages with me. Sometimes it's months before a message is collected, sometimes just days. When one of them calls, I ask how they're doing – if they're safe, if they're happy. Felicity told me something about her career, and I told Penny. I trusted her to keep it to herself, and she did.'

'Did James tell you where he's living now?'

'London. He's working as an accountant in some big London company.'

'What name does he go by?'

'I don't know. I haven't asked, and he hasn't told me.'

'Can you contact him?'

'I can't contact either of them. I wait until they contact me.'

'Excellent,' said Hazel tartly. 'That is entirely sound practice, recommended in all the best manuals. Unfortunately, while we're waiting for them to call you, the people who traced Felicity to Norbold Quays are still looking for her. It won't take them another seventeen years to find her again.'

'I understand your concern,' said Wade calmly. 'But they've got pretty good at this, Felicity and James both. They've stayed safe all this time by adopting new identities and not letting anyone know who or where they are. What can you offer that's better than that?'

Which was a very good question. Hazel could see why the Chos felt that running and hiding was their best chance of escaping Jerome Harbinger's everlasting fury; but she was a police officer, and though she knew it was an imperfect system, she believed that keeping people safe was the job of the police. She understood why the Chos felt disinclined to trust their lives to a force which had served them so poorly in the past, but she still thought it was their best chance of a future.

'I don't want them to be running scared for the rest of their lives,' she said simply. 'I want this resolved. That's something they can't do for themselves. It's something you can't help them with. It's going to need resources only the police can provide.

'You're going to tell me,' she went on, forestalling Wade's interruption, 'that we haven't distinguished ourselves up till now in protecting the best interests of either family, the Harbingers or the Chos. And I have to admit you have a point. There could be a number of reasons for that – incompetence, malice or just bad luck. But we are the duly appointed authority, and if we're not doing our job well enough, the answer is to make us do it better, not to look for some way of getting it done without us. The hand-crafted version may look as good at first glance, but sooner or later it will unravel and there'll be no one to pick up the stitches. That's where we are now.'

Wade was watching her levelly. 'Incompetence, malice or bad luck. Where are you putting your money?'

Hazel actually shivered. 'Honestly? I don't know. Could be

any of them; could be a bit of all three. I hope – I *hope* – no one took a deliberate decision to turn a blind eye to murder. That no one considered the deaths of Edward and Mary Cho a price worth paying to cover up police culpability in the death of Mrs Harbinger. That's the worst-case scenario. Incompetence? Well, that's sometimes just a word for good intentions having bad outcomes. And sheer bad luck can play a bigger role than any of us likes to admit.

'But even this long after, things can be put right. Bad decisions can be revisited. Corrupt officers, if that's what we're dealing with, can be made accountable. The police service is nobody's private army: if the chief constable himself is implicated, he won't be able to prevent a proper investigation once we start throwing all the doors and windows wide and shaking out the carpets.'

Hazel took a much-needed breath. 'I can see how lies and secrecy kept James and Felicity safe for a time. But now, secrecy is on the side of their enemy. The shadows that sheltered them for so long are now protecting the man threatening them. We need to bring the whole sorry business out into the light of day, and state publicly what's been going on and who's to blame. That's where their long-term safety lies. I think it's the only way they'll ever be safe again.'

'You want them to trust you.'

'That's exactly what I want. I want them to trust *me*. Maybe they can't trust something as big and faceless as a police force, but they can trust *me*. And I trust DI Gorman. We will figure this out. We will give them a better option than cutting themselves adrift from their lives every few years. In the meantime' – she pushed a card across the table to the sometime vicar of Pip & Jim's – 'if you hear from either of them, please – *please* – ask them to contact me. We can protect them if they'll let us. If they won't, someone else may find them before we can.'

Wade nodded, and took the card and left. Hazel thought he would do as she asked, if he got the chance. But there were so many imponderables. Whether either of the Chos would call him in the near future. Whether they would be willing to entrust their safety to a provincial detective inspector and an even lowlier uniformed constable. Whether she could keep her promises.

We can protect them . . . Was that even true? Could Hazel count on the professional skills and goodwill of her superiors? Edward Cho had thought he could, and his mistake had cost lives and might yet cost more. Why *had* the police stormed the handover, the climax of delicate negotiations, with such devastating effects? A misunderstanding? A cold-blooded lie? Had someone in a comfortable office at Division decided it was more important to prevent thieves from prospering than it was to protect the innocent parties involved?

And if that person *still* occupied a comfortable office at Division, he had a vested interest in how these events played out. He might prefer to keep the file at the back of the Cold Case cabinet rather than see it cleared up, at least – he was seventeen years older now – until his pension came through. He might be able and willing to obstruct any inquiries that would expose that old decision to new scrutiny.

Hazel sipped her tea while a notion formed. Then she took out her phone. When it came to technology, she was an early adopter. She used her mobile as a pocket computer, would have felt hamstrung without Internet access.

It took her half a minute to find the information she was looking for. 'Oh you *bastard*,' she swore softly.

Two middle-aged ladies at the next table glanced sternly her way. Swearing is still disapproved of by middle-aged, middle-class ladies in tea-rooms. But Hazel was too intent on the miniature screen, and the mental arithmetic that made the disparate facts add up to one unwelcome whole, even to notice. So she went on, *sotto voce*, oblivious of her audience.

'You *utter* bastard. What's the reason this time – a CBE? You only need to stay out of trouble long enough and the country will express its gratitude in the usual way? But not if the Harbinger case makes it back onto the front pages. Not if the media blame you for what happened to Jennifer Harbinger. As long as no one starts digging up the old controversy, you can complete your service and take your pension and wait for the envelope with the royal monogram on it. And if that means turning your back while one man you've wronged takes his vengeance on the family of another, well, he's rich and they're outsiders, and with luck no one else will ever know.

'You think your reputation is worth people's lives? How dare you? How *dare* you? You took the same oath I did, you bloody, bloody man!' And with that she shoved herself back from the table and stalked out of the café, trailing startled looks in her wake.

'ACC-Crime.'

DI Gorman had the attentive look of a spaniel that's heard someone load the shotgun and is waiting for the bang. He went on waiting. He was, he thought, reasonably good at putting two and two together. Even so, he needed more than three letters and a word to sink his teeth into.

Hazel tried to bridle her impatience. Talking to Dave Gorman wasn't like talking to Ash. He didn't pick the thoughts straight out of her head while she was still hunting for the words. Of course he didn't: no one else did either. It was her job to explain what it was that her quick trawl of the Internet had confirmed.

'He's been a dragging anchor on this inquiry since it started. He wouldn't believe that Elizabeth Lim was the target until she disappeared; and when she did, he was determined to consider the matter closed. He ordered us to waste no more time on the case. I think he also put pressure on Gabriel to keep him from helping us.'

Gorman was nodding slowly. 'OK, maybe he did all those things. So?'

'He was so worried about what a proper investigation would turn up that he dropped every obstacle he could think of in your way.'

That too seemed a tenable interpretation of the facts. 'Why?'

'Because if Elizabeth Lim leaves Norbold voluntarily and is never heard of again, and if some London accountant whose name we don't know is fished out of the Regent's Canal after an unfortunate accident with his concrete water-skis, those are two incidents no one has any reason to connect – with each other, with Norbold, or with an art theft seventeen years ago. But if someone joins the dots, that file isn't going back in the cabinet.'

'Why would ACC-Crime care?'

Hazel gave a brittle smile. 'I don't suppose you know off-hand where he was working seventeen years ago. But I wonder if you could guess?'

She saw the thought splash down in his eyes and sink through his brain. She saw understanding gain a hold, and after understanding an indignation to match her own. 'It was his decision to send in the snatch-squad?'

'I can't prove that,' Hazel admitted. 'But he was working at Division, and he was one of the handful of officers who might have made that decision. It could have been one of the others; it could have been a joint effort. But he's the one who has been actively trying to draw a veil over what happened that night.'

'So . . . he found out about the exchange, and his decision to crash the party resulted in the deaths of three innocent people.' Gorman's voice was a low growl as he mentally ticked the boxes. 'He'd expected plaudits and promotion for what he confidently expected would be seen as a major coup. Instead it turned into a disaster and somebody's head was going to roll. He thought his career was over.

'But then the storm-clouds parted and Edward Cho drove into the Clover Hill dam. So hey, guys, there's our scapegoat – if we all agree it was his fault, who's going to argue?'

'Only maybe Edward Cho didn't drive off the road. Maybe he was driven off it,' said Hazel softly. 'By Jerome Harbinger, or by someone acting for him. A month later, someone got at Mary Cho too. This time it was made to look like suicide.'

'You do know what you're saying?' breathed Gorman. 'That the man who is now the senior detective of this force, and probably other senior officers who were part of the decision-making process, opted to ignore two murders because they were afraid of being blamed for the death of Jennifer Harbinger. They started a fire-fight, and Mrs Harbinger was shot dead by a member of the ARU.'

He saw the shock-waves crash through Hazel's expression. 'You didn't know that. Jocelyn Harbinger told me. Everyone who agreed to sending an Armed Response Unit was in a potentially career-ending situation if all the facts came out. It seems they cared more about protecting themselves than the Chos. Seventeen years later, ACC-Crime is still covering his own back rather than doing his job and letting me do mine.'

'At least he arranged new identities for the Cho children,' said Hazel, looking desperately for a silver lining.

'Like hell he did,' snarled Gorman. 'That would have meant admitting that Edward and Mary were murdered. If they did that, quietly closing the file and tiptoeing away was no longer an option. They had to maintain the fiction that Edward died in an accident and Mary killed herself, and therefore the children were in no danger.'

'Then who . . .?'

'Cho worked for a security firm, didn't he? His employers must have done it. That's why we have no record of it.'

'We need to talk to them. What was their name?' Hazel flicked through her notes. 'Cavendo Security.'

Gorman lowered one bushy eyebrow at her. 'Why didn't I think of that? Oh, that's right – I did. There's nothing left of the company. They never recovered from the Harbinger episode. Their negotiator was held responsible for the deaths of Jennifer Harbinger and her chauffeur, and the loss of a valuable painting – none of the big insurers wanted to use them after that. They staggered on for three or four years, then quietly shut up shop and the partners retired to various *costas*. I haven't managed to locate anyone who was on the staff at Cavendo seventeen years ago.'

There was a lengthy pause. Finally Hazel said, 'What are we going to do about Sir?'

'Ask him if it's true.'

'He won't admit it. And we don't actually have any evidence.'

'What else can I do?' Gorman stared at her angrily. 'The genie won't go back in the bottle. I can't pretend we never figured this out. There are still two lives at stake. Harbinger found Elizabeth Lim – Felicity Cho – though it took him seventeen years to do it. He'll find her again. And then he'll find her brother. We cannot stand back and do nothing.'

Hazel felt a great surge of respect for him. Dave Gorman wasn't a man of remarkable intellectual talents. He was just an ordinary decent man who'd achieved a modest success by dint of hard work and long hours; and now he was going to risk it all trying to undo the harm that had been done by more senior, better-paid officers a generation ago. Hazel had no doubt what would happen then. ACC-Crime would call in some favours and his colleagues at headquarters would close ranks to protect him, because he'd do the same for them. They'd hold the line, and hold out for their pensions and their Birthday Honours, and DI Gorman would be remembered – when he was remembered at all – as a detective with a promising future behind him.

Hazel knew this because it had almost happened to her. She knew that Gorman knew it too; and she also knew that knowing how it had to end wouldn't alter his view of what he had to do.

'If you're going to see Sir,' she said, her voice husky with trepidation, 'I'll come too.'

ACC-Crime had a name, although no one used it and many actually forgot it. His name was Thomas Severick, he was fifty-eight years old, and he'd been born in the shadow of Pendle Hill. He spoke with a strong northern accent, though it had taken some effort to maintain it this long. He told people that if they sawed his leg off, it would have *Lancashire* written through it, like a stick of Blackpool rock.

He was the kind of northerner who took a pride in the poverty of his forebears that he would not have taken had they been well-to-do. 'Call that hardship?' he was wont to hoot at startled Londoners. 'We'd have thought a digestive biscuit with a candle on it was a smashing birthday cake. I mind the day twelve of us shared a pea . . .'

Because he was large, and loud, and inclined to boast about things most people would prefer to keep private, it was easy to overlook the most important thing about him, which was that he was very good at his job. You don't become an assistant chief constable without being. You particularly don't become Assistant Chief Constable (Crime) without impressing people time and again with your abilities, your dedication and a track record for making lucky guesses. This may be described as intuition, it may be described as instinct; whatever you call it, it means that when the chips are down and there's nothing to tell you which way to go, more often than not you make the right call. It's not something that can be taught, it's not even something that can be learnt, but it's a priceless talent for a police officer. Tom Severick had it. He had always had it.

He made one of his lucky calls as recently as this week, when he accepted an invitation to speak to students at Hendon Police College. It was a last-minute decision that had his wife hastily pressing his dinner jacket, his driver apologising to her boyfriend, and his secretary shuffling the bookings in his diary like a Mississippi gambler. But it also put him eighty miles away when DI Gorman from Meadowvale Police Station in Norbold arrived at headquarters, seeking an urgent interview.

For a moment Gorman thought it was a lie, that the man had somehow guessed his number had come up and was cowering in his office, making desperate *Don't send him up* gestures at his secretary. Then reality intervened. It was unlikely that ACC-Crime knew why Gorman wanted to see him. He had no reason to think his actions of seventeen years ago were coming back to haunt him now.

The secretary offered Gorman an appointment the following week. Gorman took it, but only to avoid further discussion. His business with ACC-Crime wouldn't wait till next week. If he didn't do this immediately, two really bad things could happen. One was that Elizabeth Lim, who needed the protection that was currently being denied her, could be found dead. The other was that he might find a reason not to do it at all. Dave Gorman worried sometimes, late at night in the privacy of his own head, that he wasn't good enough, strong enough or brave enough to do all the things he expected of himself.

He checked his diary. There was nowhere he had to be tonight. Hendon was a couple of hours down the motorway. If anything trivial came up, DS Presley would deal with it; if anything urgent came up, he could race back. Fighting the desperate hope that something urgent would come up, he let Presley know he was going out – he did *not* let Hazel know – and headed for the M2.

SIXTEEN

Hazel found out later that afternoon, when she called to ask when Gorman meant to beard the lion and learned that he was out and not expected back until after the weekend. She tried his mobile, but he didn't answer, and by then she didn't expect him to. Fuming, she went round to Rambles With Books.

'Dave Gorman's gone to have it out with ACC-Crime.'

'Yes?' Ash was ringing up a sale. It wasn't a big sale, but any sale was still a bit of an event and he liked to squeeze the full measure of enjoyment out of it.

'I told him I'd go with him.'

'Ah.'

Her jaw jutted pugnaciously. 'Ah what?'

'If he'd wanted you to go with him, he'd have told you he was going. If he didn't, that's because he wanted to go alone.'

'But why?'

Ash sighed and put his ledger down. 'I'm only guessing, but it could be because you've developed a habit of spreading troubled waters on oil. I know you think you're right about this. You may well be. But Dave Gorman is more likely to get at the truth by talking to Severick calmly than if you march in there full of righteous indignation.'

'I don't . . .' she mumbled; but she knew that she did.

'What are you afraid of? That Dave will let himself be shouted down? You know him better than I do, but I know him better than that. If he has enough evidence to confront Severick, he'll be ready for whatever response the man makes. Be patient, Hazel. Dave will sort it out, regardless of whose toes he has to tread on.'

'What if we're wrong?' But that wasn't honest either, and she amended it. 'What if *I'm* wrong?'

'About ACC-Crime? That'll be pretty embarrassing. I don't suppose either you or Dave will be on his Christmas card list this year. But what else is he going to do? Sack you? If police officers got sacked for interviewing people who turned out not to have committed crimes, there'd be no one left to direct the traffic. If it's all a series of unfortunate coincidences, that's what Severick will say, and he'll produce either the evidence or a good enough explanation to prove it. Then he and Gorman will get their heads together and find a way to help the Chos.

'But if you're right, nothing Severick says will matter – he won't have the power to damage either of you for very much longer. Be patient, Hazel,' he said again. His dog, thinking she heard her name, pushed her long nose into his hand and he stroked her automatically. 'The world turns, even without you pushing it.'

'I know. It's just . . . there must be *something* I could be doing. I can't just wait for the phone to ring so Dave can tell me if I've made an idiot of myself. Not that I have,' she added robustly. 'This is not the craziest thing I've thought that turned out to be right. You know what they say about women.'

Gabriel Ash hadn't had a very liberal education: a lot of the things they say about women had entirely passed him by. It explained a great deal about him. 'Deadlier than the male?' he hazarded.

Hazel scowled. 'I *mean*, women's intuition. Sometimes we know stuff even when we can't prove it.'

'Courts rather like you to prove it,' Ash pointed out. It was six o'clock on a Saturday evening: there was no sign of a mob preparing to wedge his door open so they could shop for second-hand books out of hours, so he turned the lock and pulled down the blind.

'Preparing a court case and solving a crime are two different things,' said Hazel, a shade pompously. 'Once you know who did what, you can find the evidence for how they did it. Getting the right face in the frame, that's the trick. And intuition can do that when nothing else can.'

'Sergeant Mole?' Hazel was given to quoting her earliest mentor.

'Mm . . .?' Her mind was no longer on the conversation. Her fair brows had drawn together and her forehead wrinkled pensively. 'Gabriel . . . what did you say?'

'Oh Lord.' He tried desperately to remember. 'About what?'

'About the female of the species being more deadly than the male.' She had the quote more accurate than he had.

Ash nodded. 'That. Why?'

After half a minute when her attention was tuned inwards, following new connections through the synapses of her brain, she looked up at him. Her voice held the slight, wondering unsteadiness of someone who'd been blindsided on the road to Damascus. 'Because Jerome Harbinger wasn't the only one who lost someone dear to him that day. Well, maybe he isn't capable any more of taking the revenge he aches for. But his daughter is.'

Tom Severick was on his way down to the hotel bar when he glimpsed, just for a moment, a face he thought he knew. Not one of the ACCs and chief superintendents he'd spent much of the day with and now, after a shower and a change of clothes, he was going to have dinner with, but someone younger and not in possession of a dinner jacket. Someone who looked familiar and out of place at the same time. By the time he looked again, eddies in the crowd round the bar had spoiled his line of sight. But he'd been a police officer too long to dismiss it as a trick of the light. He knew what he'd seen, and he knew that in another minute he'd know *who* he'd seen.

And then he had it. Detective Inspector Dave Gorman, from Meadowvale Police Station in Norbold. It had taken him a moment because, although he'd shouted at him over the phone several times, he'd only met Gorman on a handful of occasions. He hadn't expected to see him here because, frankly, the gathering was several grades above his pay-scale.

It was getting to be a long time since Tom Severick had pounded the beat. But the instincts he'd honed on the streets, that had served him so well on his ascent of the greasy pole, were as strong now as they ever were. Startled as he was to see Gorman here, he immediately knew two things. That the DI was looking for him, and that he meant trouble.

So when Gorman reappeared out of the throng at his side, wearing a ruffianly sports jacket and an expression of dogged determination, he'd barely opened his mouth to say, 'Mr

Severick, I'm DI Gor—' before Severick had him by the elbow, steering him firmly towards the vestibule.

'I know who you are, son,' he growled softly. 'I don't know what the blue blinding blazes you're doing here, but these people are looking forward to their tea and they don't need you making a scene and putting them off their prawn cocktail.' Tom Severick might have left Pendle but Pendle hadn't left him: in Lancashire you have your dinner in the middle of the working day and your tea when it's done.

There was a little conference room off reception. Severick shoved Gorman inside ahead of him. He was twenty years older than Gorman, but he was quicker on his feet than he looked. Gorman found himself in the empty room almost without knowing how he'd got there.

'I'm not here to make a scene,' he said. 'But I do need to talk to you about Elizabeth Lim, I need to talk to you now, and I need you to be honest with me.'

Severick stared at him in open astonishment. 'You pompous little gobshite! What makes you think you're important enough to be worth lying to?'

Which perhaps wasn't a convincing assault on the moral high ground, but Gorman knew he was more likely to get the truth out of someone who despised him than someone who was afraid of him.

'You know who Elizabeth Lim is.' It wasn't a question.

'Of course I do.'

'And you know she's in danger.'

'I know you've *told* me that. I haven't seen much evidence for it.'

'Two men tried to kidnap her outside her own school!'

'No, they didn't. They tried to kidnap a woman who was there collecting children. The children of a man with, let's say, a curious history. If you want to know what it was all about, don't come pestering me, talk to Gabriel Ash.' He glanced at his watch. 'And while you're doing that, I'll go and get my tea.'

Dave Gorman wasn't easily intimidated. But it's one thing to face down the upper echelons of the criminal fraternity, another to stand up to your own boss. Even so, and knowing that this time next week he could be reading the ads in the Job Centre window, he moved in front of the door. 'I'll buy you a sandwich later. I'm sorry, sir, but I've come too far' – he meant that both ways – 'to be fobbed off. We sort this out now, or I go through channels. It might have been hushed up for seventeen years. It isn't being hushed up any longer.'

ACC-Crime was staring at him as if he was mad. 'Seventeen years? What are you *talking* about? Seventeen years ago you were breaking in your first set of boots. And I . . .'

Then something happened, in his face and behind his eyes. The sort of thing that Gorman might have seen if he'd been standing in the right place when someone was hit by a train. The eyes widened and narrowed and widened again. The mouth formed shapes but no words came. Colour moved up Severick's cheeks in bands: red then white then red again, like the Latvian flag.

When he finally found a voice, it was quieter, shorn of its habitual bombast; he sounded out of breath. There was no doubting the man had suffered a genuine shock. 'Elizabeth Lim. Who is she?'

'You said you knew.'

A flicker of the old arrogance. 'I said I knew who you were talking about – the head teacher of your local high school who resigned over the phone. But that's not what you meant, is it?'

Gorman shook his head carefully. As a police officer, he thought he was pretty good at knowing when he was being lied to. But he'd been a police officer long enough to also know that you could never be sure – you could be wrong both ways. Fail to recognise the truth, and fall for a lie. 'If you don't know who she is, really is, why were you so anxious for me to drop the case?'

'Because there wasn't a case!' insisted Severick. 'Only in your head, and the head of that daft girl you spend far too much time listening to. Competent adults who choose to disappear are not police business. You know that. There are all sorts of reasons why people want to slip out of their old lives and start afresh somewhere else. Unless we have reason to believe they are criminals or vulnerable, they have every right to do so without some under-employed detective inspector waving bits of their clothing in front of the nearest bloodhound!

'We look for missing children. We look for people who are mentally frail or physically ill. We look for old people who might have got on the wrong bus and ended up in Carlisle. We do not look for people who phoned their office to say they wouldn't be coming in any more, and packed a bag and left town. What Elizabeth Lim did might have seemed out of character, but she's an intelligent woman and it must have made sense to her. If she'd wanted our help, she'd have asked for it.'

'What if she'd a good reason for *not* wanting our help?'

'Like what?!'

'Like,' said Gorman through clenched teeth, 'our mishandling of a situation seventeen years ago cost her both her parents, the right to her own name, and any chance of feeling safe ever again. Like, we threw her to the wolves once, she probably expects us to do it again.'

There was a long pause then. Severick appeared to have mastered the shock. Gorman could see him thinking: fragments of expressions raced across his face like wind-shadow, no sooner there than gone. Finally the ACC said, 'You're talking about Felicity Cho.'

Gorman raised a sceptical eyebrow. 'And you never guessed till now.'

The older man bristled. 'Don't get smart with me, sonny, or I'll feed you your own entrails. You said it: it's been seventeen years. I talked to her after her mother died. I don't think I've given her a thought since.'

'You're serious? You want me to believe that you didn't know Felicity Cho and Elizabeth Lim are the same person?'

'Frankly,' snarled Severick, 'I don't care *what* you believe. It happens to be the truth, so you're wasting your time and taxpayers' money believing anything else, but hell, I wouldn't want to be the man who came between you and a good conspiracy theory. Let me guess. I'm somehow responsible for what happened to her mum and dad, and now I want to shut her up too and that's why she's taken to the hills.'

Reduced to a single sentence, it sounded absurd. But it had made sense when he and Hazel had worked carefully through it, and Dave Gorman hadn't heard anything yet to prove they'd been mistaken. A bit of ridicule he could cope with. 'Something like that, sir, yes.'

Severick stared at him angrily. For the first time, the knowledge that he was being accused of something significant, something that wouldn't go away if he shouted loudly enough, showed in his eyes. 'Please,' he said, '*please* tell me you're joking.'

Gorman shook his head. 'No. I'm not.'

ACC-Crime took a careful step backwards and lowered himself onto the edge of the conference table. For a moment he just sat there, breathing deeply and holding Gorman in a wounded but still predatory gaze. Then he said, 'Do we need to get IPCC in here?'

'We might.' The Independent Police Complaints Commission automatically took over investigations into police officers. 'But right now, the priority is to find this woman and make sure she's safe. After that, we can talk about who did what when.'

Exasperation and perhaps a little fear twisted Severick's words into a plaint. '*I* don't know where she is. I've only just found out *who* she is! I wouldn't know where to begin looking for her.'

Gorman didn't want to believe him. This would be so much easier if all he had to do was convince his ACC that giving up his secrets was now the best way forward. If he really couldn't help, Gorman didn't know where else to turn. 'I think her new identity was provided by Cavendo Security, the firm her father worked for. You were at Division then. Did they inform you of what they'd done?'

Severick shook his head. 'No. If anything like that had come in, it would have crossed my desk. If Cavendo acted on their own initiative, they never told us about it.'

'And you didn't see anything odd about both of Edward Cho's kids disappearing? After Jerome Harbinger had threatened to wipe his family out?' Gorman's voice rose in disbelief.

'I didn't know they'd disappeared. I had no reason to contact them again. Anyway, they were always likely to move on – to move in with relatives, to start new careers. They were that age.

I'll tell you again, and after that I don't intend to repeat it: I didn't know that Elizabeth Lim used to be Felicity Cho.'

'Well, *somebody* knew. And made a determined attempt at carrying out Harbinger's threat.'

Severick's hoot of derision almost had to be genuine. 'Jerome Harbinger's an old man! He hasn't been seen in public for years. You think he even cares what became of Edward Cho's daughter?'

'Actually, I do,' growled Gorman. 'I think he meant it, literally and absolutely, when he threatened the whole Cho family. Family annihilation is pretty unusual, but it's a recognised phenomenon in circumstances where passions are running high enough. And Harbinger was, by all accounts, about as angry as a man can get without exploding.

'I think he had Cho run off the road, and I think he probably had someone drown Mary Cho and make it look like suicide. And I think that, if Division hadn't been so anxious to whitewash its own involvement, you'd have come to the same conclusion. If you had, Jerome Harbinger would have grown old in a prison cell, and Elizabeth Lim would not now be running for her life.'

The small conference room was big enough for a dozen desks, or twenty chairs if people took notes on their knees. It was nowhere near big enough for two substantial men, each angry and indignant, each convinced of the superiority of his position and the stupid intransigence of the other's. The amount of testosterone flying round the room would have sent a chimpanzee into hysterics.

'You're blaming me for that?' Severick had often been accused of shouting when he thought he was merely being firm. Now even he realised he was raising the roof, and that there were important people beyond the closed door. He made an effort to rein it in. 'You think *I* sent the ARU that interrupted the exchange? And that, having got his wife killed, letting Harbinger have the Chos was the price of keeping him from coming after me?'

That was pretty much exactly what Gorman thought, so he said so. 'Yes.'

There was nothing refined about Tom Severick. His language

was habitually as fruity as a greengrocer's window. But when he was really shocked he fell back on an old Lancashire expression his father used. 'Well, I'll go to the foot of our stairs!'

Gorman – who was born under the flight-path of Gatwick Airport – wasn't sure if that was an admission or a denial. 'Er . . . yes?'

Severick took a deep breath. In the hall outside, the diners were moving towards their meal. He was hungry too, but this mattered more. 'Right,' he said after a moment. 'Let's make this really simple. You're wrong. The ARU wasn't my call – it couldn't have been, I wasn't working that weekend. That's a matter of record. I was there on the Monday, when the guys whose call it was looked like aristocrats waiting their turn for the guillotine.'

'And yet,' said Gorman tersely, 'no heads rolled.'

'That's right. And do you know why? *Because nobody did anything wrong.* Everybody acted in good faith on the information available to them. That's not me saying that: it's the conclusion reached by the internal inquiry – we didn't have the IPCC then. Due to what the report described as certain weaknesses in strategic leadership, there was no one available at Meadowvale who was both competent and willing to deal with a dangerous and fast-developing situation. Information was coming in quicker than they could process it. Somebody called Division, and we took over. We sent the ARU. Our best guess at that moment was that an armed robbery was in progress.

'We were never informed, officially or otherwise, that an insurance exchange was going down. Cavendo chose to handle the matter on their own. If it had all gone smoothly, everybody would have said it was a good decision.' Severick gave a weary sigh. 'But if Edward Cho had let us know, even on the QT, we could have given them the space they needed until Jennifer Harbinger was safe. Specifically, we could have made sure that no one despatched an ARU because a man wanted in connection with a Post Office raid four months earlier had been seen driving into a supermarket car park.'

Gorman was staring at him, literally open-mouthed. 'The beat officer who spotted a face from a wanted poster? I thought that was an urban myth. You really expect me to believe that everything that followed, including the deaths of four people, was down to good eyesight and bad luck?'

'You don't have to take my word for it,' said ACC-Crime, in a tone that suggested it might nevertheless be a good idea. 'It's all on record. Call up the file. In fact, why haven't you called up the file before now?'

But while Gorman, avoiding his fierce gaze, was formulating a response, Severick had the reason. 'You thought the request would warn me what you were up to. Give me time to – what? – buy a one-way ticket to Venezuela?'

'Pretty much,' muttered Gorman rebelliously. The problem was, he didn't believe it any more. Severick *could* be lying to him – but he couldn't expect to get away with lying for much longer, and Gorman detected no signs of alarm or desperate machination in the man's demeanour.

And coincidences did happen, all the time: it was only when the consequences were startlingly good or devastatingly bad that it started looking like a conspiracy. Someone on routine patrol had spotted a face he'd been told to watch out for, had radio'd it in, and fifteen minutes later the Armed Response Unit had been mobilised. There was nothing intrinsically improbable about a Post Office blagger being recruited for an art raid on a wealthy household.

'Whose mug-shot was recognised?'

Severick's eyes widened. 'Hell's bells, now you're asking. It was seventeen years ago. Harry something. Harry . . . Harry . . . Clark! Harry Clark. Form as a shooter, hence the ARU rather than just the usual half-dozen lucky sods who happened to be nearest.'

'Clark was driving the car?'

'He was. There were two others with him. Clark and another man were taken down at the scene; the third man escaped.'

'With the painting.'

'With the Caravaggio.'

'And Edward Cho never tipped us off? He kept his word?'

'He did,' said Severick, 'more's the pity.'

Gorman thought some more. 'And all this is in the inquiry report?'

'Read it for yourself. There's no reason not to, now,' Severick said heavily.

Gorman shook his head in despair. 'I thought . . . it seemed to make sense . . . I thought you could help me find her. Elizabeth Lim.' His tone hardened. 'But if Harbinger found her, we should be able to, too.'

'Harbinger – if it was Harbinger – found her hiding in plain sight, working in a town twenty miles from where she grew up. Which was *too* close, but she probably felt that the events of seventeen years ago weren't a threat to her any more. Well, now she knows different, and she's gone where she thinks he won't find her again. That makes it harder for us as well. Have you tried talking to Cavendo?'

'It no longer exists. Hasn't for fifteen years. Anyway, what more could they tell us? We know now who Felicity Cho became.'

Tom Severick regarded him with disfavour. 'We *don't* know who her brother became, and he's in the same danger she is. That, presumably, is why the men in the van were told to abduct her rather than kill her – in the hope that she'd lead them to her brother. Well, the same applies to us. Finding one is probably our best chance of finding the other.'

Gorman was silently kicking himself. It was easy to forget that, before he'd attended posh dinners for a living, ACC-Crime had been an experienced and effective investigator. 'How do we even look for the brother? At least we know where Felicity Cho was ten days ago. It's seventeen years since we know where James Cho was.'

Severick shrugged. 'Nobody said it would be easy. Find a line of inquiry and I'll try to help. But not right now. Right now I'm ready for my tea.' He headed determinedly for the door and Gorman moved aside to let him pass. 'I have it on good authority it's Black Forest gateau for afters. I'd invite you to stay, but . . .'

'But what?'

'You might accept.'

SEVENTEEN

Hazel was itching to confront Jocelyn Harbinger. She wanted to put her suspicions to Jennifer Harbinger's daughter because, although she knew they would be denied, she wanted to watch her face as Jocelyn denied them. She believed she could tell when she was being lied to.

Most people think that. Most people are wrong. Many police officers think it as well, and they're mostly wrong too. If they weren't, there would be no miscarriages of justice. Throughout her training, it had been impressed on Hazel that the only way to know if someone was lying was to identify the inconsistencies that broke their story apart. That listening carefully was much more effective than watching their eyes, or their lips, or the way they scratched their nose.

Ash managed to dissuade her from driving out to the Harbingers' home in Spell. 'All you'll do by throwing accusations at her now is warn her she's under suspicion. That won't matter if you're wrong and she has nothing to hide, but suppose you're right. You can't arrest her on the basis of women's intuition. You couldn't even if you weren't on holiday. All you can do is warn her, and give her the chance either to make tracks or to cover them.

'If it is Jocelyn who's threatening Miss Lim, she could put herself beyond pursuit in the time it would take Dave Gorman to get back here and make it official. She could be on an airliner going anywhere. Or she could stay right there in Spell, arm herself with lawyers and defy you prove anything. She could even bring forward her plans to hurt Miss Lim and her brother.'

'I can't do *nothing*,' whined Hazel.

'Yes, you can. Right now, doing nothing would be a really good idea. Doing nothing won't risk compromising a murder investigation. Doing nothing won't bring Dave down on your head, or Division down on his. Doing nothing won't risk your suspect getting out her chequebook and fireproofing herself. In fact, Hazel, right now nothing is much the smartest thing you could do.'

Ash wasn't sure he'd convinced her. He went to make coffee, half expecting she'd have gone when he came back with the mugs. He was wrong: he came back and found her talking on her mobile. Her eyes were wide with astonishment.

It isn't polite to listen to other people's phone-calls. Actually, it isn't polite to answer your phone when you're under somebody else's roof either, but sometimes good manners have to take a back seat. Gesturing with her empty hand, Hazel indicated that she wanted Ash to listen in. He put down the mugs and leaned closer, but the call ended abruptly before he could make any sense of it.

Hazel went on staring at the mute phone for ten seconds before finally putting it back in her pocket and looking up. 'Well.' Surprise had left her breathless. 'You'll never guess who that was.'

Ash considered. 'If I'm patient, I bet you'll tell me.'

'Elizabeth Lim.'

Astonishment is contagious: Ash felt his own jaw dropping. That raised many more questions than it answered. The first was: 'How did she get your number?'

'From Martin Wade. The prison chaplain – I told you about him. They stayed in touch. Lim and her brother used him to pass messages. She called him earlier today, and he told her to call me.'

'Where is she?'

'She wouldn't say. Well, London – but that's the same as not saying.'

'What does she want?'

Hazel didn't answer directly, which wasn't like her. 'Did you get a morning paper?'

'Yes.' Ash and Patience had got in the habit of walking into town to open the shop, picking up the paper, jars of coffee and dog treats on the way. 'It's here somewhere.' He found it on the long table, half hidden by a history of the British royal family.

Hazel found what she was looking for. It hadn't made the front page, but that didn't mean that it wasn't – at least for Elizabeth Lim – the most important item in the paper. Hazel refolded the page and passed it back.

Dockland killing

The body of a young Chinese man was discovered by two schoolgirls walking home through Bermondsey yesterday evening. Police say he was the victim of a sustained knife attack.

Although they are still attempting to identify him, Scotland Yard detectives believe the killing is connected to a recent upsurge in violence between rival gangs operating in the area.

'They found her brother.' Ash's voice was thin, colourless.

Hazel nodded. 'Yes.'

'It was nothing to do with gang warfare.'

'No.'

'And if the Harbingers found him . . .'

'It's only a matter of time before they find her too.'

'What does she want to do?'

Hazel shook her head. 'She doesn't know. She thought she was safe – that they both were. She thought that breaking her trail, and not telling anyone where she was, would be enough to keep her safe. But it didn't keep her brother safe, and now she doesn't know what to do.'

'What does she want *you* to do?'

Hazel gave a wan smile. 'I think she wanted me to tell her what to do. Whether she should come home and ask for police protection, or vanish again and try to buy herself a few more years. I didn't know what to tell her. I said to give me half an hour and I'd call her back.'

'Did she give you her number?'

'No, she rang off.' She gave a little grimace. 'She wants to trust me, she just doesn't know if she can. After what she's been through, I'm not surprised.'

'She was distressed.'

'Of course she was distressed, Gabriel!'

'If she was upset, she may not have remembered to withhold her number.'

Hazel's eyes flared wide with understanding. She snatched her phone out again. Then she looked up. 'So I *can* call her back. If she answers, what do I tell her?'

'You can do more than call her. Or if you can't, Dave Gorman could. He can trace the location of that phone.'

But Gorman wasn't in his office, was thought to be in London, and wasn't expected back until Monday. Hazel dialled his mobile number again. It went straight to voice mail.

'Dave, it's Hazel. I need you to call me as soon as you get this. If you're in London, stay there till we've talked.' She couldn't say any more without compromising herself, or him, if Gorman's phone fell into unsympathetic hands.

Ash was looking at his watch. The boys had bought it for his birthday: it wasn't an expensive one but it gave him more pleasure than if it had been. 'I'd better let Frankie know I won't be home till late.'

Still, now and again, he managed to surprise her. 'We're going to London?'

'If that's where Dave is, and that's where Miss Lim is, it makes sense to meet him there. We'll take him your phone.'

'But I don't know where he is! London's a bit bigger than Norbold, you know?'

'You *will* know where he is, when he phones you. In the meantime, we can be halfway there.'

'Dave isn't the only one who could have Lim's phone traced. Superintendent Maybourne could do it.'

'If she does it, Division will hear about it. If Dave does it, he'll go through Scotland Yard. I bet Miss Lim would rather deal with the Yard.'

Hazel leaned back against the wall of books, regarding him. 'Where is my friend Gabriel, and what have you done with him? The last time we talked about this, you were dead set against us getting involved.'

'The last time we talked, I believed Elizabeth Lim was probably safe. Now I don't.'

Hazel nodded. 'Your car or mine? Mine's outside, but we'll have to drop Patience off at Highfield Road before we leave anyway.'

Ash caught his dog's indignant glance. 'Actually, I don't think we should waste any more time. Will you drive? Give me your phone – I'll talk to Dave when he calls.'

They were barely onto the motorway before the phone rang

– or at least, played the opening bars of the 'Policeman's Song' from *The Pirates of Penzance*. If Gorman was surprised that Ash answered, it didn't show in his voice.

He had left ACC-Crime to his Black Forest gateau and checked his phone before heading back to Norbold. He listened without interrupting as Ash explained the situation. The case for meeting in London rather than at Meadowvale was not spelled out, but was understood as well as if it had been. 'Where shall we find you?'

There was only one answer to that. 'Scotland Yard.'

Gorman had a head start on them: he was coming out of Scotland Yard as Hazel and Ash were coming in. For a moment his focus tripped over the sight of Patience leading the way, a picture as improbable here as it was familiar in Norbold. 'Er . . .'

Hazel gave a weary sigh. 'Don't ask. What's the state of play? Can we get our phone tapped?'

'Technically speaking, it's a phone hack,' said Gorman, who'd been corrected on the same subject half an hour earlier. 'And yes, we can. Of course, Lim may have realised her mistake and dumped the phone after talking to you. But before we start the ball rolling . . .' There he hesitated. He almost seemed to be embarrassed.

Hazel was curious. 'What?'

Gorman grimaced. Screwed up like this, his homely face appeared positively Neanderthal. 'I know this is a stupid question. But before we put ourselves in the hands of the boffins, I suppose you have tried calling her back?'

There was a lengthy pause. Then Ash admitted, 'No, we didn't. I suggested tracing the phone, and we never got round to trying the blindingly bleeding obvious first.' His frustration with himself was evidenced by the uncharacteristic invective.

'She won't answer,' said Hazel quickly. 'I mean, that's how she's stayed safe this long – by avoiding contact with almost anyone who could link her to her old life. She's not going to change that now. Why would she?'

'Because what worked in the past isn't working any more,' said Ash. 'If the Harbingers found James, she has to assume they may be close to finding her. She may be rethinking her strategy.'

'Actually,' said Gorman, 'the strategy worked just fine. The Harbingers didn't find James. The Chinese boy in Bermondsey is not and never was James Cho.'

Hazel stared at him in astonishment. It had never occurred to her to wonder. Elizabeth Lim had told her that her brother was dead, and there was the evidence in the paper. 'Are you sure?'

'Absolutely sure,' said Gorman. 'I talked to the SIO. It was a nineteen-year-old kid caught pushing drugs in the wrong nightclub. His mother's down at the morgue now, identifying him. James Cho will be in his mid-thirties now. There's no way it could be him.'

'Elizabeth saw the same report we did, and jumped to the same conclusion,' guessed Ash. 'And she has no way of discovering the truth, unless the newspaper follows the story up in more detail, but that could be days from now. She still thinks her brother has been murdered.'

'Call her,' said Gorman.

'She won't answer.' But Hazel was already looking for the number.

At least Lim had not destroyed her phone; nor did it go straight to voice mail. But it went unanswered for so long that Hazel was about to ring off when suddenly there was a silence at the other end that meant her call had been picked up. She nodded at Gorman, who moved closer.

'Elizabeth? Elizabeth – don't ring off. It's Hazel Best. I have some really good news for you. That wasn't James who was murdered in Bermondsey, it was a teenage drug pusher who fell foul of a rival gang.'

She thought she heard an intake of breath; nothing more.

'Did you hear me? It wasn't James. I'm at Scotland Yard now with Detective Inspector Gorman, and he's spoken to the senior investigating officer. He knows who the victim was, and it wasn't your brother.'

Gorman was gesturing for the phone. 'Miss Lim? DI Gorman. Hazel's telling you the truth. Unless you have some other reason to believe he's come to harm, James is as safe today as he was a week ago.

'What we don't know is whether either of you is safe enough. You made a mistake when you called Hazel – if you hadn't answered your phone we could have traced it. And what we can do legally, other people can do illegally. It's hard to disappear completely if someone's determined enough to find you. You may have left other clues, or James may have done. I want you to consider coming back with me, letting us keep you safe. Next time your brother calls your vicar friend, I'll tell him the same thing.'

Hazel heard the snort, half derision, half despair, from an arm's length away. 'Back to Norbold? Are you mad? They found me there once already. They know who I am.'

'But we *didn't* know who you are. Now we do, we can protect you.'

'The way you protected my parents? I'm sorry, Inspector, but you must understand how little confidence I have in Norbold police!'

'I do understand that,' said Gorman, his voice low. 'You were badly let down. You may think it was worse than that – that you were sold out. I thought so too, for a time. That's how it looked: as if people whose job it was to protect you took the conscious decision to protect themselves instead. But I don't think that's what happened. I've looked into it, I've talked to people who were directly involved, and I honestly think that circumstances conspired to make a succession of wretched coincidences look like dereliction of duty. And then the people who should have been looking after your family's interests got scared and defensive, and hoped that if nobody rocked the boat, the storm would blow over.

'Maybe you don't want to gamble your safety on my best guess. All I can do is assure you that I haven't finished asking questions – that I *won't* finish until I'm satisfied I have the whole picture, and that no one's managed to airbrush themselves out of it. In the meantime, I don't think you have any reason to be afraid of Norbold police. I *know* you have no reason to be afraid of me.'

More silence. Perhaps she was thinking it over. Or perhaps she'd quietly dropped the phone into a bin and walked away.

'Can we at least meet and talk about it?' asked Gorman. 'Hazel and Gabriel Ash are here. We could all get together and figure out the best thing for you to do next. Name a place: we'll meet you anywhere. If I can't convince you that you'll be safer coming back with us, I won't stop you leaving and I won't try to find you again.'

She hadn't walked away. After a long moment she came up with a name. 'It's a coffee shop in Great Russell Street, opposite the British Museum. I'll see you in there at nine.'

Gorman drove, with Ash giving directions. 'We used to bring the boys here, when they were . . . well, far too young to appreciate it, actually. There's the coffee shop.' He sounded a little surprised. 'It's had a bit of a makeover since I was here last.'

Gorman found somewhere to park. 'Let me do the talking, will you?' He was looking rather pointedly at Hazel. 'I don't want to scare her off. I just need her to listen to reason and make a rational decision.'

'And if her rational decision is to go on trusting her own skills to keep her safe?' Hazel raised an interrogative eyebrow.

'Then that's her choice. I won't like it. I'm pretty sure it'd be a bad idea. But I shan't try to force her to accept our help.'

The golden rule of rendezvous is, Always be the first to arrive. And it was as well they were early, because the first problem presented itself on the pavement outside the coffee shop.

'I can't take Patience inside,' said Ash.

It might have occurred to one of them that this would be a problem before now. But in an odd way they almost forgot she was a dog. She was so much a part of what they did together that both Ash and Hazel tended to think of her more as a dog-shaped person, and not comment on the difference just as well-brought-up people didn't comment on another's lack of stature, excess of substance or eye-popping acne.

Hazel peered round anxiously. If Lim arrived and didn't see them, she would leave and they might never manage to contact her again. 'Can't you . . .?'

If she suggests tying me to the railings, Patience said for Ash's ears only, the answer is No.

But Hazel was looking at Gorman. '. . . Deputise her or something? Make her a temporary acting police dog?'

Gorman treated the suggestion with the disdain it deserved.

'You go ahead,' said Ash. 'Patience and I will wait out here. It's you two Lim needs to talk to anyway. It's you who have to gain her trust.'

So Norbold's finest headed into the café, taking their time, scanning the customers who were already inside. Elizabeth Lim wasn't among them.

Ash looked across at the museum and gave a nostalgic little sigh. It was years since he'd been in London with enough leisure to stand in one of the great hubs of civilisation and observe the city orbiting around him. Because the forecourt of the British Museum is not merely an entrance, it's a venue in its own right. Any time the museum is open, and quite often when it's shut, it's filled with Londoners, with tourists, with students, with many-accented voices struggling to be heard, with the cut-and-thrust of intellectual debate, with bus-loads of excited children who've crossed England to see the mummies, with mummies hunting in panic for mislaid children. If you haven't time enough to see much of London, you can do worse than sit on the steps of the British Museum and let London come to you.

That's what he did now. Though the galleries had closed three hours earlier, there was still a buzz of activity on the plaza outside. Patience at his side, Ash crossed the road and strolled through the forecourt to the broad stone steps where, heedless of his clothes – even at the peak of his earning capacity he'd tended to look as if he dressed from a rummage sale – he sat down to watch London being sociable on a summer evening.

Elizabeth Lim, formerly Felicity Cho, came and stood in front of him. 'Good evening, Mr Ash.'

Ash stood up quickly, brushing grit from his trousers. 'Miss Lim. Or . . .?'

She heard the unspoken question, darted him a fleeting smile. 'Elizabeth Lim has been my name for a very long time.'

'Detective Inspector Gorman and Constable Best went into the coffee shop.' He gestured at Patience. 'We thought we'd wait over here. Shall I phone Hazel, tell her you're on your way? Or ask them to join us here?'

'In a minute.' She leaned her back against the handrail and turned her face to the sky. She looked very tired. Fear will do that. 'How much do you know, Mr Ash?'

'Most of it, I suppose. Except who's doing this to you.'

That made her look at him. 'Jerome Harbinger, of course. Who else would it be?'

He gave an apologetic little shrug. 'It is the likeliest explanation. What we're short of is proof. He's angry enough, but frail.'

Lim's dark almond eyes narrowed. 'My father didn't get the chance to grow old and frail.'

Ash winced as if she'd accused him of something. 'I know. I heard what happened.'

'Which version?' Her voice had a steel string running through it, vibrating with the rage she'd learned to contain. 'The one where he was murdered because of someone else's mistakes? Or the convenient one, where he drove off a steep road on a frosty night?'

'Both,' admitted Ash. 'Whose mistakes? The police?'

Lim shook her head. He'd never seen her with her hair down before; it made her look like a different person. 'The police, yes. But also the people my father worked for. They put him in an impossible position.'

Patience lay down, curled like a stone greyhound on a gate-house pillar, as if she knew they weren't going to be moving soon. Ash thought the same, and sat down again, spreading his handkerchief as a somewhat inadequate picnic rug for Lim. After a moment she took it.

Ash said, 'What happened?'

EIGHTEEN

'You'll have been told my father wasn't very good at his job,' Elizabeth Lim said softly. 'That isn't true. In fact he was very good at his job. He was an accountant. The auditors who reviewed the accounts of Cavendo Security after his death said they were exemplary. Exemplary.' She said it again with quiet satisfaction.

'But he was not just an accountant. He took over much of

the work of the office, leaving the security experts free to do the job they knew. He made such a contribution to the success of the company that he was offered a partnership.'

'He didn't take it?' Ash thought she wouldn't have put it that way if he had.

'He intended to take it,' said Lim carefully. 'But he wanted to learn every aspect of the business first, not just the financial side. He began working with the various specialists. He learned about financial fraud and identity theft, and insurance fraud, and insider trading – all the competencies Cavendo had amassed over the years. And now he was learning about hostage negotiation.

'This is not a major part of security work in England,' she explained. 'Mostly Cavendo were consulted about personnel and assets seized abroad. There were parts of the world where hostage-taking was – probably still is – an important local industry.'

'I know,' Ash said quietly.

'So my father was shadowing Cavendo's chief negotiator, learning how he worked, how he resolved situations. Not with the intention of doing that work himself, but so that he would understand the issues that came up at directors' meetings. So that he would know what he was voting for or against. He wanted to do a good job. He always only wanted to do a good job.'

She took a deep breath. 'Things happen quickly in the security industry. You cannot always know who will be needed and when. Cavendo undertook to have specialists available twenty-four/seven.' She leaned forward then and began to stroke Patience. The dog lifted her head, pressing against the woman's hand.

'It was a family wedding. The chief negotiator had gone to a family wedding. He'd followed protocol and told the office where he'd be, and there shouldn't have been a problem. But people drink at family weddings. They meet people they haven't seen for years, and spend long enough with them to remember why they've been avoiding one another, and there are bottles on every table for the toasts, and when they run low, others appear . . . When the call came in, the chief negotiator wasn't drunk, but he was too drunk to drive and too drunk to work. He had the office call my father.

'It wasn't an unreasonable thing to do,' Lim conceded. 'It should have been a simple negotiation. It concerned property rather than persons, and the exchange would be conducted in England rather than halfway round the world. Even if the negotiation failed, it should only have meant the insurers meeting a bill they'd expected all along. It must have seemed a safe enough task for a less experienced negotiator. And my father had been working with the specialist for some time by then. The company was happy to entrust the matter to him.

'Only after the police interrupted the exchange, starting a train of events which ended with the deaths of Mrs Harbinger and her chauffeur, did the directors of Cavendo decide that my father's handling of the task had been misguided from the beginning. They all remembered advising him to do it differently. They reported finding him stubborn and intransigent. They accused him of having informed the police of the proposed exchange in the hope of both regaining the painting and retaining the ransom, and then lying about it.

'In short, Mr Ash, his colleagues used my father as their scapegoat. They abandoned him to the fury of Jerome Harbinger.'

Ash hesitated for a moment, unsure whether what he was proposing to say would make her feel better or worse. But he thought she would want to know, and that anyway it would come out soon enough now, and she deserved to hear it from him rather than reading it in a newspaper. 'He didn't tell the police. DI Gorman can confirm that. They had no idea what was going on at the supermarket that night. One of the gang was recognised by a routine patrol as a person of interest in a previous robbery: he was followed to the car park where the exchange was to take place, and an Armed Response Unit were sent to make the arrest.'

One great tear gathered in the corner of each almond eye as Elizabeth Lim stared at him. 'Truly? You can prove that my father kept his word? That he didn't gamble with Mrs Harbinger's life in order to safeguard the insurers' profits?'

Ash nodded. 'It was a terrible coincidence. Your father promised Harbinger the police wouldn't be informed, and they weren't. They stumbled on what they thought was an armed robbery, and acted accordingly.'

'Then why didn't they *say* so? Why did they let Mr Harbinger believe that my father betrayed him?' Her voice broke with the pity of it.

All Ash could offer was an apologetic little shrug. 'Because they were only human. The outcome was so disastrous that the officers who despatched that ARU thought they'd be crucified. They were afraid public opinion would forget who was really responsible – the thieves who brought firearms to the exchange – and blame the police for the deaths of two innocent civilians.

'They wanted to focus attention on the fact that they'd broken up a criminal gang and recovered most of the items stolen from a valuable collection. They didn't want to admit that it was random chance that brought them to the car park at the critical moment, because dumb luck doesn't look as good on your annual report as clever detective work.'

'But allowing people to think they'd been tipped off left my father to take the blame!'

'I know,' murmured Ash. 'I don't suppose anyone anticipated what happened next. No one could have guessed how Jerome Harbinger would react.'

'He murdered my father!' cried Elizabeth Lim. Her clear voice, her audible distress and the words themselves turned heads for five metres all round. 'And then, four weeks later, he murdered my mother as well. He said he was going to, and he did. When my father told the police we were all in danger, they told him it was just the grief talking. They told him there was nothing to worry about. That Mr Harbinger would apologise when he calmed down.' She gave an empty little laugh as deep as despair.

Ash gave her a moment to collect herself. Then he said, 'And then you and your brother disappeared from the record, and turned up as two other people. I imagine Cavendo helped with that.'

She nodded, the fall of her black hair curtaining her eyes. 'They said it was the least they could do. I have to say, I agreed.'

'And you went to university as Elizabeth Lim. Who did James become?'

Lim shook her head. 'I don't know. He didn't share his new identity with me, and I didn't share mine with him. If Mr Harbinger found one of us, it was necessary that we didn't know enough to betray the other. All I knew was that he'd gone into banking, that he'd married and had two children, and that he lived in London. All *he* knew was that I was a teacher working in the Midlands. Our only point of contact was through Martin Wade, and we always called him – he didn't know how to contact us.'

'You did well,' said Ash. 'It's easy to disappear – it's not easy to *stay* disappeared for seventeen years. Most people can't resist the temptation to go back at some point. That's when their past catches up with them.'

'I suppose I made that mistake as well,' said Lim thoughtfully. 'Norbold was too close. I should have done what James did: bury myself in a big city in another part of the country. But I thought seventeen years was long enough for Felicity Cho to have gone for good. And I really wanted that job. I told myself that I'd been away long enough for the trail to go cold, that no one could recognise me as the frightened sixteen-year-old girl I was last time they saw me. It seems I was mistaken.'

'We'll get this sorted out now.' Ash couldn't imagine what gave him the authority, or the confidence, to promise her that, but he meant it absolutely. 'This won't be hanging over your head very much longer.'

'Mr Harbinger was very rich,' Lim observed sadly. 'I believe he still is.'

'I don't think that had as big a bearing on the investigation as the fact that he was himself the victim of a tragedy. Did you know that his wife was killed by a police firearm? There were so many regrets and recriminations flying round, I think the police felt they owed it to Harbinger to cut him some slack. They downplayed his outburst instead of recognising it as a genuine threat to your family. Even after your parents died, there was a reluctance to believe that Harbinger was responsible, because they knew what the actions of the police had cost him.

'Well, all the facts will come out now. Those officers who

accepted a convenient fiction – your father's accident, your mother's suicide – rather than conducting a thorough investigation will be held to account. A comprehensive inquiry will establish how your parents died, and who's been threatening you, and bring him to justice.'

He smiled at her. 'And then you can go back to Norbold Quays, and pick up where you left off, and all you'll have to worry about will be remembering the birthdays of your nieces and nephews.'

Lim regarded him steadily over the top of Patience's head. 'You really think it's all over?'

'I think it will all be over very soon.'

Elizabeth Lim rose gracefully from the stone steps, and Ash retrieved his handkerchief, as Hazel and DI Gorman hurried across Great Russell Street. A detached portion of Ash's brain noticed with amusement that Hazel hadn't wasted the time she'd been waiting in the café: there was a blob of cream on the tip of her nose.

'Mr Gorman, Miss Best.'

'Miss Lim. Or . . .'

She smiled. 'We've been through that already.'

Dave Gorman wanted to know what else they'd been through while he was buying espressos and chocolate éclairs. But Ash warned him off with a fractional shake of the head.

'Miss Lim's coming back to Norbold with us,' he said. 'I suggest she rides with you. You can talk on the drive.'

Hazel wanted to hear the story too, so Ash and Patience had Hazel's car to themselves. Ash drove more slowly than Gorman, but he left London first: Lim had to collect her belongings from the small hotel where she'd been staying.

Patience took the front passenger seat, a concession she met by agreeing to wear her seatbelt. As they reached the motorway she said, You didn't tell Hazel she had cream on her nose.

Ash barked a little laugh. 'No, I didn't.'

You should have done. She'll be cross when she looks in a mirror.

'I know.' Ash was still chuckling as he drove through Watford Gap.

* * *

'Why didn't you tell me I had cream on my nose?' demanded Hazel.

'Had you? I didn't notice.'

Hazel sniffed, unconvinced.

They were in Ash's kitchen at Highfield Road. It was gone midnight, and the boys and even Frankie had long ago retired to bed. Patience was sleeping too, curled like a croissant on the sofa with her long head on Ash's knee.

Ash said pensively, 'I hope we've done the right thing.'

'Bringing her in from the cold?' Hazel had a certain fondness for spy fiction. 'Of course we have. We couldn't leave her in London, with no friends and nowhere to turn for help. Sooner or later . . .' She didn't finish the sentence.

'I suppose. But it's risky, bringing her back to Norbold. Harbinger knows she's spent the last five years here. Maybe it would have been better to send her off north, somewhere she had no connections.'

'She had no connections in London,' Hazel pointed out. 'We were worried he'd find her anyway. And then the sheer anonymous scale of the place would make it easy for him to get at her and get clean away afterwards. If we've finally persuaded the top brass to take the risk seriously, she's better where people who understand what's been going on can keep an eye on her.'

'Assuming the top brass really are taking the risk seriously now.'

Hazel shrugged. 'Dave Gorman reckons Sir was telling the truth. That there was a toxic combination of bad luck, bad decisions and moral cowardice, but there never was a conspiracy to throw Elizabeth Lim to the lions. We're putting her up at a safe house in town. Dave wants to interview her again before he has another go at the Harbingers.'

'Meadowvale has a safe house in Norbold?' Ash sounded surprised.

Hazel nodded. 'Well . . . kind of. It's more of a safe flat, at the back of Derby Road. We don't have the funds to staff it permanently, but she'll be OK there for the moment.'

Ash remembered how long Meadowvale had been able to provide protection when it had seemed that his sons were in danger. 'It's not a long-term solution. Dave needs to make arrests. One or both of the Harbingers, and whoever they've been using for muscle. Then Miss Lim can return to her own flat and go back to work. The longer that takes, the harder it will be to keep her safe.'

'We *will* keep her safe,' insisted Hazel. 'We have to. Whatever it takes.'

'Whatever?'

Hazel said nothing. After a moment Ash tilted the reading light for a better look at her. She avoided his gaze.

'What are you not telling me?' As soon as he'd said it, he knew. 'Oh *Hazel* – you didn't?'

She gave a negligent shrug. 'She has the flat for a few days at least. But when Maybourne can't provide full cover any longer, she'll be better moving in with me. She can have Saturday's room' – her last lodger had left no more belongings than would fit in a cardboard box under the stairs – 'and I'm still on holiday so I can be with her round the clock. They'll do drive-bys, too – lots of them. She'll be safe until Dave can wrap things up.'

Ash was appalled. 'You are not trained in close protection!'

'No, but I am a trained police officer, I'll have the ARU on speed-dial, and an old lady with an arthritic knee could hobble from my house to Meadowvale in three minutes. I know, it's not a perfect solution. But you said it: close protection is only ever a short-term option. I can keep her safe long enough for Dave to end the threat permanently.'

Ash's voice rose enough to disturb his dog, who lifted her head to look at him. 'You can't fight off armed men, you can only get hurt trying. Three minutes is more than enough for a professional to break down your door, run upstairs, fire two shots into your bed and two shots into hers, and be on the motorway before the ARU reaches Railway Street. You'd never know what hit you.'

Hazel was not unimaginative. The picture he painted glimmered in her mind's eye. But everything he'd said, she had already considered. She'd weighed the risks, to Lim and herself, and accepted them. She thought she could make a better job of protecting Lim, and Gorman could do a better job of stopping the Harbingers, than anyone else who was both willing and available. No one would look for Felicity Cho in Railway Street. She could be brought in the back way, under cover of darkness, and stay out of sight until Gorman could make his arrests. It wasn't a perfect solution. She thought it was the best they could do.

'Gabriel,' she said quietly, 'we owe it to her. The police. We let her down. We let her down when her parents were murdered, and we let her down again after Harbinger found her. You can blame ACC-Crime, you can blame the old boys' culture at Division, you can blame poor information-sharing; you can blame anyone and everyone who had a duty to help her and didn't. But what matters right now is that Elizabeth Lim has broken cover because we said we could look after her better than she can look after herself. So we have to. If that means having her as a house-guest until Dave brings the Harbingers to book, I'm good with that.'

'If they find her, you standing in the way will not stop them.'

'It won't come to that. Even if the Harbingers somehow tracked Lim to my house, they aren't stupid. They know we're onto them. They know that if they move against her again, we'll be round their place before the ink's dry on the warrant. Whether it's the old man or his daughter who's keeping this vendetta alive, they don't want to spend the rest of their days behind bars.'

Ash thought she was being naïve. 'This is a small town. You can't keep secrets for long. People notice things.'

Hazel lifted her head and pinned him with her gaze. 'Nobody noticed you living above Laura Fry's office when you were supposed to be dead. And you weren't even careful. You wandered round the town at night, peering in at my windows to make sure I was looking after your dog!'

He had no answer to that: it was true. Anyway, no answer he made, no argument he advanced, would change her mind. She wanted to do it because she took a broad view of her duties as a police officer. Partly because of her pride in public service, but also because she got an adrenalin rush from taking a gamble and getting away with it.

This was something new, something that had happened

in the last year. It had happened as a consequence of things that they had done and been through together.

When Ash first knew her, Constable Best was an essentially conventional girl learning the book by heart so she could go by it in all conceivable circumstances. But there are times when the book doesn't work; or, if it works, times that there are quicker, surer or more satisfying means to an end. That was something she'd learned from Gabriel Ash. Not because he was a natural rebel, but because he'd been forced into situations where the book was no help – where risky options were the only options.

And the thing about taking risks is, if the gamble doesn't work you don't get a second chance; but if it does, there's no going back. No one stops gambling because they've won. Ash had a great many regrets about his life, and this wasn't the least of them: that he was responsible for the adrenalin junkie that his friend was fast becoming. He was afraid for her. Sooner or later, every gambler loses. The lucky ones only lose money. But Hazel was starting to gamble with her safety; and, like all gamblers, she was starting to enjoy the game.

Anxious as he was, Ash couldn't think what he could do, what he could say, to change her mind. He could only hope that DI Gorman would make his arrests before Elizabeth Lim's lease on the safe house expired.

NINETEEN

Dave Gorman was no happier about the arrangement than Ash was. He saw no likelihood of bringing charges before Hazel moved her new house-guest in at Railway Street. He had tried to argue against it but found himself outmanoeuvred. Before she put the plan to him, Hazel obtained approval from Superintendent Maybourne.

'It's only for a few days,' she said reassuringly. 'Until you can get the Harbingers locked up.'

'*Days?*' Gorman exploded. '*How* long have you been a

police officer? *Nothing* happens in days. This could drag on for months.'

'No, it really can't,' Hazel told him severely. 'I don't want a third career running a B&B. Plus, Saturday could come back at any time and want his room.'

Privately, Gorman didn't expect any of them to see Saturday again. If it comforted her to think otherwise, she could – but that wouldn't make the machinery of justice run any faster. Like the mills of God, the law grinds slowly but it grinds exceedingly fine. At least, he corrected himself, it grinds slowly.

But concern for both women put an edge on his hunger to see justice done. He wasn't a religious man, but even if he had been, the urgency of the situation precluded taking Sunday as a day of rest. He lifted his phone to organise a formal interview with Jocelyn Harbinger, here at Meadowvale. Then he put it down again. Summoned to the police station, she would arrive with her solicitor, and the two of them would have spent the drive discussing exactly what she should and shouldn't say in answer to his questions, and at what point they would challenge him to charge or release her. If he turned up on her doorstep, she might decline to speak to him without her solicitor present. But she might take the view that refusing to co-operate would only feed his suspicions.

He went alone – there was no longer any reason not to involve his team, only that he'd have to waste time explaining why he hadn't involved them before – and he spent the twenty-minute journey planning the interview. In particular, he drummed it into his head that he must not – must *not*, under any circumstances – give away the fact that he knew where Elizabeth Lim was. That he'd spoken to her. That was all someone as smart as Jocelyn Harbinger would need. Someone with enough connections could find out about the flat behind Derby Road.

The housekeeper answered the door. 'Detective Inspector Gorman,' he said. 'Mrs . . .?'

'Fisher,' she said stiffly. She was a woman in her fifties, wearing little or no make-up and the trademark black dress of her profession. Dave Gorman was no expert on women's fashions, but he recognised that particular severity of style that came with a price-tag attached. Of course, as a senior member of staff to a wealthy family, she probably earned more than he did. 'You can't see him.'

Gorman blinked. 'Mr Harbinger? Why, what's happened?'

'He's had a turn.' There was a note of disfavour in her voice. 'The doctor's been. He says no one's to be admitted – *especially* the police. He says it was your questions that brought it on. Raking everything up again.'

'I'm sorry Mr Harbinger isn't well,' said the DI woodenly. 'Is Miss Harbinger at home?'

'She's with him. I'm not disturbing them while she's with him.'

Gorman made an effort to hang onto his patience. 'Mrs Fisher, there's no need for us to disturb Mr Harbinger. If you'll ask Miss Harbinger to come downstairs, we can talk in the . . . in the . . .' He looked round the hall in search of something he recognised.

Dave Gorman was born in a two-up, two-down identical to Hazel's house in Railway Street, so his familiarity with the domestic arrangements of the super-rich was minimal. He seemed to remember that country houses had libraries. And possibly orangeries. But his nerve failed under the withering scorn of the housekeeper's eye, and he simply picked a door and pointed. 'In there.'

Mrs Fisher regarded him with ill-concealed triumph. 'Miss Jocelyn Harbinger does *not* conduct interviews in the broom cupboard.'

Gorman was almost – *almost* – certain that the houses of the gentry, even those which had originally been built as farmhouses, did not have the broom cupboard opening off the central hall. Another moment under that brittle, hostile gaze and he'd have felt compelled to establish the fact, one way or the other; so it was with relief that he heard a step on the stairs, and looking up he saw Jocelyn Harbinger looking down at him over the baluster rail.

'Mr Gorman? I'm afraid you've had a wasted journey. My father isn't fit to answer any more questions.'

'So Mrs Fisher was telling me,' said Gorman. 'I'm sorry he's not well. Will he be all right?'

'I expect so. He's had these episodes before. He just needs to be quiet for a few days. Can your inquiries wait?'

'In fact, Miss Harbinger, it was you I wanted to speak to. Is there somewhere we can go?'

'Of course.' She walked past him and opened the very door he'd chosen – not a cupboard but a small, comfortable sitting room. 'We won't be disturbed in here.'

Gorman caught the edge of a chilly smile as the housekeeper disappeared through a door opposite.

'Now.' Jocelyn Harbinger took one oversized armchair and gestured Gorman to another. If his presence here made her anxious, it didn't show. 'How can I help you this time?'

'I need to ask you about the night your mother died.'

'Why?'

He'd been prepared for annoyance, for anger, even for tears. But that took him aback. 'Because I'm a detective.'

She gave him an impatient glance. 'I mean, why are you raking all this up again? It's been seventeen years. All the healing that we're capable of has taken place. Why do you want to reopen the old wounds again?'

'You know why. Someone *hasn't* healed. Someone has held onto their grudge so doggedly that even after seventeen years they're still looking for their pound of flesh. And not from someone they can conceivably blame for what happened, but from that man's son and daughter, who weren't much more than children when it happened.'

'I wasn't much more than a child, either, Inspector.'

For the most fleeting of moments he thought that was a confession. But it wasn't. Her expression was calm, slightly quizzical; she was reminding him of something she thought he'd forgotten.

'I know that, Miss Harbinger. But you're not a child now. You're a successful businesswoman, and I imagine that took equal quantities of intelligence, application, hard work and sheer bloody-mindedness. The same qualities that would enable someone to conduct a campaign of murderous persecution over nearly two decades.

'Now, maybe you didn't start this. Maybe that was your father, when he was physically stronger and his world had just been ripped apart. But as he got old, you got older. If he'd asked you to finish what he couldn't, I don't think anything that's happened to the Cho family would have been beyond you.'

'You're serious?' But nothing in her tone now suggested that she thought he was joking. She was quiet and focused, watching him with a directness that Gorman found faintly disconcerting. And still nothing resembling alarm, which troubled him even more. 'You think we've made a family business of persecuting the Chos?'

'Have you?'

'Detective Inspector Gorman,' she said with a trace of impatience, 'it's perfectly true that my father started something and I'm carrying it on. It's called Harbinger Transport; it's a twenty-four/seven operation involving a hundred and twenty-two lorries, ninety-three drivers, and delivery routes from the Isle of Wight to the Outer Hebrides. It doesn't leave me much time for hobbies!

'Of course, if I was determined to pursue this supposed vendetta, I could have saved up my holiday entitlement and spent it looking for Edward Cho's children. But why would I want to?'

'Your father threatened to wipe out the whole family,' said Gorman. 'Now both parents are dead, and an attempt has been made to kidnap the daughter. We don't know about the son – nobody knows where he is, not even his sister.'

Jocelyn sighed. 'I know what my father said. *You* know the circumstances in which he said it. He'd just lost his wife because someone he trusted tried to recover the valuables without spending the ransom money. The most generous assessment is that Edward Cho wasn't competent to handle the negotiation, and by informing the police he cost my mother her life. You're surprised that my father was so angry he didn't know what he was saying?'

'Are you telling me that, when he calmed down, he forgave Mr Cho?'

Jocelyn bit her lip. After a moment she shook her head. 'No, I can't tell you that. He has always bitterly resented the way we were let down. He loved my mother, and he shouldn't have lost her that way. It may be true to say he wouldn't have pissed on Edward Cho if he was burning. That's not the same as saying he'd have started the fire.'

Gorman was nodding slowly. 'He *was* let down, but not by Mr Cho. Cho was doing the best he could in difficult circumstances. He was put in a situation he had limited experience of, and he took it on because, if he hadn't, someone even less well equipped would have had to. He didn't notify the police. I know that for a fact. It was sheer fluke that we got involved. Someone on routine patrol recognised someone in the thieves' car as a wanted person and followed them.'

Jocelyn was staring at him. It was the first time she'd heard this: Gorman thought it would be a while before she knew how she felt about it. It took her long moments to find a voice. 'Why didn't anyone *tell* us this?'

'I don't know,' Gorman said wearily. 'I think, because the whole thing was a disaster. Police intervention had caused the death of an innocent civilian, and both your needs and those of the Chos were trampled in the rush to avoid the responsibility. The senior officers who should have stood up for the truth and dealt with the criticism decided instead to keep their heads down and let Mr Cho take the flak.

'Since no one took your father's threat seriously, when Cho drove off an icy road into a reservoir those same officers wanted to believe it really was an accident. And that, a month later, Mrs Cho's death was suicide. They could have been right. But it was their job to be sceptical and investigate thoroughly, and they didn't do it.'

He sighed. 'Now it's seventeen years later, and someone's *still* trying to hurt the Chos. Someone sent a snatch squad to Felicity's school; and if they find her again, they'll have another go. That's why I need to figure out who's behind it, and stop them.'

There was a pause while she considered. Then Jocelyn Harbinger said, 'Two innocent civilians.'

Gorman frowned. 'Sorry?'

'Two innocent civilians died. Everyone remembers my mother,' said Jocelyn quietly, 'and everyone forgets her driver. But his death was important too. Jeremy worked for our family for over ten years. He didn't have to drive her that evening. He knew it was risky, and my father said he was under no obligation to do it – that he had his own family to consider. But he thought he could look after my mother if things got nasty. He was mistaken, and it cost him his life, but he was a brave and honourable man, and he wasn't just collateral damage.'

'No, he wasn't,' agreed Gorman after a moment. He was impressed that it was her saying it, but telling her so would have been both patronising and unprofessional. 'Jeremy? That's not the name on the file.'

Jocelyn smiled, impishly. 'No. His name was John. We called him Jeremy because of Beatrix Potter. It started as a joke and ended up being absolutely routine. I don't think he'd have responded to anything else.'

Seeing that he wasn't following, she glanced at his left hand. No wedding ring, so probably no children to read bedtime stories to. 'Beatrix Potter?' she said again. '*The Tale of Jeremy Fisher*?'

He answered with a slow grin of his own. 'I see.' Which meant . . . 'Your housekeeper is his widow?'

Jocelyn nodded.

'Then it was her who was injured the night of the robbery.'

'Yes. She was alone in the house that night – we all had Christmas functions to go to, and Jeremy was driving my parents. Even the Fishers' son was out with friends.'

'Was she badly hurt?'

'Bad enough. She tried to keep the robbers out, and they knocked her about. She was badly concussed. There were terrible headaches that went on for weeks afterwards.'

'Who drives for the family now?'

'Their son John. You've already met him – he looks after the gardens as well. He was still at school when it happened, but my father always intended him to have the job when he was old enough. He deliberately hired an older man to drive for us for a few years. He was happy to retire when John was ready to take over.'

'That was thoughtful,' said Gorman.

Jocelyn shrugged. 'We had to look after Jeremy's family. In the circumstances, of course we did. It wasn't much of a sacrifice. Mrs Fisher was always an excellent housekeeper, and John's been a great success too. This house would fall about our ears if it wasn't for the two of them.'

'Mrs Fisher certainly seems . . . *protective* . . . of your father.'

'They have a lot in common. Not just what happened – their way of looking at the world. They're kindred spirits. If she didn't work for him, they'd be best friends.'

'You told me about the chess.'

Jocelyn smiled. 'That's only one of the ways she looks after him. I don't mean just making his meals and ironing his clothes: she genuinely cares about him. I think it fulfils a need that both of them have, that was left vacant when they each lost the person they loved most. So he relies on her, and she puts all her energies into caring for him. I love my father, Inspector, but I don't think he'd miss me as much as he'd miss Mrs Fisher.'

Gorman nodded his understanding. 'So . . . a hundred and twenty-two lorries. Any grey vans?'

'No,' Jocelyn said immediately.

He cocked an eyebrow at her. 'You're sure about that?'

'Absolutely sure. We have vans – of course we have. They're all painted in burgundy and gold. Fleet colours.'

'All of them?'

'*All* of them,' she said firmly.

TWENTY

Of all the people Hazel *didn't* expect to hear from any time soon, her friend at the PNC was high on the list. 'Everton? I thought I was out of favour with you people.'

'I thought so too,' said Everton Woods with disarming honesty. 'Except, apparently not today. Today one of our inspectors wandered by – not officially, you understand, just in passing – and said if I happened to be talking to you, you might be interested in something that came in yesterday.'

All Hazel's instincts sharpened like the quills on a porcupine. 'What came in yesterday?'

'A DD found up the Angel.'

'DD?'

'Discovered Deceased. In the rear of an antiques shop in Islington. There was a sign on the door saying *On Holiday: back next month*. The neighbours only started worrying when they noticed a smell in the back alley. They called the council and the council called the Met. Turned out he wasn't on holiday, and he isn't coming back. BFT.'

Blunt force trauma. 'Someone beat his head in?' Everton grunted confirmation. 'Who was he?'

'Lester Pickering, aged fifty-four, divorced, no children.'

'I'm guessing Mr Pickering is known to the Met as more than an honest antiques dealer.'

'Oh yeah. Not much actual form – a bit of petty theft twenty years ago, a conviction for handling stolen goods ten years ago that he put his hands up for on the basis that it was criminal carelessness rather than criminal intent, nothing since. General feeling round the Yard, though, is that he didn't become a better person, just a better con.'

Hazel grinned at that. 'He was a fence?'

'Perfect cover, an antiques shop. It's cash business, you don't get a registration book with a Victorian sideboard, and if you can pass the gear through an auction you're probably safe even if it is identified later.'

'Market overt,' Hazel said sagely. It was one of the curious loopholes in English law that she'd gained extra points in her exams for remembering. 'You think he was murdered over a Victorian sideboard?' When Hazel was growing up, people were paying other people to take away their grandmothers' sideboards.

Unseen at the other end of the line, Everton Woods frowned. 'Don't be silly. That was just an example. The late and largely unlamented Lester was more into the art side of the business.'

Hazel felt the fine hairs on the back of her neck stand up. 'Paintings?'

'Among other things.'

'And he'd have been doing this, say, seventeen years ago?'

'Probably.'

'Do we know who killed him?'

'No.'

'Any suspects?'

'*Lots* of suspects,' said Everton judiciously. 'No evidence.'

'Then, do we know *why* he was killed?'

'Also no evidence, but probably a falling-out with someone he'd done business with.'

Hazel pursed her lips. 'Why do you say that?'

'*I'm* saying it because that's what it says in the crime report. The SIO said it because of what was missing from Pickering's shop.'

She waited, but he wanted prompting. 'What was missing from his shop?'

'Almost nothing,' said Everton smugly. 'Whoever killed him walked past trays of jewellery and cabinets of silver, and a Fabergé-style egg (slightly damaged), and all he took was a picture off the wall of the back office.'

'A picture? What kind of a picture?'

'He said that would interest you,' said Everton with quiet satisfaction. 'The inspector who just happened to be passing. He said you'd prick your ears up at the mention of a picture.'

'Everton, what *kind* of a picture? A painting, a photograph – what?'

'Dunno. No one they've questioned so far remembers seeing it. All we know is the size of the white patch on the wall where it used to hang: fifty-eight centimetres by seventy-two.'

Hazel wrote it down. She had no idea how big the Harbingers' missing Caravaggio was; and anyway, what would it be doing on someone's office wall seventeen years after it was stolen? More likely, it was a photograph taken on a boozy night out showing Lester Pickering with someone who, now, didn't want the moment memorialised. But if there was even the outside chance that the measurements matched . . .

'And he didn't take anything else?'

'Hard to be sure what was in the shop at any given time. What we do know is that he left behind antiques worth thousands. So far as the SIO could tell, the only thing he was interested in was the picture in the office.'

'Was the blunt instrument recovered?'

'Yes, he dropped it on the floor as he left. A brass-headed walking stick with a price-tag on it. Looks like the cheeky beggar lifted it from a rack by the door as he went in.'

'Any prints apart from Lester's?' She knew there wouldn't be.

'Gloves.'

Hazel had grabbed a pad and was scribbling notes. 'So Lester was murdered in the back of his own shop, and the killer left a note on the door so the neighbours wouldn't report him missing. Have we anything resembling a time of death?'

'He opened mail postmarked a fortnight ago, and didn't open mail postmarked twelve days ago.'

'Then, sometime between twelve and fourteen days ago, someone went to the shop of Lester Pickering, known fence and possible art thief, killed him with an implement he found at the scene, and left with nothing but a picture that was hanging not in the shop but on the office wall. So it wasn't a robbery – he could have come back with a van and emptied the place at his leisure. Any CCTV?'

Everton checked the information on his screen. 'Nothing helpful. We have people in the street – there's a pub across the way – but we don't have the front of the shop so we don't know who was the last to go inside.'

'I don't suppose the neighbours remember exactly when the note went up on the door.'

'Around twelve or fourteen days ago,' said Everton.

Hazel needed to talk it through with Gorman. But she needed to know something else first. 'Everton – *why* are you telling me this?'

'Because someone I call Sir told me to.'

'OK. But why *me*? Why not contact DI Gorman if he had information that might help his investigation?'

'Sir thought telling you was pretty much the same thing, just a bit less formal.' He meant, Untraceable. Plausible deniability.

'Well, thank Sir from both of us. Whether it leads anywhere or not, it's another piece in the puzzle. I'll have to check the size of our painting, but if it *was* hanging on Lester Pickering's wall until a fortnight ago, that must mean something.'

'He couldn't get his hands on a Pirelli calendar this year?' hazarded Everton Woods.

The measurements of the Caravaggio were in the file. 'Forty-six centimetres by sixty,' said Dave Gorman.

It had always seemed a long shot. But somehow, this wasn't what Hazel had expected. Her hopes sank. 'It isn't the same picture.'

Gorman leaned back from his desk, discouraged. 'Of course, that doesn't mean Pickering *wasn't* involved in the Harbinger robbery. We're pretty sure art theft was his field of expertise at the relevant time.'

'And he got himself killed a few days before the attempt on Elizabeth Lim. The two incidents could be connected,' said Hazel. 'Everton's Sir must have thought so, or he wouldn't have wanted us to have the information.'

Dave Gorman had a face made for scowling. He scowled now. '*Why* did he want us to have the information? Who's playing silly buggers *now*?'

Hazel didn't know either, but she was willing to make an educated guess. 'ACC-Crime?'

The DI considered. 'Maybe. He said he'd help if he could. Maybe he's put the word out that anything potentially relevant should be sent my way.'

'It wasn't, though – it was sent *my* way.'

'So Severick' – Gorman was working this out as he went along – 'wants us to have thc information, but he doesn't want his fingerprints on it, because he doesn't want anyone thinking he was forced into a corner by a couple of loose cannon pinging round the decks of HMS *Meadowvale*. Most of all, he doesn't want *us* thinking that.'

In all probability they would never be able to prove it. And possibly it wasn't necessary for them to know why sources of information dammed up a week ago were now starting to leak. It was enough that they were back in the loop, that people who handled a lot of information were suddenly aware of what might interest them and felt able to pass it on.

'If it wasn't ACC-Crime, it was someone working to the same agenda,' Hazel surmised. 'Someone who's decided that seventeen years is long enough for a murderer to go free. Someone who thinks the Cho case can be cleared up now but doesn't want to do it himself. Possibly because he could have done it before if he hadn't been protecting people that *he* calls Sir.'

Gorman sniffed sourly. 'Someone who thinks it could still be a poisoned chalice, and he'd rather someone else took the first sip.'

That was entirely possible. Hazel chuckled ruefully. 'I suspect there's a big red stamp on our personnel files – yours and mine – saying *EXPENDABLE*. Well, maybe that's what we're best at: taking flak. And – and this is important – keeping going. We'll crack this, Dave. The information is out there. And now there are higher-ups willing us to succeed, even if they're not ready to announce the fact. We just have to put it together.'

'That's all?' said Gorman weakly. 'Oh good.'

They pushed ideas between them for another hour, without making much progress. Then Gorman was called out to deal with an attempted robbery at knife-point – the teenage perpetrator, his identity disguised by one leg of a pair of tights because his mum didn't wear stockings, was locked in a storeroom: he'd panicked and rushed through the wrong door when the seventy-year-old shop assistant set about him with a mop – and Hazel took the scenic route home, via Rambles With Books.

The boys were there too. Frankie had dropped them off after school while she visited her dentist. Ash had set them to rearranging the display on the long central table.

'Find me one on art theft,' Hazel said in passing, and Gilbert – sounding exactly like his father – said, 'I'm sure we'll have one here somewhere.'

Ash noticed the new purpose in her manner and raised an eyebrow. 'Developments?'

'Maybe. Not sure.' She told him about her conversation with Everton Woods.

'So what are you thinking?' asked Ash. 'That this man Pickering fenced the Harbingers' Caravaggio?'

'Possibly. He seems to have been in that line of work.'

'Is there any reason to suppose that's why he was killed?'

Hazel shrugged. 'He seems to have been killed by someone who also wanted what was hanging on his office wall. We've no way of knowing what that was, except it was too big to be the Caravaggio.'

'His office wall? Not in the shop?'

'No, it doesn't seem to have been part of his stock. So far the Met haven't found anyone who remembers seeing it.'

'So, whatever it was, it was for his own private satisfaction. Or . . .' The rest of the sentence failed to materialise, and when Hazel looked sharply at him his face had gone still and his eyes had turned distant and unfocused.

Recognising the expression, she didn't want to interrupt his thought processes. But when a couple of minutes had passed and he was still peering intently at some internal landscape, her patience ran out and she prompted him. 'Or what?'

'Hm?' He came back to her then, and there was a new clarity in his eye that suggested he'd brought something with him. 'Art theft is a specialised field. Stealing a painting isn't like stealing a diamond necklace or a stack of gold sovereigns. It has no intrinsic value – you can't cut it down or break it up or melt it and recast it as something else. A painting is only worth something when it can be identified. When it can be attributed to a good artist. Otherwise it's just a bit of old canvas and flaking paint.'

'All right,' said Hazel. 'So?'

'So what do you do with a stolen painting? There's an international art theft register: the moment something is reported stolen, no reputable museum, gallery, private or institutional buyer will look at it. And if you render it unrecognisable, you destroy its value anyway.'

Hazel tried to follow his train of thought. 'So you . . . hang it in your private office for seventeen years?' She hoped, she really hoped, Jennifer Harbinger hadn't died to provide Lester Pickering with wallpaper.

'In a way, yes,' said Ash. 'Paintings like that – like the Harbinger Caravaggio – *do* have a value when they're used in a particular way. They're used in crime circles – serious crime circles – as a kind of hostage to fortune.

'It works like this. Suppose I need money to set up a bank robbery. It's an expensive business – like any other enterprise, you need to speculate to accumulate. There's information to buy, people to buy off, equipment to get hold of. I know I can repay these sums from the proceeds of the crime, but I can't go into the Credit Union and ask for a loan, can I? I need someone to bankroll me. And he wants some guarantee that he'll get his money back, with interest. He doesn't want to take my word for it – he's not sure I'm entirely honest.'

'Whatever would give him that idea?' murmured Hazel.

'Plus, even if I'm not out to cheat him, things can go wrong. Like a bank lending money, he doesn't want to share in the risks of the enterprise, only the profits. Fortunately, I know Lester Pickering, and Lester has a painting which is probably worth more than the bank has in its vaults. Lester will lend this painting to the man with the money, to hold as ransom until the loan is repaid. When the job is successful, the money man gets his money back, together with his cut; Lester gets his painting back, together with *his* cut; and I keep what's left.'

He became conscious of her open-mouthed stare. 'What?'

'Gabriel – how do you *know* this stuff?'

'You know what I used to do for a living.'

'You were a spy.'

'I was *not* a spy,' he retorted sharply. 'I was a security analyst. And before that I was an insurance investigator.'

'You worked on this sort of stuff?'

'Sometimes. And I worked with people who did it all the time. Who knew the workings of the criminal underworld better than the criminals themselves.'

Hazel gave herself a little shake. Occasionally, he still amazed her. After months of playing with absolute conviction his role as the archetypal middle-class householder, small businessman and parent, the stage curtain had twitched aside for a moment and given her a glimpse of this other life he'd had before she knew him. She knew he was a clever man. She knew his professional skills had been in demand. Somehow, evidence of why still managed to surprise her.

'All right,' she said after a moment. 'Suppose that is what Pickering was doing. And suppose the Harbingers' Caravaggio is what he was doing it with. Who would want him dead?'

'Not the people who used him to guarantee their loans. Now he's gone, they'll have to find someone else to underwrite their projects.'

'What if one of them went wrong? If someone took the money and didn't do the bank robbery?'

'Then the money man would keep the Caravaggio until the bank robber could put together another job. That's what it's for. But neither party would blame Pickering. He's the one who would have restructured the loan for them. He'd have to, or he'd never get his painting back.'

Hazel shook her head. 'If it *was* the Caravaggio, everything would fall into place. Then it would be the Harbingers who killed him. They found out he was involved in the theft of their art collection, and they finally caught up with Pickering just as they caught up with Elizabeth Lim. Unfortunately, it isn't. It isn't the right size.'

'Bigger? Smaller?'

'Pickering's picture was bigger. And while you might conceivably cut a painting down – if it got damaged, for instance – you couldn't make it bigger.'

'How much bigger?'

She consulted her notes. 'Twelve centimetres in one direction, and . . . OK, twelve centimetres all round.'

Ash was looking at her as if she'd just said something very foolish, and for the life of her Hazel couldn't think what.

He said, 'It's a frame.'

TWENTY-ONE

Hazel still didn't understand. 'Nobody's trying to frame anybody, Gabriel. But if the picture's too big—'

Ash shook his head gently, trying not to smile. 'The extra twelve centimetres – that's the picture frame. The insurers' report would give the size of the canvas. The white patch on Lester Pickering's office wall would be the size of the framed picture. Twelve centimetres all round would be a nice baroque frame, just the thing for an Old Master.'

Hazel put her hand to her mouth and closed her eyes for a moment. It was so obvious, now he'd pointed it out. 'It never occurred to me. I compared the measurements, and they weren't the same. I have to tell Dave.'

But Gorman wasn't answering his phone. He was too busy preventing the elderly shopkeeper from beating up the teenager who'd tried to rob her.

Hazel turned back to Ash, an expectant glow in her face. 'If that *was* the Caravaggio, surely we're right back to the Harbingers as prime suspects. They killed Pickering because he was involved in the robbery that led to Jennifer Harbinger's death. Maybe he was actually there – maybe he was the one who got away, with the thing tucked under his arm. He certainly had it long enough to produce a mark on his office wall.

'When they tracked him down, the Harbingers beat his head in and took the painting because it was theirs to take; and they didn't take anything else because, whatever else they are, they're not thieves. They don't have to steal antiques when they can simply buy them.'

'Jerome Harbinger is a frail elderly man,' Ash reminded her. 'Jocelyn Harbinger is a woman. But beating a man's skull in with a walking-stick requires physical strength.'

'Or maybe just a lot of pent-up anger,' said Hazel. 'It's amazing what people can do with enough motivation. Anyway, the Harbingers could hire someone to do their dirty work. It wasn't them at the school either. That doesn't mean they weren't responsible.'

Clearly that was true. Perhaps the two men in the grey van paid Lester Pickering a visit. Which meant – Ash paled visibly – a cold-blooded killer had laid hands on his sons. If Hazel hadn't weighed in when she did . . . Involuntarily, he glanced out into the shop, to check they were still there, still safe.

'You're pretty confident it's them, aren't you?' he said. 'One of them, or both of them.'

'Means, motive, opportunity,' Hazel enumerated. 'They had all three. We don't know of anyone else who had. That's not the same as proof. But what are the odds that there's someone else out there with a vendetta against both the Chos *and* a known fence of stolen art?'

Put that way . . . 'Not high,' Ash admitted. 'So Jerome Harbinger meant every word he said. And when he got too frail to finish the job himself, he got someone to help. Possibly his daughter, as well as two men with a grey van. And Elizabeth

Lim is still in danger, and will be until that vicious old man and those he's either bought or suborned are behind bars.'

'Exactly.' Hazel seemed to remember telling him this days ago.

Ash must have sensed what she was thinking. 'I'm sorry I haven't been more helpful. I was wrong to tell you not to get involved. This needs clearing up, now, so Miss Lim can go home. She's been a victim long enough.'

She'd heard that note in his voice before. That little hint of steel, that was how he spoke instead of shouting. Her heart quickened. It was as if he'd been away and now he was back. This was what she'd missed: this sense of being part of a team. She almost had it with Dave Gorman, but not quite. The ranks got in the way. When push came to shove, if Gorman said, 'Jump', either she jumped or she started looking for another job. What she had with Ash was a meeting of free minds, kindred spirits with a shared purpose, two people trying to do the right thing not because they were paid to or because they had to but *because* it was the right thing. Since his boys had come home, Ash had been too busy, too preoccupied, to be her wingman. She knew she'd missed him: she hadn't realised just how much.

'Yes,' she said. 'Oh yes. What do you suggest?'

'I'll go and see Superintendent Maybourne. She needs to put more people on the case. Even with your help, even now Dave can use the rest of CID, there aren't enough bodies for an investigation on this scale. She may need to bring in detectives from neighbouring forces.'

And *that* was as if he'd used a very fine needle to prick a tiny hole in her balloon: not big enough to burst it, just enough to let all her hopes leak quietly away, leaving her heart an empty bladder.

'That's it?'

He looked surprised. 'It should help, don't you think? I know manpower is always stretched, but this is a murder investigation. And the longer it takes to wrap it up, the more likelihood there'll be another murder. It isn't just a major inquiry, it's an urgent one. If no one else has spelled that out for Superintendent Maybourne, I will. Any member of the public has the right to express concern about policing matters, and it may make it easier to drum up extra help if she can tell Division she's getting complaints about the lack of progress.'

Hazel was looking at him not so much with disappointment as suppressed indignation.

'What?' asked Ash uncertainly.

'I have to tell you, Gabriel,' she said tersely, 'you were more fun when you were mad. Now you're sane again, you're just like everybody else. Conventional. Predictable. *Safe*.' She made it sound like an insult.

He was genuinely taken aback. He didn't know what he'd done to upset her. 'But Hazel . . . what more can I do? Borrow a Stetson, stick a tin star on my lapel and meet Jerome Harbinger at high noon on ground level enough that his wheelchair won't run away? I am not and never have been a police officer. You are, but – I'm sorry to be blunt – you don't have the seniority to do what needs doing. Dave Gorman is the senior detective in this town. Tom Severick is the senior detective of this force. What can we possibly do that they can't?'

'Care?' suggested Hazel acidly.

Ash frowned. 'That's unfair. Dave is doing his best to resolve this. If he can get the help he needs from headquarters now, he'll get on top of it.'

The criticism in his tone stung. 'I know that. I know how far Dave was prepared to stick his neck out for Elizabeth Lim. He went up against ACC-Crime knowing Severick had the means and believing he had the motive to cut the legs from under him. And I was ready to go with him. He didn't want me to, but if things had gone the way we fully expected, I'd have been right there beside him.

'Because that's what the job requires. We keep the peace, we protect the innocent, we hold the guilty to account – and we do these things not just when it's convenient and makes our superiors smile benevolently, but also when it's going to raise hackles and lower eyebrows all the way up the corridors of power.'

She thought for a moment. 'They say the job of a free press is to tell truth to power. I've always admired that. Someone has to, and it takes courage to stand up to people with more bullets in their gun than you've got. However this ends up,

Dave Gorman comes out of it with honour, because he tried to do the right thing even when it looked like costing him everything.

'But what about you, Gabriel? A lot of people have stuck their necks out for you in the last couple of years. Don't you feel it's your turn now? To help someone else who's afraid and in danger, and has run out of people to turn to? Or did you stop being interested in justice once you'd got yours?'

The unexpected fierceness of her attack stunned Ash into silence. He hadn't seen this coming, hadn't realised it had been building for days. That her frustration at the lack of progress had created a head of steam that, sooner or later, was always going to blow the kettle off the stove.

His soul recoiled as if scalded. His first instinct, when he could find a voice at all, was to protest. To say that she was being unreasonable; that she was venting her anger on him only because he was handy; that she was expecting more of him than any man with a small business and two children to look after could hope to deliver.

What stopped him was the realisation that her assessment might, at least in part, be justified. Working together these last fifteen months, their achievements had been broadly satisfactory but their motivations had not been the same. Ash thought he was, on the whole, a good man, but he lacked Hazel's perfect altruism. She was right: what good he had done, he had done from essentially selfish motives. To protect himself, his family and his friends. To fend off the recurring questions about his mental equilibrium.

He had not done what she had done: taken up the cause of complete strangers simply because no one else would. And one of those complete strangers had been him, and he wouldn't be here – right here, in his shop, with his two sons on the other side of a flimsy partition wall – if she too had kept her compassion close to home.

He knew it, and felt a sudden surge of shame. Unfortunately, it had the effect that shame so often has on people: it made him defensive. 'I'm not Superman,' he gritted. 'I have never felt the urge to wear my underpants on the outside. I have only so much to go round: so much time, so much passion, so much strength. And yes, I look after my own first. I'm sorry if that seems selfish to you. Perhaps when you have children, you'll understand.'

Hazel barked an incredulous laugh at him. 'Oh dear God, you're playing the fertility card! The last refuge of the man losing on points. Gabriel – everything has babies. Goldfish have babies. Earthworms have babies. Mice do almost nothing their entire lives but have babies. Having the physical equipment and the psychological urge to pass on your DNA does not turn you into a higher life-form! It just messes with your hormones so you *think* it has.

'Having children is not a get-out-of-jail card for when difficult decisions have to be taken. If anything, your family gives you a vested interest in having a civilised world to raise them in. You can't opt out of your duties as an intelligent, compassionate human being because it's time to help with the homework!'

The gibe struck home. Fair comment always does. Ash muttered resentfully, 'You used to be more understanding . . .'

'And you used to care about people you weren't directly related to,' snapped Hazel. 'Now you hardly care what happens, as long as it doesn't happen here or at Highfield Road.'

'I'm sorry to be such a disappointment to you,' retorted Ash. Beyond the kitchen door, the bitterness of his tone made the boys look up from their books. 'But everyone grows up eventually. This is what being an adult looks like. Having responsibilities, and having to meet them even when you're not sure how or even if you can. Having to put everything else on the back-burner because nothing, *nothing*, gives you the right to mess up children's lives. Not being too tired, not being too busy, and not being distracted by other people's problems.

'Those children out there' – he gestured jerkily – 'exist because we made them. Cathy and I. They are about the only good things either of us ever did. And their mother deprived them of their father for four years, and then their father deprived them of their mother. I can't undo any of that. I can't wave a magic wand and give them nothing but happy memories. But I can be here for them now: always, every day. If that means not being available to play Batman and Robin with you, I'm sorry. I really am sorry, Hazel. I know how much I owe you.

Maybe I don't say it often enough, but I haven't forgotten. Everything I have today, including those boys, I owe to you.

'But don't you see, having them is what ties my hands now. I'm not a free agent in the way that I was twelve months ago. It's not that I think Elizabeth Lim's problems aren't important. It's just that I'm pretty well fully committed – mentally, emotionally and in terms of hours in the day. However much I might like to help, I don't have the spare capacity for projects.'

As soon as the word was out, he knew it was the wrong one. And if he hadn't, the dark flash of Hazel's eyes would have told him. '*Projects?* You think that's what this is – a little hobby for me? Like needlework or stamp collecting: something to occupy my pretty little head and keep me out of mischief.'

'I didn't mean that,' Ash said miserably.

'You meant *exactly* that,' insisted Hazel. 'That someone with a family, or perhaps a more important job, would have better things to worry about.'

For a moment she teetered on the brink of pointing out how much he owed to her penchant for a project; and if she had, their friendship might have never entirely recovered. Some things can never be unsaid, or forgiven, or forgotten. At the last, though, she rowed back from rubbing his nose in her moral ascendancy. The essential kindness that underlay everything she did reasserted itself, and she just shook her head with a quiet regret that drove blades between his ribs.

She passed through the shop. 'All right. You get on with being a responsible member of society, and I'll go see if there's anything trivial enough for me to waste a bit of time on.'

Both boys' heads swivelled to watch her go. When the door had closed between them, the quiet click jolting Ash's heart as a resounding slam would not have done, Gilbert left the book table and joined his father in the kitchen. 'I suppose you know, Dad, you could have handled that better.'

'Tell me about it,' muttered Ash. Then, because he had a desperate need to strike out at someone, if only verbally, he growled: 'Who are you, my mother?'

Don't shoot the messenger, Patience said calmly, regarding them both from the kitchen doorway; and Gilbert cast her a puzzled look as he went back to his books.

TWENTY-TWO

By the time she reached her car, Hazel was having to stoke her anger to keep from crying. It wasn't the first time she'd exchanged harsh words with Gabriel Ash. There were times when he'd behaved badly, there were times when she had. This was different. There was a sense of finality she had not had before. She was aware that things had changed which could never change back, and that in consequence the friendship she had so valued must either change too or break. There were no other options. The sense of loss ached in her throat.

Nor was she blind to the inevitability of this moment. Its seeds had been sown when he discovered that his sons, long feared dead, were in fact alive and well. Hazel had thrown herself into the campaign to bring them home with a determination and an energy matching their father's, and this was what it had earned her: to be pushed aside as an irrelevance by someone who, it turned out, mattered more to her than a lover.

Hesitating on the pavement, with the car door open and the sights of downtown Norbold – the slab-sided concrete pillbox that replaced the pretty Victorian town hall back in the 1970s, the closing-down sale in the town's one department store, some of the finest potholes in the county – blurred by unshed tears, for a moment she considered going back to Rambles With Books and trying to salvage something from the wreck of their friendship. What stopped her was pride. She was reluctant to admit how much it meant to her when it clearly meant so much less to Ash.

Pride has its uses. But Hazel was a realist: she knew that it destroyed more than it built. She would have swallowed hers if she could have seen a way that their next conversation could end on a more positive note than the last one. She would have apologised, except that apologising for misdeeds she hadn't committed and statements she believed to be true could only make matters worse. If they weren't going to be honest with one another, perhaps nothing they shared was worth saving.

Perhaps it was time to admit that whatever they'd had, it had run its course and come to its natural end. Perhaps she was behaving like a jilted ex, refusing to believe that someone she had once been close to had moved on. Was that what Ash saw when he looked at her now – a clinger? Someone desperate to turn the clock back?

She hesitated on the pavement no longer, but got into her car and drove out of Norbold with no clear idea of where she was going, only what she was leaving behind. A couple of miles into the leafy lanes of Warwickshire, however, she knew where she was heading.

The Harbingers' housekeeper greeted her with as little enthusiasm as is consistent with common politeness, or slightly less. 'Not again!'

A police officer goes many places where she isn't welcome. It had never worried Hazel much. But she was surprised to be so instantly recognised, even out of uniform, by someone she'd never met. 'Possibly,' she said carefully. 'Assuming I am who you think I am.'

Mrs Fisher sniffed disparagingly. 'You're from the police.'

'Well, yes,' admitted Hazel, 'and no. I *am* a police officer. I am not currently on duty.'

'Detective Inspector Gorman didn't send you?'

At least Hazel was able to answer honestly. 'No.'

'Detective Inspector Gorman,' said Mrs Fisher darkly, 'has spent so much time in this house recently that I'm beginning to wonder if I should make up a room for him and set him a place at dinner. He has strained the patience of this family severely.'

Hazel kept her expression blank. 'I'm sure he'd be sorry to know that. But you do understand, he's trying to save someone's life.'

'What a pity he didn't try harder seventeen years ago!'

Seventeen years ago, Dave Gorman had even less seniority than Hazel had now, and no responsibility for policy or tactics. At the time the housekeeper was alluding to, he was doing foot patrols in a wooden-top helmet, seeing old ladies across busy roads and chasing truant children out of shopping centres. Hazel forbore to mention this, partly because of collective responsibility – an individual police officer and The Police were essentially the same in the eyes of most citizens, which was actually fair enough – and partly because the widow of Jennifer Harbinger's chauffeur had every excuse for feeling bitter.

'It must be very difficult for you,' she said quietly. 'That whenever these events are discussed, it's Mrs Harbinger's death that people talk about. As if she was the only innocent victim that night.'

Margaret Fisher looked quickly at her, and Hazel couldn't tell what was going through her head. 'Yes,' she said after a moment. 'It was. It's a long time ago now.'

'I'm not sure that injustice is something that time heals.'

'I've had a lot of support from my employer,' said the housekeeper. 'It helped.'

Hazel nodded. 'I imagine he feels the same way. The rest of us can only sympathise. But you know exactly what he went through, and he knows what you did. That's a bond between you that no one else shares.'

'Except family.'

'Of course. He has a daughter.'

'I was referring to my son,' said Mrs Fisher coldly.

Inwardly, Hazel winced. That momentary lapse had cost her ground in gaining the housekeeper's trust. Honesty was probably the only thing that would help her now. 'Yes, of course you were. I'm sorry, I'd forgotten you and Mr Fisher had a son. He works here too, doesn't he?'

'He's the gardener.' A flicker of a smile suggested forgiveness. 'Really, he's more like an estate manager. Any decisions regarding the house, Miss Jocelyn and I take together. Any decisions regarding the outside space, Miss Jocelyn and John take together.'

'They must have known one another most of their lives.'

'They grew up together. There's only a couple of years between them. And of course, they too have something in common that they don't have with anyone else. There's never a good age to lose a parent, particularly in circumstances like that, but I think perhaps your teens is the worst time of all.' Mrs Fisher frowned. 'Is it Miss Jocelyn you're here to see? I should have asked.'

'Actually, it was you,' said Hazel. 'It occurred to me that we've talked to everyone else who was affected by these events, but I don't think anyone's asked if you remember anything helpful.'

'Helpful . . .?' The woman was clearly stunned. 'You want me to talk about Mr Harbinger? About this foolish threat he's supposed to have made when his heart was breaking on a daily basis? Do you imagine he told me he'd pushed the man responsible for Mrs Harbinger's death into a reservoir – and because nobody asked me, it never occurred to me to mention this? Miss Best, if there had been a conversation like that, and I'd decided to keep it to myself out of loyalty to my employer, do you suppose I'd change my mind just because you asked about it?'

'Mrs Fisher, I'm expressing myself very badly,' Hazel apologised. 'That's not at all what I was thinking. I'm sure Mr Harbinger would never put you in that position. No one who thought as highly of you as the Harbinger family obviously do would ask you to choose between protecting their interests and protecting your own.

'But seventeen years is a long time. It's hard to understand now just how these events transpired, who knew what at what point, what they did about it, what they said to other people. After so long, people's best recollections may be unreliable. Their memories may have been coloured by subsequent discoveries. They may honestly believe they saw or heard or said things which they didn't, or not until later.

'To be frank, Mrs Fisher, we're not getting on top of this in the way we need to. That may be because someone's lying to us, or there may be a degree of confusion because people's memories aren't as good as they think they are. If so, then the more people we talk to, the more cross-referencing we do, the sooner we can complete this investigation. I'm sure that's what you want, too.

'After seventeen years, there are only so many people we

can ask. You're one of them. You were intimately involved with the original events, and you're still in daily contact with two other people who were. I'm not asking you to betray any confidences. I'm asking you to help me understand what happened, the effect it had on all concerned, and whether we're even right in assuming that the robbery is the reason a woman who never did anyone any harm is now in fear for her life.'

Mrs Fisher looked doubtful, then she looked suspicious. 'The Cho girl? She'd be – what? – mid-thirties now. I haven't heard her name for years. Who knows where she ended up?'

Hazel bit her lip. But if the kidnappers knew, there was probably no reason to keep the truth from the Harbingers' housekeeper. 'She ended up in Norbold, as head teacher at the local school. After her parents died, she changed her name.'

The older woman was staring at her. 'So close? I had no idea. And the son?'

'That we don't know. London, we think, but his sister has no way of contacting him.'

'And you say she's in danger?'

Hazel nodded. 'Some men tried to kidnap her. It looks as if whoever murdered her parents finally tracked her down.'

'Her parents weren't murdered, Miss Best! Her father was unfortunate, or possibly careless, her mother was weak. No one is responsible for their deaths.'

'That's what the police thought at the time,' agreed Hazel. 'But *somebody* tried to snatch Felicity Cho from outside her school. I know that for sure: I was there. I would really appreciate any help you can give me.'

'I suppose, if you have some questions, I could try to answer them.' The housekeeper seemed to hear the reluctance in her own voice and felt the need to justify it. 'You'll appreciate, Miss Best, I don't harbour any great fondness for the Cho family. That man's actions resulted in the deaths of my husband and the lady I worked for.'

'I know that's the impression you were given. In fact, Edward Cho didn't tip off the police. One of the thieves was recognised by a patrol officer. The Armed Response Unit thought they were rounding up a Post Office blagger, not a gang of art thieves.'

It was impossible to judge what was going through Mrs

Fisher's head, whether this information made the events of the past easier to bear or harder. She had spent years coming to terms with an account of her husband's death which now seemed to have been inaccurate. It would take her more time again to process this new version and figure out how she felt about it.

Finally she said, 'Does Mr Harbinger know this? Or Miss Harbinger?'

Hazel didn't want to have to admit that she didn't actually know. 'DI Gorman has talked to both of them. But the details of what happened that day are still being put together.'

'And you're sure? You're not going to come back in another week and say, "Actually, there's more information again and *now* we think something different"?'

Hazel spread her hands helplessly. 'I can't guarantee that, no. This is what police work is like – we're always working on the last best guess. But I think this is the full story. The bits of the jigsaw were always there, only no one took the trouble to put them all together. Now we have, this is the picture we've got. If someone killed Edward Cho because they thought he'd put the insurers' financial interests above the safety of Jennifer Harbinger and your husband, they were mistaken. If the same person is trying to hurt his children, he'll only stop if we can convince him it was a mistake.'

'A mistake? *A mistake?* People have *died*.'

'Yes,' said Hazel sombrely. 'Mr and Mrs Cho were probably murdered, and we may be able to prove it now. But that was seventeen years ago, when the wounds were still very raw. I think there would be a degree of understanding if someone who'd just lost his wife struck out at the man he blamed. I don't think there'd be the same understanding if, all these years later, he attacked a woman who was only a schoolgirl when all this began. You talk about Jocelyn and your John being too young to lose a parent – well, Felicity lost both hers. And now she's being hunted herself. If you can tell me anything – *anything* – to help us protect her, you must see it's the right thing to do.'

Mrs Fisher fixed her with an accusing glare. 'You are. You're asking me to betray Mr Harbinger. To remember something that points the finger of blame at him. He's a sick old man! He doesn't need to be harassed like this.'

Hazel had a sense of matters balancing on a knife-edge. Whatever she said next could tip the housekeeper into grudging co-operation or obstinate resistance, and the stance she took now she would maintain under the assault of anything less than dynamite. Hazel picked her words carefully.

'He *is* an old man. And if he's done something wrong – even something very wrong – that will be taken into account. He isn't well. Losing his wife like that must have done terrible things to his mind. What happened seventeen years ago – to his family, to yours, to the Chos – is in the past and, sadly, there's not much we can do about it. But we can prevent him – save him, if you like – from doing something wicked *now*. I think a real friend would want to do that, even if there was a cost involved.'

'He'd go to prison?' asked the housekeeper in a low voice. 'In his condition?'

'I don't know,' Hazel said honestly. 'Some of this is speculation – we may not be able to prove what he did or didn't do seventeen years ago. A slippery country road, a distraught widow – we may suspect, but we'd have to be able to *prove* that Mr Harbinger was responsible, and the ability to do that falls off dramatically even after a few days, never mind years. But if something happens to Felicity Cho now, the evidence will be fresh. We'll know what we're looking at, and what we're looking for. We'll find the man responsible. Someone who cares about that man needs to keep him from committing a crime *now*.'

She waited.

It was impossible not to see, and not to sympathise with, Mrs Fisher's dilemma. The conflict was etched in her face. She would have walked over coals to protect Jerome Harbinger from anyone who threatened him. But what would she do to save him from himself? Still Hazel waited. She'd made the best pitch she could. Either it would succeed or she'd be shown the door.

Finally the woman said, uncertainly, 'It's not as if I *know* anything. I know what you know: that that poor man had his life ripped apart, and that he blamed the security company's negotiator for selling us out. I know he threatened Edward Cho and his family. I understand, and I think you do too, that he wasn't himself when he did that. Nothing that he said to me subsequently, and nothing that I overheard or saw, proves that he carried out that threat, or even attempted to.'

'And yet?' Hazel prompted gently.

Mrs Fisher sighed. 'And yet, I cannot put my hand on my heart and tell you I never suspected. There *were* things. Things he said, sometimes just looks, that were slightly out of place. Things that suggested he was – I don't know – thinking about something other than what we were talking about. When I heard what happened to Mr Cho, then when I heard about Mrs Cho, I can't say I didn't wonder.

'Unless I was imagining it.' She raised a supplicant face to her visitor, as if looking for reassurance that that was the explanation, that she'd simply let her imagination run away with her. Hazel could offer no such reassurance, so after a moment she continued. 'Of course, physically he was still strong then. Even as he grew older, he employed a lot of people. A lot of men have worked for him for a lot of years. They're not all . . . well, let's say they're not all choirboys. If he'd wanted that kind of help . . .' She shrugged unhappily.

'What about his daughter?' asked Hazel. 'Do you think she suspected too? Perhaps she was even involved. She may have felt the same compulsion he did.'

Mrs Fisher looked away. 'As time went on, Miss Jocelyn took over all her father's responsibilities. I'm not sure how much they actually discussed it – I think, very often, she just spotted something that was being neglected and worked it into her schedule. But within five or six years, she was running the company.'

'That's not really what I'm asking.'

'I know what you're asking!' The sharpness of her tone came from the pain these questions were causing her. 'And I've told you, I don't *know* anything. I'm just saying, when Jocelyn took over the business, she may have taken on everything that was important to her father. They were always very close. They're two very similar people. The same things matter to them, and they deal with problems the same way.'

'Did you ever hear them discussing the Chos? Or anything that, with hindsight, *could* have been a discussion about the Chos?'

'*Could* have been – yes. I don't listen in to their conversations, but neither do they wait until I've left the room before they talk to one another. There have been times when I've wondered what they were talking about. I've always assumed it was something to do with the business. I could have been wrong. John said once . . .' And there she stopped.

'Your son John? What did he say?'

Her brows drew together as she debated with herself. Finally she said, 'I told you, he doesn't just work in the garden. When they need a chauffeur, he puts on his father's old uniform.' She managed a thin smile. 'Metaphorically speaking – John's a much bigger man. And they don't need driving as much as they used to when Mrs Harbinger was alive. Mr Harbinger hardly goes out, and Miss Jocelyn usually prefers to drive herself. But . . .'

'But it happens sometimes,' suggested Hazel. 'And once when he was driving them, he overheard . . . what?'

But Mrs Fisher was close to shutting down the conversation. She'd already said much more about her family than a loyal housekeeper normally would. Hazel thought it wasn't concern for past crimes that motivated her so much as the hope that she might protect the Harbingers from the consequences of any future actions. She didn't think Mrs Fisher cared very much, even now, about the persecution of the Cho family, except as it might impact on her employers.

'I don't know,' said the housekeeper yet again; now her whole manner was closing down. 'I wasn't there. I may have misunderstood what John said; and he may have misunderstood what he heard. You can ask him yourself, if you want to. He's working in the garage this morning. Shall I call him and tell him you're coming?'

'Unless you want to come round with me, so we can all talk it through together?'

'No thank you,' said Mrs Fisher coldly.

TWENTY-THREE

You should call her.

'Call who?'

Even for a man doing his accounts, this was disingenuous. Even a man doing accounts much more demanding than Ash's would have known exactly who his dog was referring to.

Patience rolled her toffee-coloured eyes and sighed. You should call her.

'There's no point. She wants me to do something I've no intention of doing. If I call her, we'll only argue again.'

Better to argue than to pretend that hurting one another doesn't matter.

Ash put down his pen and turned to look at her. They were in the kitchen at Highfield Road. Ash had started bringing his books home to do at the kitchen table while the boys did their homework. It had seemed a nice, companionable thing to do. But first Gilbert and then Guy got bored with keeping him company after their own work was finished, so now they raced upstairs as soon as Frankie brought them home, did their homework at the playroom table, and spent the summer evenings either in the garden or in front of the trashiest television programmes they could find.

'She doesn't understand that I have other obligations now. Other responsibilities.'

She understands. But she misses you. She wonders why she fought so hard to give you a life in which she would no longer have a place.

Ash stared at his dog. She lifted one ear – the speckled one – and scratched delicately under it with a back paw. There was no doubt about it: she was a dog. It had occurred to him to wonder if she was actually an alien from the planet Zog, who by some kind of cosmic joke just happened to look like a dog. It would explain her use of telepathy. Of course, that would also be explained if his trolley had finally jumped the rails and was merrily hurtling downhill on the path of least resistance.

He blinked and cleared his throat. 'I don't actually need any help to feel guilty. Not about Hazel – not about any of it. It's the one thing I can do really well all by myself.'

Patience said primly, Feeling guilty is a self-indulgence until you've done everything in your power to make amends.

Ash snorted. 'Did you find that in a fortune cookie?'

You know where I found it, she said gnomically.

And he did. She could read him like a book. Now, as so often, Patience spoke the inconvenient truths that he tried to bury in the deep damp cellar of his consciousness, behind the Victorian furniture stored for long-deceased aunts and the boxes of orphan crockery that would come in useful sometime although they never had yet.

He muttered, 'What kind of amends?'

Call her, Patience said again. Better still, let's go round and see her. Apologies should always be made face-to-face if possible.

'I don't think Hazel's in the mood to apologise.'

Not her, you muppet – you.

'Me?' Ash was genuinely surprised. 'I haven't done anything to apologise *for*!'

All the more reason, Patience said firmly.

He dismissed that with a sniff and returned to his accounts. But he wasn't running Amazon, and there's a natural limit to how long anyone can spend writing up the sale of – it had been a good day – twenty-two second-hand books. When that limit had been reached, and he could tell from the quizzical tilt of her eyebrows that Patience knew it as well as he, Ash gave in.

'*All right.* All right. We'll go and see her. I'll apologise. Maybe, on the walk over, I'll figure out what I'm apologising for.'

There's a good boy, said Patience approvingly.

Railway Street, where Hazel lived, was a world away from Highfield Road, but only a twenty-minute walk. Since acquiring a dog, Ash had done a lot of walking, and they still did a couple of miles together most days. It was when he did a lot of his thinking. The roads around Norbold were too busy for day-dreaming behind the wheel, so if he wanted peace to think he would take Patience's lead down from the hall rack, wait while she fetched Spiky Ball, and set off for a ramble round the park or up the canal towpath.

Patience made a point of not interrupting him, but trotted quietly at his side, Spiky Ball held precisely in her narrow jaws; and people who would once have crossed roads to avoid Ash now smiled at them as they passed. When he noticed he smiled back; but mostly he thought, hunting the elusive notions through the labyrinthine pathways of his mind.

Hazel's car was missing from its usual spot under her front window. There was nothing odd about that: the likeliest explanation was that she'd gone to Meadowvale, to pester Dave Gorman some more. Ash phoned to ask if he should wait for her, but the call went straight to voice mail.

That wasn't unusual either. There are many junctures in the career of a police officer when the jingle of an untimely phone-call could be embarrassing, others when it could be dangerous. But Hazel was supposed to be on holiday. Perhaps she'd got in the habit of turning it off. Now he thought about it, he hadn't phoned her for so long he couldn't be sure. They talked – when they talked – when she called him, or when she came round to Highfield Road or the shop.

He looked down at Patience, and Patience looked back, smugly. See?

She had a point. It doesn't take long to make a phone-call. There were plenty of quiet moments in his schedule when he could have asked Hazel about her day and told her about his. 'We'll wait,' he decided. 'Maybe she won't be long.'

'Cooee!'

That wasn't Hazel. Hazel had never cried 'Cooee!' in her life. Ash looked round for the source of the hail and spotted the next-door neighbour waving at him from an upstairs window.

'Hello, Mrs Burden.'

'It's Mr Ash, isn't it?' Ash had to acknowledge that it was. 'If you're looking for Hazel, she went out.'

He nodded. 'Do you know when she'll be back?'

'Couldn't say,' said Mrs Burden. 'I just saw her driving off.'

'When was that?'

'About tea-time. Half-past five or so.'

That was when she'd come to the shop. He glanced at his watch: nearly five hours ago. He'd thought, when she left him, she was coming home. 'She hasn't been back since?'

'I don't think so, dear. I generally hear the front door.'

It was gone ten o'clock, and the long summer twilight was well advanced. Hazel had left the bookshop soon after six; and she had left angry with him. Where had she gone instead of coming home? She might have met friends, or gone to a local pub, but the worry beads chafing softly in the pocket of Ash's mind suggested another possibility. She'd thought of a way forward, seen a way to hasten matters towards a conclusion. If so, there were two places she might have gone.

DI Gorman's number was one of a small, select circle on Ash's phone: with hardly a moment's hesitation he called it.

Gorman answered immediately. 'Gabriel? Is everything all right?'

'I expect so. Is Hazel with you?'

'No.' He sounded surprised.

'Has she *been* with you?'

'No. Have you tried her home?'

'I'm there now,' Ash said tersely. 'Her car's gone, and her phone's switched off. Dave, I saw her earlier. She was angry with me – she wanted me to do something about the Harbingers. I refused, and she stormed out. I think that's where she's gone.'

DI Gorman was done playing games with these people. He turned into the Harbingers' drive at speed, spitting the carefully raked gravel onto the carefully manicured lawn, with two squad cars behind him. This was as near going in mob-handed as Meadowvale could manage with three constables on holiday and Sergeant Murchison off with his trouble.

Nor had he sought permission. He had informed Superintendent Maybourne what he intended to do and why; and while he was still marshalling his arguments for when she said no, she nodded and reached for her jacket. 'I'll follow you down.'

Hurrying home for his car, Ash found himself trailing the police convoy by a mile or more. Gorman had a search organised by the time he reached the Harbingers' farmhouse. The doors to all the outbuildings were standing open and uniformed and CID officers were working methodically through a range of garages, potting sheds, boiler houses, empty stables and disused pigeon lofts.

Hazel's car was not in front of the house, not in the yard that ran down the side and round the back, and now, with the doors ajar, it was plainly in none of the garages either.

Jocelyn Harbinger stalked down the kitchen steps and looked for a moment as if she was going to take a swing at the detective inspector. Instead she said, in the clipped tones of someone who is only just not shouting, 'I take it you have a search warrant?'

Gorman eyed her implacably. 'Do I need one?'

'Yes!'

'Then yes.' He shook it out and slapped it into her hand. 'Where's your handbag?'

She stared at him. 'Inside. Why?'

'You're going to need it. And your father's going to need any medications he ought to take in the next six hours.'

'Six hours?' Jocelyn's voice ran up in anger and alarm. 'I don't understand. What . . . where . . .?'

'You're both going to accompany me to Meadowvale Police Station, where I will be conducting formal interviews into the attempted kidnapping of Elizabeth Lim and the actual disappearance of Constable Hazel Best. If you'd like your solicitor present, now's the time to call him.'

Jocelyn was shocked by the change in his manner. She'd had him down as a fairly affable, reasonably competent small-town copper, promoted to or possibly just beyond the limits of his ability, working on not enough evidence and generally a shade out of his depth. She wasn't sure what had turned him into this hard-eyed, sharp-tongued, infinitely determined officer – new information he hadn't had before, mislaying one of his officers? – but the transformation left her breathless and off balance. 'Are you arresting us?'

Gorman leaned closer and his eyes were fierce. 'Do I need to?'

'Er . . .' Perhaps it was a bluff. But she didn't dare call it. 'No . . .'

'Good. Get your father. If you need help with him, bring your housekeeper.'

The search party split up, half its number following Jocelyn into the house while the rest finished inspecting the outbuildings before moving off into the grounds.

A thorough search of even a modestly sized property is a more time-consuming affair than members of the public ever realise. It can take a couple of days to be quite sure that any and all evidence of wrong-doing has been collected. An evidential search of a building as old, large and randomly extended as the Tudor farmhouse could easily take a week, and leave the place looking like a bombsite. But they weren't, at this point, looking for fingerprints and bloodstains. There was no attempt to lift carpets and rugs, no shifting of furniture, no application to suspicious stains of Luminol and ultra-violet light. They were just looking for a missing person, and after forty minutes DI Gorman was as confident as he could be that, if Hazel had come here, she had also left.

Only at that point did he ask Jocelyn Harbinger if Hazel had paid her a visit.

'Who?'

Gorman breathed heavily at her. 'Constable Hazel Best. Tall girl, fair hair – full of questions. We know she came here.' This was stretching the truth a little, but he felt justified.

'Well, I haven't seen her.'

'Ask your father.'

Jerome Harbinger was in the back seat of the second police car, looking both lost and angry. Jocelyn glanced at him, and back at Gorman. 'Inspector . . .'

'Ask him.'

But before she could, the housekeeper who had been putting a somewhat superfluous blanket around her employer's knees straightened up and said primly, 'Excuse me, Miss Harbinger, but I saw the young lady the policeman's talking about. Earlier this evening. About a quarter to seven?'

She looked to him for confirmation, and Gorman nodded. 'That might fit.'

'She seemed to think I could tell her – tell the police – things that the family either couldn't or wouldn't. She was, of course' – she looked directly at Jocelyn – 'mistaken. We talked for a little while. She asked if she could also talk to my son, and we went out into the gardens to find him. But he'd gone over to a neighbour for some vermiculite. She said she might pop back tomorrow, and she left. A little after seven, I suppose.'

'Did she say where she was going next?' Gorman was keeping an open mind about Mrs Fisher's account. He didn't have to decide whether or not to believe her just yet. All he had to do at this point was keep asking questions.

Mrs Fisher frowned as she sifted her memory. 'Yes. Well, no, but she asked the best route to Coventry from here.'

'Coventry?' He turned to Ash, who was standing at his elbow. 'You know any reason she'd want to go to Coventry?'

'I don't think so.' A suspicion tugged at the corner of Ash's mouth. He looked past Gorman to the housekeeper. 'Which *is* the best way from here?'

'This time of year? The hill road – through Beominster, up Clover Hill and past the reservoir. I wouldn't send anyone that way in winter, but it's a good enough road in good weather.'

Mention of the reservoir flared Gorman's eyes wide. 'That's where . . .'

'Yes,' said Ash flatly. 'She wanted to see where Edward Cho died.' He was halfway to his car before the sentence was out.

Gorman went to follow. But Jocelyn Harbinger stopped him with a hand on his sleeve. 'So . . . what? Are we coming with you? I should tell our solicitor to meet us at the reservoir?' She'd had a couple of minutes to recover something of her old self-possession.

Gorman thought for a moment, then shook his head. 'No. The interview will have to wait. I'll send a car when I'm ready to see you.'

TWENTY-FOUR

It wasn't the shortest way to Coventry, and it wasn't the fastest road. But the shortest road was via one small village after another, none of them with bypasses, most of them occupied mainly by old ladies on sticks and young children on tricycles, all confident of their right-of-way over vehicular traffic. And the fastest road, the motorway, was eight miles in the wrong direction. In summer, the Clover Hill road was the obvious choice.

In winter it was a series of frost pockets linked by sheet ice. Edward Cho wasn't the first motorist to end his journey in the reservoir, fifteen metres below the road, and he wouldn't be the last.

Some reservoirs are miracles of the water engineer's art, beautiful as well as useful, indistinguishable from natural lakes and drawing trippers from miles around. The Clover Hill dam wasn't in that category, mainly because of its underlying geology. Warwickshire is a county of rolling hills, green pastures and picturesque spinneys; Clover Hill was unusual in the steep ravine that fell away from its western flank, providing the perfect opportunity to dam a watercourse. If the art of dairy farming is to extract the maximum amount of milk with the minimum of moo, the skill of reservoir building is to hold back the maximum amount of water with the shortest possible dam. Water engineers have wet dreams about ravines.

So even on a sunny day there were no campsites on its steep banks, no painters poring over their easels, no windsurfers exploring its chilly depths between occasional brief excursions on their boards. But it did have a certain bleak charm, and a small car park had been constructed close to the spillway. Sometimes, in nice weather, people brought kites to fly over the dark and enigmatic water, but by the time the police convoy arrived dusk had all but given way to darkness and the car park was empty.

Ash was not a police driver and his Volvo was not a police car: he was overtaken on the first hundred-metre straight. As he pulled into the car park he saw headlights and torches, and Gorman hurrying up the bank towards him. Behind him, the last of the day extinguished by the towering hills, the surface of the water was oily black. Ash lowered his window. 'She's not here?'

DI Gorman bit his lip. 'Gabriel – there are tyre-marks on the grass.'

For a moment he didn't understand. 'Going where? There's nothing down there but . . .' And there he stopped.

Gorman gave a fractional nod. 'Yes. Going into the water.'

If they'd got here an hour earlier, DI Gorman would have called for police divers. That was what Ash expected him to do, and he waited impatiently to hear that they were on their way. Gorman took him aside.

'It's too dangerous in the dark, Gabriel. If her car's down there, and if she's still in it, we know she's not coming out alive. I can't risk men's lives for what can only be a recovery operation.'

Ash stared at him. He couldn't believe what he was hearing. It made perfect sense, it was the only possible decision, except that this was Hazel they were talking about. Except that his friend could be trapped in her car under fifteen metres of cold black water, and Gorman wanted to leave her there until it was safe to send someone down to take a proper look. Ash wanted to shout and scream at him, to swear that it wasn't so, it couldn't be, but if it was they had to do something now, right now. But deep inside him an emotional black hole was opening up, hollowing him out, feeding on his gut and then his heart and then his voice. When he opened his mouth, for a moment no sound came. Then he managed, 'What are we going to do?'

Gorman was gutted too. But he had more experience at putting his emotions on hold while he did what was necessary. He said gently, kindly, 'You're going to go home, and go to bed and try to get some sleep. I'm going to stay here, and at first light tomorrow, which should be about four o'clock in the morning,

I'll have divers ready to go into the water. I'll call you as soon as I know anything.'

It was midnight before Ash and Patience returned to Highfield Road. But Frankie, hearing the door, came downstairs, got the salient facts in a few brief sentences, and took over.

She didn't think Ash would go to bed, but she made him lie down on the kitchen sofa and put a warm quilt around him for the shock. Then she made hot chocolate and buttered toast, and told him to eat, and went upstairs for another quilt, meaning to spend the night in the chair beside him. If she could do nothing to help but wait with him, that was what she would do. But returning a minute later she found that fear and exhaustion had caught up with him and he was asleep, the white dog pressed into the small of his back. She sat down quietly, finished the toast, and drowsed intermittently as the night wore on.

At ten past four the phone rang. It was DI Gorman. 'The divers are in the dam now. There's a car down there. But it's deep – it's going to take time to recover it.'

'Hazel's car?' Ash needed him to be clear.

'It's too soon to say, Gabriel. It could have been there for years. They can't even tell me what colour it is. Best guess is, it's a small dark hatchback.'

There was nothing else to be said. Both men knew what Hazel Best drove.

'When will you know if . . . if . . .?' He meant, If she's still in there.

Gorman knew what he meant. 'Soon. I'll call you back.'

'Don't bother,' said Ash, throwing off the quilt, 'I'm on my way.'

By the time he reached the Clover Hill, the divers had attached a rope and airbags to the sunken car, and borrowed a JCB to lift it onto the bank. Ash hurried down the grassy slope to where Gorman was watching the rope arrow into the depths. Something was becoming visible: not the car but the yellow airbags raising it. The seconds ticked slowly by. The shape of the vehicle began as a suggestion and hardened to a certainty. Finally there was no more room for doubt. It was a small navy-blue hatchback, still showing the scars of its last off-road venture. Hazel had nearly drowned in a roadside ditch that night.

Ash had to know but it took all his courage to look. He let out a gusty sigh. 'There's no one inside.'

'No,' agreed Gorman. 'But Gabriel, don't get your hopes up. The windscreen's broken. She could have gone out that way.'

Ash didn't understand. He looked urgently round the hillsides, half now in sunshine and half in shade. 'You mean, she could be trying to walk home? We need to look for her – organise a search. We need—'

'Or,' Gorman interrupted him, 'she never made it to the surface.'

Ash gave a little moan like an injured animal. All the strength drained out of him, like the black water draining out of the drowned car. So this was how it ended. He'd never thought he would lose her. He'd always thought that, when he needed her, she'd be there.

When she'd needed him, he wasn't.

Only an effort of will kept him on his feet. 'When will you know?'

'When we find her. We've got four men in the water now, there are more on the way.'

'And if they don't find her?'

'Then we won't know until we find her somewhere else.'

It wasn't what he needed to hear. He needed to hear that no news was good news; that while they didn't know she was dead, there was a chance she was alive. He wanted Gorman to promise that there had been time for her to get out before the car sank, and that with luck she was steaming gently in front of the Aga in the nearest farm kitchen right now. He wanted someone to tell him that she hadn't died the way Edward Cho died, scared and alone with the cold waters of the Clover Hill dam closing over her head.

DI Gorman couldn't do that. But he reached out a clumsy hand and clasped Ash's shoulder. 'If this wasn't an accident . . .'

'Of *course* it wasn't an accident!' Ash's voice broke with grief.

'. . . We'll find out. This one isn't going to the back of the filing cabinet.'

After a moment Ash nodded, mutely, and Gorman went back to work.

Someone was tugging at Ash's sleeve. He looked down and met the golden gaze of his dog looking up.

She wasn't in the car.

Ash blinked several times in quick succession. But he hadn't imagined it. Trying not to move his lips he whispered, 'How do you know?'

Patience gave him a deeply cynical stare. Is this nose ever wrong?

'The car's been in fifty feet of water!'

I'm telling you, she was never here. I know what Hazel smells like. She wasn't the last person in that car.

Hope burgeoned in Ash's breast like a sob. 'But that means . . .'

. . . She's somewhere else, agreed Patience. All these policemen are looking for her in the wrong place. You have to tell them.

And that was going to be a problem. 'Excuse me, officers, my dog says . . .' Ash had *never* been sufficiently insane to tell the local constabulary that his lurcher spoke to him. When they saw *him* talking to *her* they called him Rambles With Dogs. He hated to think what they'd call him if he said she talked back.

He sidled up to Gorman. 'Dave – I don't think she's dead.'

The DI turned sharply on his heel and fixed Ash with a penetrating gaze. 'Is that hope talking, or have you some reason for thinking it?'

Ash gave his awkward, bear-like shrug. 'I don't know. Maybe I'm kidding myself, but I think I'd know if she'd died here.'

Gorman looked deeply unconvinced. But he said, 'Well – that's good, isn't it?'

'It would be great,' agreed Ash, 'if I could think of some way that her car ended up in fifty feet of water but she wasn't in trouble.'

When Dave Gorman frowned, his hairline came down to meet his eyebrows. 'You're serious about this?'

'Yes. I'm worried that we're all standing round here when we should be out looking for her.'

'Gabriel – the likeliest explanation—'

'I know,' Ash cut in quickly. 'I know that, usually, things are exactly how they look. But *you* know that sometimes they aren't. I know what I feel. I can't explain it, I can't *prove* that she's alive. But just suppose I'm right. Can't we cover the possibility? We should go back to the Harbingers'. That's the last place where we know she was.'

All Gorman's experience told him Gabriel Ash was clutching at straws. That he was hunting desperately for some alternative explanation because he couldn't deal with the evidence in front of him. But experience isn't everything: there's such a thing as instinct too, and Gorman's instincts were telling him that, until they found the body of Hazel Best, they should not treat her death as a fact.

He reached a decision. 'Give me another half-hour. If they haven't found her by then, I'll leave Superintendent Maybourne to oversee things here and I'll take my people back to Spell. I don't think she's there, Gabriel. We'd have found her if she was. But I can talk to the Harbingers again, and SOCO can look for trace evidence.' He meant bloodstains.

Ash nodded his gratitude. 'What would you like me to do?'

'Honestly? I'd like you to go home. You can't be part of the investigation, and that means you're just in the way. Leave it to us now. You don't want to be here if we find a body. And if we find her alive, you'll be the first one I call.'

That made sense. 'All right. We'll leave you to it. But you will call . . .?'

'Of course I will. Whether there's anything to report or not.' He watched Ash shamble back to his car – his late mother's car, that predated electric windows and parking assist and computerised diagnostics, and was thus likely to remain road-worthy until someone actually drove a steamroller over it.

Only as the buff-coloured Volvo headed back down Clover Hill did Gorman get an echo of what Ash had said. Puzzlement made his forehead vanish again. 'We?'

TWENTY-FIVE

It was cold where Hazel was, and dark, and damp. The words bounced queasily around inside her aching skull. They were accurate, so far as they went, but as her mind started to clear a little she recognised that they didn't explain very much.

It was summer: there should have been nowhere this cold anywhere in England. It was like the cold at the bottom of a deep well where the sun never reaches. The stones she lay on – stones? Yes, apparently, setts or blocks of stone tightly butted with fine gritty lines between them – radiated cold, transfixed her with penetrating fingers of it. She couldn't remember what she was wearing, but it wasn't enough.

The dark wasn't the dark of a dark night, when you might have trouble distinguishing a friend from a stranger close enough to touch. There were no shapes of deeper darkness silhouetted against the almost black of an overcast night. There was no light of any kind. The darkness was absolute. She blinked, consciously, to make sure her eyes were in fact open; and establishing that they were, confronted the possibility that whatever had happened had blinded her. The throbbing pain at the back of her skull was the only evidence she had, and it wasn't reassuring.

The stones she lay on weren't just cold, they were damp. Dank. So was the air she breathed. It smelled of deep earth and neglect, like an abandoned mine. Were there any abandoned mines in Warwickshire? She didn't know.

She considered, briefly, the possibility that she was dead. She hoped not – it would be disappointing to learn that you took your headaches with you – and on the whole decided it was unlikely. She tried to approach the puzzle logically. But she hadn't got much further than cold, dark and damp when a wave of nausea rolled over her, putting a stop to any more productive thinking for now. She lay with her cheek flat against the cold, damp stone, and cold salt tears rolled slowly down her nose.

*   *   *

We're not really going home, are we? asked Patience as soon as a bend in the Clover Hill road hid the little car park from sight.

'Of course we're not,' said Ash. His voice was steely.

Good. Where are we going instead?

'Harbingers'. We know Hazel was there – we need to find out if she ever actually left. Let's see if that nose of yours is as good as you claim.'

One of my forebears was a bloodhound, said the slim white lurcher loftily.

Ash wasn't entirely convinced. 'Well – maybe. In any event, any dog's sense of smell is vastly more powerful than a person's. The time has come to establish whether you're as smart as you say you are, or just a dog like any other dog and everything else is my imagination working overtime. Have a prowl round those outbuildings, see if Hazel was there. See if' – he didn't want to say it out loud, but it was what he was thinking – 'she came to any harm there.'

There was a pause then. Ash drove. Patience sat on the front seat beside him, wearing the seatbelt Hazel had insisted she needed. After a little while she said, We will find her, you know. She'll be all right.

'From your mouth to God's ear,' swore Ash.

To dog's ear, Patience amended complacently.

Jocelyn Harbinger was still in bed, though she hadn't done much sleeping that night, when she heard the hiss of tyres on gravel. Her heart turned over. She had known DI Gorman would either return or send for her, and she'd prepared herself for the interrogation that would follow. She didn't know what evidence he was working on, had persuaded herself there couldn't be anything worthy of the name. But if he was back here at – she glanced at the clock, already clear in the brightening day – quarter past five in the morning, he must have something substantial. It looked as if she was in for the fight of her life.

Well, that was all right too. She had been sitting on her hands to stop her doing what she had always done in difficult times: grabbing control of the situation and bending it to her advantage. This was different because today she wasn't the de facto head of Harbinger Transport but a suspect in a murder inquiry, and trying to force the pace would only make the investigating officer wonder why. But she wasn't sorry if matters were finally coming to a head. All her life she had fought for what she wanted. Fighting came more naturally to her than waiting. She rolled out of bed, dashed water in her face and quickly dressed.

When she heard voices in the hall she went downstairs. But it wasn't Gorman. It was the big, slightly unkempt, shambling man in the old beige Volvo, accompanied by his slender white dog. 'Mr Ash. Did you catch up with Miss Best?'

He wasn't sure how much he should tell her. But if she was involved in Hazel's disappearance – for now, that was the label he was sticking with – she already knew, and if not she might be able to help. 'We found her car. Where they found Edward Cho's, at the bottom of the Clover Hill dam. There was no one in it.'

The colour drained from Jocelyn's face, the timbre from her voice. 'Have you found her?' Ash shook his head. 'So she might still have . . . gone into the reservoir?'

'She might,' agreed Ash. 'We don't know.'

'Oh, dear God.' There was an oak blanket-box at the foot of the stairs. Suddenly weak, she lowered herself onto it. 'Are they – I don't know – looking for her?'

'Of course. There are divers in the water now. If she was in the car when it went into the dam, there's little chance of finding her alive. So I'm pinning my hopes on the possibility that she wasn't.'

'That she got out before it sank, swam ashore and wandered off into the hills?' It didn't sound very likely, but if he wanted to cling to a chance in a hundred, Jocelyn wasn't going to argue.

'Or else she wasn't in the car at all, in which case someone's gone to a lot of trouble to make it look as if she was.'

'Who?' She bridled. '*Me?* Now I'm being accused of kidnapping police officers? Tell me, are there any outstanding crimes on the books at Meadowvale Police Station that I'm *not* in the frame for?'

'Right now, Miss Harbinger,' Ash said wearily, 'all that interests me is finding Hazel. If she is in the dam I'm already too late: if she's anywhere else, there may still be time. Have you any objection to me searching your outbuildings?'

'The police have already looked there!'

'I have a dog.'

Jocelyn regarded Patience. Patience regarded Jocelyn.

'That dog?'

'She's in plain clothes.'

Jocelyn Harbinger rolled her eyes despairingly. 'Go anywhere you want to. Look – sniff – anywhere you want. You won't find her. You won't find anything.'

As the nausea subsided, Hazel supposed she ought to make an effort to move. Nothing much happened, but the attempt was itself instructive. Trying hurt her wrists and her ankles. Even in her current state, it was no great leap of intuition to conclude that someone had tied her up.

In an odd way, this was reassuring. Criminals, even violent criminals, she could deal with. She could figure out their motives, predict their actions, hope to out-think them. Well, perhaps not just now, but when this headache subsided a bit more. Dealing with criminals was part of her job, and she was *good* at her job. She clung onto that thought as if it were the only floating debris after a shipwreck.

Against people, even people who'd do this to her, she had a chance. Half an hour ago – maybe: she had no way of accurately tracking the passage of time – she'd thought she might be dead, and she didn't fancy her chances against the Grim Reaper at all. As recently as five minutes ago, when she'd first tried to move, she had thought that the injury which had caused her headache might also have paralysed her. Compared with that, a bit of rope round her hands and feet was a problem on a much more human scale. She made a determined effort to calm her thinking, plan her next move – well, *metaphorical* move. Someone had gone to considerable efforts to bring her here and make sure she stayed. He – or she: Hazel believed in equal opportunities – would be back. She needed to know what she would do, what she would say, then.

It would help to understand how she'd got here. She was pretty sure she'd been unconscious for a while, possibly quite a while, so what was the *last* thing she remembered? What was she doing, where was she doing it and with whom, immediately before the world went away?

She screwed her eyes up tight – out of habit, there were no sights to distract her – and forced her mind to retrace its steps. She was in the country somewhere. She remembered driving through countryside: trees, and dappled shadows under them. It had been a nice day for a drive. No, a nice *evening.* Where was she going? And did she get there?

Big house, she thought ponderously. Bigger than Railway Street; bigger even than Highfield Road. And . . . lorries?

That was the key that opened the floodgate. It all came back then. She'd driven out to Spell, to the Harbingers' farmhouse; but it wasn't them she'd been speaking to, it was their housekeeper. Who'd been helpful up to a point, but Hazel had left knowing little that she hadn't known before.

But she had left. She remembered that. She was going to talk to . . . to the gardener . . . to John Fisher, who was the son of the Harbingers' murdered chauffeur, but he'd gone somewhere, for something. Vermiculite. What the hell *was* vermiculite?

So she'd got back in her car and . . . And that was where the memory ran out. Which didn't mean that it was then that someone took a blunt instrument to the back of her head. It could have happened then, but it could have happened later. Brains are complex and mysterious organs, and it was possible that her recollection ended where her problems began, but it might simply mean that concussion had interfered with her ability to retrieve stored memories.

If she didn't know what *did* happen, could she theorise about what *might* have happened? She might, or might not, have left the farmhouse. If she didn't, then it was probably one of the Harbingers who was responsible for her current situation. By all accounts Jerome was too frail to be hauling sturdy young women about, even if he'd managed to take one by surprise; but he was a man who employed other men, who was used to giving orders and being obeyed.

What about his daughter? She could have wielded the blunt instrument, but again, was likely to have needed help to move Hazel from where she fell to where she was now. So what about the gardener? He could have returned with his mysterious vermiculite in time to stop her leaving. He would have had no difficulty throwing her into the back of his vehicle, and perhaps not much compunction about it. They were as thick as thieves, the Harbingers and the Fishers. If they guessed she'd worked out what they'd done, seventeen years ago and since, they might have seen her visit – alone, apparently unsanctioned by Norbold CID – as an irresistible opportunity to bring her meddling to an abrupt and conclusive end.

So why had they tied her up instead of – she swallowed – killing her? They couldn't let her go after this, so why take the risk that she might escape or be discovered? Because . . . because . . . because she had information they needed. They thought she could lead them to Elizabeth Lim. They wanted to know what she knew: everything she knew. They had hurt her to bring her here, they would hurt her again to get the information they wanted, and then they would kill her.

Would they believe her if she said that everything she knew, DI Gorman knew as well? Probably not. It happened to be the truth, but it was exactly what she *would* say even if it wasn't.

He'd find her. Sooner or later Gorman would find her, however carefully the Harbingers disposed of her; or, if he didn't, Ash would. Neither of them would give up until they did. But it was going to be too late to do her any good. They probably didn't even realise that she was missing yet.

Which meant that, if she was going to come through this, she was going to have to rescue herself. The thought should, she was sure, have sent a warm tingle down her spine and a wine-like draught of courage to her heart. Where there's life there's hope. She was fit and strong – well, normally she was – and not stupid, and reasonably cool under fire; and she was a trained police officer with skills at her command that could tip the balance in her favour.

But she was also a realist. She was concussed, disorientated, chilled, tied up, and a fit strong *woman* when whoever had brought her here was almost certainly a fit strong man. All the sex-equality legislation in the world wouldn't alter the fact that her assailant was more powerful than she was. He might also be armed. If he thought for a moment that he was losing control of the situation, he would kill her on the basis that nothing she knew, nothing she could be persuaded to tell him, was worth the risk that she might get away.

She was so dead.

If she couldn't overpower him, could she out-think him? It would be helpful to know who she was dealing with. Not who was paying the piper, but who was playing the pipe. She kept coming back to John Fisher. She couldn't remember if she'd ever actually met him – although she had an image of him in her mind, big and broad-shouldered, so maybe she had. Maybe he got back with his horticultural necessity before she left the Harbingers'. Maybe they met on the driveway, and she stopped to speak to him, and . . .

Maybe it was before that. Could he have been one of the men at the school? On the whole she thought not. That was the sort of job you brought people in for. You didn't do it yourself, and you didn't give it to someone who worked at your house. Norbold was too close to home: there was too great a risk of recognition. Harbinger Transport employed a lot of men all over the country – if there was dirty work to do, there'd be someone willing to do it and able to disappear afterwards.

The chill of the damp floor was working its way into her bones. Hazel humped and wriggled herself onto her other side. It wouldn't make any difference in the long run, but her morale took a tiny boost from being able to do something, even something so minimal, to improve her situation.

Of the various people who *might* have decked her, the likeliest candidate was John Fisher. She'd been looking for him. His mother had said he'd be back shortly. They'd both worked for the Harbingers for years. Was that reason enough to commit murder for someone?

Hovering on the edge of her memory was something else someone had said. It might have been her. She'd said . . . she'd said . . . she'd said to Mrs Fisher, 'Mrs Harbinger wasn't the only innocent victim that night.' She'd acknowledged the housekeeper's loss, and the hurtful way her husband had been almost airbrushed out of the story.

But Mrs Fisher wasn't the only one to suffer that loss, that hurt. The same applied to her son. Her fit, strong son who worked for the Harbingers and had as much reason to resent Edward Cho as his employers had.

He hadn't threatened the Cho family. That didn't mean he didn't share the purpose of the man who had.

Jocelyn Harbinger had been twenty when her mother died, the chauffeur's son a couple of years younger. Suppose . . . suppose . . . Jerome Harbinger meant every word when he said he would wipe the Chos off the face of the earth. Suppose he killed Edward and Mary himself, alone and unaided. But as he grew older and frailer, who more natural to turn to for help than his employee, the strapping son of the other murder victim?

It made a kind of sense. The crimes perpetrated on the Cho family had required strength of purpose, strength of body, and money. Strength of purpose, to keep a vendetta alive for seventeen years. Physical strength, to do what had been done to Hazel, what had been done to Lester Pickering. And money, because if someone kills people for you, the last thing you want is for him to feel undervalued. Jerome Harbinger and John Fisher made a credible partnership in all the deeds that had been done.

Better than Harbinger and his daughter? Yes, because a gardener, a man who used his muscles every day, would always be stronger than a woman. Better than Harbinger and someone else she hadn't yet thought of? Also yes, because John Fisher had a motive that no one else could match.

When the door opened – there had to be a door, even if she couldn't see it – it wouldn't be Jerome Harbinger coming for her, and it wouldn't be his daughter. It would be John Fisher. He'd want to know how much the police knew, and where Elizabeth Lim was hiding. Some of the things she knew, she could *only* have learned from talking to Lim. That might not prove that Hazel knew where she was now, but Fisher would believe that she didn't only when he was sure she'd have told him if she did.

Then he would kill her, and if she hadn't managed to hold her tongue, he'd kill Lim too. That was what mattered most, to him and to Harbinger. Getting away with it mattered too, but annihilating the Cho family mattered more.

An odd little sound rasped in her throat. For a moment Hazel tried to believe it was a grim little chuckle. She could have taken some satisfaction from facing her own imminent death with a smidgeon of bravado. But it wasn't a chuckle: it was a sob, and she wasn't good enough at deceiving herself to pretend otherwise. Cold, alone and desperately afraid, she cried brokenly in the dark – for all the people she would never see again, for all the things she would never do, for the opportunities she had let pass and those that could never come again – until exhaustion stilled her.

TWENTY-SIX

Gabriel Ash was wary of giving Patience commands. This was not because she was disobedient, although she had a way of treating even the clearest requests as mere suggestions. He wasn't worried about offending her: after all, no one heard what she had to say except him. He worried what bystanders might think if she declined to co-operate and they heard him engaging in a strenuous, one-sided argument with his dog.

Today, though, there was no prospect of a disagreement. They both knew what they were here for. Ash opened the doors and, one by one, Patience explored the outbuildings.

All of them smelled of many things and quite a lot of people, including some people she was familiar with. None of them smelled of Hazel.

She wasn't here.

Ash didn't know if that was good news or bad news, but he knew Patience would be right. He turned to Jocelyn. 'Do you know where she parked her car?'

Jocelyn Harbinger shrugged, raised her voice. 'Mrs Fisher, did you notice where Miss Best parked her car?'

The housekeeper came out onto the kitchen steps. 'At the front, I think.'

'We'll try there.' Ash led the way round the corner of the house.

'See if you can pick up her scent,' he said softly to the dog. 'Figure out which way she went.'

Jocelyn was looking oddly at him. 'Aren't you supposed to give one-word commands to dogs?'

'I was thinking aloud,' said Ash.

In front of the house, where the gravel was disturbed by the comings and goings of many cars, Patience lowered her long nose to the stones and began casting from side to side. Almost immediately she stopped, with a somewhat casual version of a point.

Here.

'All right. And where did she go when she got out?'

More sniffing, then: The front door.

'Did she leave the same way?'

I don't think so.

The white lurcher cast a widening circle that took her back towards the side of the house.

She came out by the kitchen door. And . . . *here! Here!*

'What?'

Something was parked right here, on the corner. She got into it. She didn't get out.

Still Ash didn't know if he was hearing good news or bad. If Hazel had got into something other than her own car, and hadn't got out, almost anything might have happened to her – except driving her car off the Clover Hill road and into the dam. The turmoil of emotions raced across his face like cloud shadows on a meadow. 'Who parked here?' he asked.

Jocelyn could not or would not help. 'Anyone? Everyone? There have been cars coming and going for what feels like days now.'

Ash could barely contain his impatience. 'There was a vehicle parked right here, and Hazel Best went away in it. Who was driving it?' But neither Miss Harbinger nor her housekeeper had an answer for him.

He turned in desperation to the dog, no longer caring who else heard or what they thought. 'Can you find that vehicle?'

I can try, said Patience uncertainly.

'Try.'

Vehicles, like people, each have their own distinctive smell.

The trouble with roads, and even driveways, is the number of vehicles that pass over them. The cocktail of oil smells and grease smells and rubber smells that make up one particular vehicle's olfactory footprint is so easily overlaid and diluted by all the others.

Sometimes fate lends a hand. While Patience was still trying to sniff her way through the nasal maze that was the Harbingers' yard, and Ash was standing well back to give her room to work, a brown pick-up came down the drive. It made a jink around the dog and pulled up at the corner of the house, a couple of metres from where Ash was standing.

Patience wasn't sniffing now. She was erect, her head up, staring at the truck. She said, Found it.

John Fisher was a few years younger than Ash, and a few kilos heavier, but they were much of a height and build. The similarity would have been even more marked if Ash had earned his living working out of doors, building up muscle and a healthy farmer's tan, and would remember to stand up straight instead of stooping slightly. It was a habit he'd picked up during what he thought of as his doolally days. Being mentally ill attracted enough nervous glances; being mentally ill and six foot two made people cross roads or wait for another bus.

Jocelyn Harbinger said, 'Making an early start, John? I'm glad you're here. We've got a bit of a crisis on. Someone's gone missing – a policewoman from Norbold. Will you help us look for her?'

'Here?' He sounded almost more offended than surprised.

Jocelyn gave a helpless shrug. 'I don't quite understand it myself. Apparently her car was found in the Clover Hill dam. But Mr Ash' – she glanced at him but her gaze didn't dwell, possibly because of what he might read in it – 'thinks she may not have been in it. She was here yesterday, he thinks she may have come back.'

'Why?'

It could have been either of two questions: why would Hazel return to the Harbingers' house, or why would anyone think that? Ash chose to answer the first. Knowing what he knew – what Patience had told him – made it hard to be civil to the man; but he had to do it and somehow he did. The alternative was to admit to the source of his information, which would be the last thing he did before men in white coats dragged him away. He said quietly, 'Perhaps she had unfinished business here.'

'If I'd just driven my car into the Clover Hill dam,' said John Fisher, 'business would have to wait while I found some dry clothes and told people I was safe.'

Ash nodded. 'If that's what happened.'

Fisher looked at Jocelyn. 'I thought you said her car was found.'

'Police divers are searching the dam now,' said Ash. 'They still haven't found a body.' Only the belief that Patience knew they wouldn't kept his voice from cracking.

'And that means she came back here?' said Jocelyn doubtfully.

'It may mean she never left.'

'So how did her car get up to Clover Hill, five miles away?' That was Fisher.

'Clearly, someone drove it. It's a small hatchback, not a B-52 bomber – it doesn't take a special skill-set to operate it.'

Finally Jocelyn understood what he was saying. 'You mean – someone may have wanted it to look as if she'd drowned, when actually . . . You think she's been *kidnapped*?'

'I think that's possible, yes,' said Ash. 'That someone wanted us to waste time dragging the dam instead of looking for her.'

'Why would anyone kidnap a policewoman?' asked Fisher cynically.

'Why would anyone try to kidnap a teacher?'

Fisher looked at him. Then he looked at Jocelyn. Then he looked back at Ash and shook his head. 'I have no idea what you're talking about.'

'He's talking about Felicity Cho,' said Jocelyn Harbinger quietly. 'Someone tried to abduct her outside the school where she worked a couple of weeks ago.'

'Cho? As in . . .?'

'Yes.'

'*That* isn't a name I expected to hear again!'

'Perhaps that's why she changed it,' Ash said softly.

Fisher's gaze darkened from puzzlement towards anger. He hadn't actually been accused of anything, but it *felt* as if he had. 'Tell me again: *who* are you?'

'My name's Gabriel Ash. I run a bookshop.' Ash waited until he saw confusion in the other man's expression. 'I'm a friend of Hazel Best's – the missing woman.'

Perhaps the name rang a bell. Fisher looked at Ash as if he knew now who he was. And knowing took a weight off his mind. 'Oh yes.' He smiled. 'I've heard of you.'

His manner made it impossible to take that as a compliment. Ash gave a surprisingly predatory grin. 'That should save time, then. When did you last see Miss Best?'

'I haven't seen her,' said Fisher.

'She was here yesterday evening.'

'Yes? I wasn't here.'

'Because you were . . .?'

Fisher frowned. 'If it's any of your business, I was picking up some vermiculite.'

'The agricultural suppliers are open at seven in the evening?'

'A friend picked it up for me earlier in the day. He needed fertiliser. He picked me up a sack of vermiculite while he was there, and I collected it from him. You want to talk to him? We discussed football and milk prices – I'm sure he'll remember.'

Ash ignored the insolence of his tone. 'And you didn't come back here afterwards?'

'No, I went home.'

'So where's the vermiculite?'

Fisher stared at him. 'In the back of the pick-up. Do you want to see it?'

Which meant it was certainly in the back of his vehicle. It proved nothing. 'No, thank you,' Ash said politely. 'Can you explain why, when my dog picked up Hazel's scent, it brought her to your van?'

Fisher's mother had been following the exchange from the kitchen steps. 'Now I come to think of it,' she offered, 'I don't think she did park at the front. The policewoman. She parked her car on the corner, just about where John's pick-up is. Maybe that's what the dog can smell.'

'That could explain it,' conceded Ash. He turned to Jocelyn Harbinger. 'Do you mind if I take her out into the grounds? She might be able to find the trail again where there have been fewer people tramping around.'

Jocelyn looked deeply unconvinced. But she nodded. 'If you think it'll help. Is there anything I can do?'

'Not at the moment. Unless . . . are there any outbuildings we should check? Barns, byres, chemical stores?' He watched Fisher for a reaction; there was none. 'If any of them are locked, and you have keys . . .?'

Jocelyn had to think. 'There's a derelict barn over in the north-east corner.' She pointed. 'We've never used it, but a previous owner used to dip his sheep there. There's no lock on the door. By now, there may be no door. Apart from that, all the outbuildings are here, behind the house.'

'Including the one where I store chemicals.' A shade theatrically, Fisher reached into the back of the brown pick-up and carried two sacks, one under each arm, across the yard. Ash didn't even glance into the outbuilding where he deposited them. Patience had already checked inside.

'How much land do you have?' asked Ash.

Jocelyn looked momentarily perplexed. 'About half a mile in every direction. There was more once, but we aren't farmers.' That was clear: any farmer's daughter would have known to the nearest half-acre. 'The previous owner sold some off, and we sold some more. Most of what's left is let out to the neighbours.'

'Neighbours with *sheep*,' Fisher said pointedly. 'Don't let that dog worry them.'

Worry them! said Patience indignantly. What does he think I'm going to do – sneak up and whisper *Mint sauce, mint sauce* in their ears?

'We won't do any damage,' said Ash, his expression a careful blank. 'I'm just looking for my friend.'

'I hope you find her safe,' said Jocelyn.

'She's probably just chilling out,' suggested Fisher, closing the stable door. 'She'll bob up sooner or later.'

'From your mouth to dog's ear,' said Ash; and with that he and Patience turned down the drive towards the road.

Jocelyn Harbinger and her gardener watched them go. After a moment, hesitantly, Jocelyn said, 'Did he just say . . .?'

Fisher nodded. ''Fraid so. I said I'd heard of him, didn't I? Do you want to hear *what* I've heard?'

'Ooh yes,' said Jocelyn.

TWENTY-SEVEN

Hazel had no way to measure the passage of time, even approximately. At one point she'd tried counting, but either she'd got bored or perhaps she'd nodded off. It seemed absurd that anyone in her position could indulge in a little nap, but there was time since she regained consciousness that she couldn't account for. Perhaps the concussion was still affecting her. Perhaps it was the absolute darkness telling her body it should sleep.

The headache was better now, no more than tenderness and a kind of lurking discomfort. On the other hand – well, on both of them, and her ankles – the ropes chafed more with every passing hour. It was the closest thing she had to a timepiece.

She had tested them before; now she did it again, in case either they had grown looser or she had grown stronger as the night – or morning, or afternoon – had worn on. But the result was the same as before. The only thing with any freedom of movement was her brain.

Fisher would come for her. He would open the door, and after so long in the dark the light would blind her. But somehow – blinded, bound, and in the presence of a man whose safety required her death – she must find a way to live. To defeat him, or evade him, or raise the alarm, or *something*. People would be looking for her. Ash would be looking for her by now, and though he mightn't know where to look, he also didn't know how to stop. Maybe Dave Gorman would be looking too.

If she could do nothing else, she could yell. She could yell like a bull-moose at the peak of the rutting season. There was always the chance that someone would hear her, once that door was open. Of course, Fisher had brought her here – wherever *here* was – because it was quiet and out-of-the-way, and he didn't expect to be disturbed; but all the same . . . When the alternative to small chance is no chance at all, you grab the small chance and try to make it bigger.

So she would yell. Not engage him in a sensible conversation and attempt to persuade him of the error of his ways. It was too late for that. His strength of purpose and fear of the consequences both required that he dispose of her. They could chat as politely as a couple of church wardens at a vicarage garden party, they could do it over a cup of tea and a plate of small iced fancies, but in the end it would be her or him. She had to die for him to live free.

Her voice was probably the best weapon she had, but there was also her poor bruised head. She didn't relish the prospect of using it as a battering ram, but if she could find some way of propelling herself, even if these damn ropes did saw at her flesh, she would. She had nothing left to lose. Actually, *that* was the best weapon she had. Having nothing left to lose made her dangerous.

She wished she *felt* more dangerous.

Then, in the cold damp darkness, there was a sound that wasn't her. It was the first she'd heard in all the time she'd been here. She wasn't sure what it was, or where it was coming from. There was an odd acoustic in here: it almost sounded to be above her. As if someone was walking on her grave.

He was coming. This was it: her last chance, her only chance. She had nothing to fight him with, except the knowledge that anything she could do was better than doing nothing. If he got close enough for her to get her teeth into him . . .

After the long silence, the grating grinding of the door was like a scream in her ears. White light exploded in her eyes, swamping her vision. She couldn't afford to squeeze her eyes shut, couldn't bear to open them. Haloed by the light, almost eclipsed by it, was a dark figure. In truth it could have been anyone, but she knew who it was.

She forced the last fragment of play out of the ropes, ignoring the whines of protest from her savaged flesh, and rocked herself into a kneeling crouch that put her head more or less at groin height. All she needed was for him to come closer. One step, two steps. Close enough to kill her. He wouldn't use a gun – however carefully he'd chosen this place, he wouldn't risk that much noise, that *distinctive* a noise. A knife, then. And all that was holding her was rope.

Come on, sunshine, she thought combatively – just a little bit closer, and then let's see if you can hang onto that knife when your balls are screaming for mother and trying to hide behind your kidneys . . .

Patience padded along with her nose on the ground. It muffled her voice slightly – which struck Ash as odd, since it didn't actually seem to come from her mouth. Perhaps he imagined it. Perhaps he'd imagined it *all*. In which case there was no reason to suppose that Hazel . . .

He couldn't go there. He listened to what the dog had to say, which was in the nature of a running commentary.

Too many cars; too many damn cars, comin' an' goin'. Oh – dat one's ours. An' dat one waf Hazel's. Can't tell if she waf innit. An' dat one's de pick-up.

She followed it all the way to the road and glanced in the direction of Norbold rather than the hill road to Coventry. He may have been telling the truth, she told Ash sadly. That he was calling on a friend.

'Maybe he was,' said Ash reluctantly. 'But Hazel's been missing for twelve hours. Maybe Fisher did visit his friend and then go home. But what was he doing before *that*?'

Patience looked at him sadly, aware that he was hurting and unable to ease his mind. At least when she lifted her long nose off the ground her voice was clear. I'm a dog, she said, not a satellite tracking system. I get the smells. Smells record a moment in time, not a video. I know that pick-up was coming from *that* direction – she pointed with her nose – before it turned in here. I know that was this morning. I don't know what it was doing last night.

Ash cast around helplessly for his next move. If Patience had done all she could, and Gorman still believed Hazel was at the bottom of the dam, whatever John Fisher had done to her or done with her, the only one who could help his friend now was Ash. And he had no idea where to look. The nearest thing he had to a plan was to go back to the house and try to beat the information out of Fisher; and that was more likely to end with Ash bleeding on the lino than Fisher. After which he'd have to explain to DI Gorman why he blamed Fisher for Hazel's disappearance, again without naming his informant. If he failed, it would be white-coat time again.

With the perspective offered by the intervening years, Ash could contemplate the mental health services with a degree of equanimity. He'd never been treated badly by them. They'd done what they could to help him. Admittedly, Philip Welbeck keeping an eye on his welfare wouldn't have hurt, but even allowing for that, Ash was grateful for their intervention. They'd got him through times when, left to his own devices, he would have lost his last shaky grasp on reality. For four years, it had been a comfort to know that, if things got that bad again, the men in white coats would have a net ready to catch him.

Things were different now. He was no longer a lost soul, anchorless and drifting. He was the custodian of two young boys. The men in white coats couldn't have him: his sons needed him more. Trying to beat the truth out of John Fisher wouldn't have been a smart move even if the man had been half his size and twice his age and had to be helped out of low chairs.

As he scanned the fields and spinneys along the horizon, desperately seeking inspiration, the approximately straight lines of a man-made structure caught his eye. He glanced at the sun, orientating himself. North-east . . . 'That must be the barn Miss Harbinger mentioned.'

Yes? From her level, Patience couldn't see it.

'It didn't sound very promising,' admitted Ash. 'And Fisher didn't seem worried when she drew attention to it, did he?'

No, said Patience. She was *good* at knowing when people were worried.

'Still, we'd better check it out. I can't think of anywhere else to look.'

Suits me. Patience thought it was *never* a bad time for a walk. Especially a walk in the country; especially the kind of country where there were rabbits. As they left the drive and struck out across the fields, her nose dropped again, filled with the beguiling scent that was fun and dinner combined.

Ash had no concerns about her chasing sheep, only that someone seeing her might jump to an unwarranted conclusion; but in spite of what Fisher had said, there was currently nothing in these fields except grass and the odd purple-headed thistle.

In the end, it was a rabbit that brought the breakthrough Ash so desperately needed. It wasn't intentional, of course. Rabbits don't take much of an interest in human affairs. In fact, the only things that interest rabbits are (a) eating, (b) not being eaten and (c) making more rabbits. It was (b) that was uppermost in the mind of the rabbit that Patience sprung in the lee of a hedge just too far from the warren for it to dive to safety underground. Instead it jinked across in front of Ash, its eyes wild with fear and the lurcher close on its scut like the blazing tail of a comet.

Ash called her name, in the doubtful tone of someone who doesn't really expect to be obeyed; and indeed, for another three or four enormously long strides, her whole body bunching and exploding to drive her forward, there was no indication that the dog had heard – was capable of hearing – anything but the manic race of the rabbit's heart.

And then she stopped. So abruptly that her back legs were still running after her forelegs weren't, with the result that she turned a somersault in the long grass. Ash watched in amazement. In his household, *no one* fell over themselves to obey him.

'Patience?' But she remained rooted to the spot, her nose delicately picking apart the scents surrounding her until she had isolated the one that mattered most. The one that was important enough to have stopped her in mid-chase.

That pick-up, she said. It came this way. Last night.

Ash hurried to join her, staring at the grass. He could persuade himself that it had been flattened in two continuous bands, long enough ago for the stems to have sprung up again, not quite long enough for all trace of the disturbance to have vanished. He would never have seen it, but there was a trail there. He raised his gaze, seeking its destination. But there was nothing to see in that direction. The derelict barn, now only a field away and clear enough in its knot of overgrown hawthorns and elder, was well to the east. He wondered if Fisher had come this way to find a gate. But no likely projection of the tracks in the grass approached the only gate he could see, which in any case was fastened with wire and probably hadn't been opened for years.

But if he wasn't heading for the barn, why come this way? There wasn't even a cart-track across the field, and there were no animals for him to check. He must have had a reason. And right now, unless Patience had made a serious error, the thing uppermost in John Fisher's mind, the thing that was even more important to him than (c) was to rabbits, was that nosy constable with her questions and her intuition and her bloody *perseverance*! He came this way because there was somewhere he could leave Hazel and know she'd still be there when he returned.

Here, said Patience. It stopped here, and then it went back.

Ash stooped to consider the sunlight falling on the lifting stems. She was right. The parallel tracks came this far and no further. He'd driven into the middle of a field, then – yes, there – done a three-point turn and driven away again.

It made no sense. There wasn't *that* much grass – if Fisher had been insane enough to dump Hazel's body a few hundred yards from where he worked, it would have been immediately obvious. And if he'd wanted somewhere quiet to interrogate her, even that decomposing barn with its defunct door would have afforded more privacy than the middle of a field.

Just chilling out, said Patience.

Ash stared distractedly at her. 'What?'

That's what he said. That Hazel was probably just chilling out. Wasn't that an odd thing to say?

Ash hadn't noticed – unless that part of his secret brain that masqueraded as his dog had, and this was its way of calling his attention to it. 'I suppose.'

He wasn't afraid of you. He wasn't afraid of the police. He thought his secret was safe enough to risk playing with you.

'It meant something?'

What do you think?

'Chilling out,' Ash said, thinking aloud. 'It wasn't very . . . appropriate, was it? With police divers searching the bottom of the dam for her, the best that can be said is that it was in pretty poor taste. Plus, is it an expression gardeners use? Isn't it a bit . . . urban cool? More city lights and loft living than violets and vermiculite.'

Which means?

'It amused him because it meant something to him and wouldn't mean a blind thing to me. That was the joke – that he was telling me where she is, and I'd never know.'

Chilling, said Patience thoughtfully. What else can it mean?

Ash looked back towards the house. Softened by the distance, the old farmhouse was wearing well, mainly because it had been extended and remodelled time and again over half a millennium to meet the new needs of new owners. There was a modern conservatory, green oak and glass glittering in the mounting sun; the kitchen wing might have been Victorian, and much of the rest had been given a thorough make-over in Georgian times. In true Darwinian fashion, it had adapted to survive. What had begun life as a working farmhouse had ended up as a gentleman's country residence, stables behind, wooded coverts to shelter the pheasants. Gracious living for the tweedy set.

A house that predated mains electricity.

Ash jerked as if he'd got a sudden jolt of electricity himself. He turned quickly, staring afresh at the grassland around him. After a moment he hurried over to a hummock in the ground and jumped up and down, experimentally, a couple of times. Then he strode to another hummock and did the same thing.

Er . . . Gabriel? ventured Patience uneasily.

'There's an ice-house here,' he explained briefly. A chord of barely contained excitement thrummed in his voice. 'Before people had fridges, people who owned country houses stored ice in stone-built crypts, half underground to insulate them. Then electricity came along, and the little stone cells weren't big enough to be useful for anything else. So they were forgotten, and briars and nettles swarmed over the top, burying them completely.

'That's where she is. There must be an entrance here somewhere. But you'd need to know it was here in order to find it. Patience, don't just stare at me like that – *sniff!*'

It took another minute, but when they found it there was no longer any doubt that they were in the right place. The grassed-over top of the structure was barely any higher than the rest of the field, but on its northern side, pointing away from the summer sun, was a low wooden door sunk another metre into the earth.

Not long ago, enough debris had been cleared away for the door to open. And then someone had fastened it with a padlock.

Most people, faced with a padlock to which they do not have the key, call a locksmith. A few people raid their mother's dressing table for hairpins. But Ash had worked in security, and he knew that there are very few padlocks that will withstand the determined application of a hammer. Ash didn't have a hammer, but he found a fist-sized stone in the roots of the hedge that would serve as well.

This one gave at the second blow, the hasp crumpling, the broken padlock pinging off the mossy stonework into the undergrowth. Undeterred by, or possibly unaware of, his skinned knuckles, Ash dragged the heavy door open and ducked under the low stone lintel.

TWENTY-EIGHT

'Fire! Fire! Help, fire!'

'What? Where? Oof . . .'

'*Gabriel?*'

'Hi, Hazel. That is you, then.' His voice sounded to be coming from a lot further away than the gritty stone floor of the little ice-house. Still squinting against the light, she made him out sprawled on his back, panting softly, winded by the violent collision of her head with his belly.

'Sorry. I wasn't expecting you.'

'No. I guessed that.' He sucked in a lungful of air. 'Are you all right?'

Skin heals, she told herself severely, fighting back tears. 'I'm fine. You?'

'Give me a minute,' he said breathily, 'and I'll be fine too.' There was a pause for consideration. 'Why did you shout *Fire*?'

'It's a well-known fact,' said Hazel, 'that people who think you're being attacked will run a mile, but everyone wants to see a fire.'

While Ash recovered his composure, Hazel had time to reflect that, if it had been John Fisher come to kill her, her countermeasures would scarcely have delayed him a minute. She was still bound hand and foot, he would have been where Ash was, between her and the door, and there was no sign of the Seventh Cavalry arriving in the person of DI Gorman.

'It was John Fisher, wasn't it?' she said. 'The gardener.'

Ash sat up and looked at her. 'Don't you know?'

'I didn't see who hit me. Or if I did, I don't remember. I must have been out cold when he brought me here. Where *is* here, by the way?'

Ash told her. 'It's on Harbinger land, about five hundred metres from the house, but unless you knew it was here you'd never find it. I was standing on top of it and thought it was just a hump in the grass.'

'Then, how did you find me?'

'Patience' – he swallowed the word *said* just in time – 'indicated that you'd been in Fisher's pick-up. Then she tracked its scent over the fields.'

Hazel was suitably impressed. 'Clever dog. Where's Fisher now?'

'I left him back at the house . . .' That, he was suddenly aware, didn't mean Fisher was *still* back at the house. 'We need to get you away from here.'

'Unless you want to carry me, you'll have to untie me first.'

Ash had nothing resembling a knife about his person. He picked the knots apart with his nails and his teeth, and by the time Hazel was free his fingertips were cracked and bleeding.

She shook the last coils off her wrists, rubbing some life back into them. 'Is Dave Gorman here?'

'He'll be here in half an hour. Right now he's dragging the Clover Hill dam because he thinks you drove into the reservoir.'

'The one where Edward Cho died?' Hazel stared at him. 'Why on earth would he think that?'

'Let's put it this way. You were going to need a new car before too long anyway, weren't you?'

Her eyes rounded as understanding dawned. 'The bastard dumped my car in the reservoir?'

'I suppose it was quite clever, really,' Ash said wryly. 'They found the car first thing this morning, in fifty feet of water. The windscreen was smashed. If they never found a body, they'd assume they just hadn't been able to find the body. But if he needed to dispose of you later, he could slip you into the dam after they'd all gone home and wait for someone to find you months or years from now.'

'Gabriel.' She took a moment to admire the restraint in her own voice.

'Hm?'

'Can we *not* waste time discussing how my body could be disposed of when the man who wanted to kill me may be close enough to hear? Call Dave, tell him where we are. Tell him it was Fisher. We can prove it later.'

Ash had got quite good about carrying his phone. He pulled it from his pocket and looked at it doubtfully. 'Will the signal carry through solid stone and half a metre of earth?'

'Of course it will,' said Hazel briskly; but she was wrong.

'We'll take it outside.' Ash was on his feet now but still bent double under the low stone roof.

He never made it. As he ducked even lower under the lintel, something coming in the opposite direction with the weight, speed and unerring accuracy of a mule's kick slammed into his temple and he dropped without so much as a sigh.

Hazel saw nothing of the cause, only the effect. Even so, it came as no surprise when first a double-barrelled shotgun and then the face of its owner appeared in the doorway. The gun was pointing her way, and the face was wearing an expression of profound irritation.

'You know, this is starting to get messy,' said John Fisher.

He made no attempt to enter the stone igloo. Hazel hoped he might, and that Ash's form collapsed in the doorway would impede him to the extent that she might snatch the gun. But Fisher saw the same danger. He sat down on the grassy bank where the door cut into the landscape, invisible from anywhere anyone might have been looking.

There was something wrong. Well – something *else* wrong. 'Where's Patience?'

Fisher frowned. 'Who's Patience?'

'Gabriel's dog.'

'The lurcher? I shot it.'

Hazel thought for a moment, then shook her head. 'No, you didn't. We'd have heard.'

'No, I didn't,' agreed Fisher with a grin. 'I ran over it with the truck.'

It's odd how human emotions work. In that moment, it was more upsetting to her that Ash had lost his dog than that the man responsible was about to kill both Ash and her. Hazel gave herself a mental shake. She couldn't afford to think like that. She was in the same position she'd been before Ash arrived. Fisher intended to kill her, but she didn't have to make it easy. Conceivably, she could make it impossible. There was at least enough hope to keep her focused. For one thing, her hands and feet were free now.

She was still facing a double-barrelled shotgun. But a gun is a little like a nuclear bomb: it can only be used in all-out warfare. In anything short of that – border disputes, say, or the assassination of minor royalty – it's more of a hindrance than a help. You can't use an atom bomb to win territory that you couldn't use for generations because of the fall-out, but having it stops you thinking in terms of weapons you *could* use. Hazel didn't kid herself that having a gun put Fisher at a disadvantage, but right now any edge was worth exploiting. For what was the worst that could happen? He was prepared to murder them both. He couldn't murder them *twice*, however much she annoyed him.

She said – and it astonished her how calm she managed to sound – 'You can't use that in here.'

Fisher raised a sardonic eyebrow. 'Wanna bet?'

Hazel kept her gaze steady. 'These are stone walls. *Curved* stone walls. The shot will go everywhere. You'll do as much damage to yourself as you will to us.'

She saw the hesitation flicker across John Fisher's face. He wasn't sure if she was right, but he wasn't confident enough to ignore the warning. 'Teach you that in plod school, did they?'

'They did better than that,' said Hazel, 'they showed us. Put a dummy where you are now, and used a string to pull the trigger. From behind a blast wall.' She waited.

He didn't want to ask. He couldn't not do. 'And?'

'Let's put it this way. That dummy was going to need a fast ambulance, blood transfusions and reconstructive surgery. It wasn't going to limp down the lane and get its mother to stick a plaster on its knee.'

Fisher couldn't help himself. His eyes left her and travelled over the walls of the ice-house. 'I don't believe you.'

Hazel shrugged. 'Suit yourself. DI Gorman will be suitably grateful. It's always a bonus when the criminal leaves *himself* at the crime scene.'

There are people who don't care about being caught in the commission of their crime. Who don't care about *dying* in the commission of their crime. Who are so hell-bent on achieving what they've set out to that even the ultimate price seems worth paying. But John Fisher wasn't one of them. He wanted to walk away from this. He expected to be able to close the door on the ice-house, and drop a few old logs or something in front of it, and never see it opened again. He hadn't signed up for the nuclear option entailing mutual assured destruction.

'OK,' he said slowly. With his left hand he reached into a deep pocket. 'Good job I've got this, then.' It was a knife, a broad strong blade that could take cuttings from a plant or gut a rabbit or cut the throat of a human being. He switched it into his right hand, used his left to pass the gun carefully out of sight behind the stone doorframe.

It might as well have been in the next county, because Hazel would have to pass Fisher to reach it. Nevertheless, she felt a quiver of hope in her breast. Now she was facing a pocket-knife instead of a double-barrelled shotgun, and she'd been taught how to disarm a man wielding a knife.

Of course, she'd also been taught that there are no guarantees. That sometimes the man with the knife declines to give it up, and even a very small knife is a potentially lethal weapon. What she needed to do next, she supposed, was persuade him to put the knife away too, and threaten her with a balloon on a stick . . .

She said quietly, 'Nobody thought of you, did they? They all assumed you were too young to have had anything to do with Edward Cho's death. That was a mistake. You *were* young – but you'd just lost your father. You were probably as angry as Jerome Harbinger was.'

Fisher sneered at her. 'I didn't kill Edward Cho.'

'No? You mean, that was Harbinger?'

'Actually, no,' he said. 'He never laid a hand on him.'

'It really was an accident?' Hazel didn't believe it. She knew what these people were capable of: it was straining credulity to think Jerome Harbinger had been prepared to annihilate Cho's entire family, but a stroke of luck started the process for him.

'That's what I was told. I wasn't there.'

'And Mary Cho, a month later?'

'Ah. That *wasn't* an accident.' He volunteered nothing more. But in a way it hardly mattered which of them – Fisher, Harbinger or Harbinger's daughter – had brought about Mrs Cho's death. If all the elements of a conspiracy were there, they were all responsible.

Hazel had to keep him talking. The longer he talked, the more chance that Ash would return to the land of the living. 'And you spent the next seventeen years trying to track down the Chos' children. When you found out that one of them was teaching a twenty-minute drive away in Norbold, you saw your chance. But you needed to talk to her before you killed her. You wanted her to tell you where her brother was.'

John Fisher dipped his head with a slow smile. 'You're good at this. You should be a detective.'

Hazel replied with a brittle smile of her own. 'Which is also why you didn't kill me when you had the chance. Why you brought me here. Well, you could have saved yourself the effort. I don't know where her brother is. I don't even know *who* her brother is.'

'No,' said Fisher softly. 'But you know where Felicity Cho is, don't you?'

Hazel froze at the core. It was all she could do to keep the fear out of her eyes and voice. 'No. What makes you think that?'

John Fisher had a kind of lazy smile that said, I know you know. I know you know I know. And we both know how this is going to end. Hazel could imagine that smile was the last thing ever seen by generations of slugs and greenfly. 'You've been talking to her. You know things you could only have learnt from her. Where is she?'

'You're wrong,' insisted Hazel. 'I've been talking to people *about* her. I wanted to find her before you did, so I asked a lot of questions. But I never did find her. No one has seen her since you tried to grab her outside the school. At least, I'm assuming that was you. It all happened so fast, I only got a glimpse of the faces.'

'Actually,' he said irritably, 'it was the hired help. If it had been me, we'd have got the right woman and not some damned nanny. I mean' – irritation barred his voice – 'you'd think it was simple enough, wouldn't you? I gave them photographs. I told them where she'd be, and when she'd be there. You wouldn't think they could get it wrong, would you?'

All Hazel could think to say was, 'You can't get the staff these days.'

Fisher looked at her as if he didn't quite understand. As if they didn't have irony where he came from. He shrugged it off. 'So where is she?'

'I told you, I don't know.'

'You know,' he said with heavy certainty. 'And you're going to tell me. And frankly, I don't care how much I have to hurt you.' The blade flickered just enough between his fingers to catch the light.

'Lester Pickering,' Hazel said quickly, snatching the name out of the air. Anything, *anything*, to distract him. To buy time. 'You killed him?'

'The fence? Yes.' Remembering, Fisher smiled again. 'With his own walking stick.'

'Why him?'

'The robbery was his idea. He put the firm together, and it was him at the house. It was him who beat my mother. And it was Pickering who handled the exchange. It wasn't him who shot my father – that was Harry Clark; he died at the scene. Pickering was already heading for the exit with the Caravaggio under his arm. It's been on his wall on and off for the last seventeen years. He couldn't sell it, it was too well known. He used it as collateral to bank-roll other jobs, but it always came back to that nail in the wall above his desk.'

He shook his head in a kind of wonder. 'Where anyone could have seen it, and no one ever did. Or no one who both knew what it was *and* was going to talk to the police. You have to assume the man didn't get many visitors. Which is why, I suppose, it took so long for anyone to find him.' The smile turned impish. 'Of course, the note I put in his window saying he was off on holiday may have helped.'

'Where is the painting now?'

Fisher grinned. He was a good-looking man, even an attractive one, except for the circumstances. 'Look, *I've* seen those films too. Where the villain confesses everything to someone he's going to kill, only she doesn't die and she puts him away for twenty years. I'm not telling you anything.'

'You think I'm going to overpower you?'

'Actually, no,' he said. 'I think you really are going to die. But why take the risk?'

'Because if you're going to kill me, you owe me some kind of an explanation. I mean – *why?* I can see why you'd be angry with Edward Cho. But what did his family ever do to you?'

'You wouldn't understand,' he said gruffly.

'I *want* to understand.'

'Because . . . because some acts of treachery are too massive to be paid for with one life alone. The stupid man killed himself, anyway. Where's the justice in that? Where was the closure? He destroyed two families, the Harbingers and mine. He could only ever pay for that with his own. They had to be . . . eradicated. Expunged. So there was never any chance of my mother turning into the bread aisle at Sainsbury's and finding herself face to face with Edward Cho's wife, or his daughter, or his son. That man ruined her life. My father would be alive today if he'd kept his word.'

'Mr Cho *did* keep his word,' said Hazel. 'I'll tell you what happened, if you like. But maybe you don't want me to. Because it would make a nonsense of how you've spent all your adult life. It would mean you killed Mary Cho for nothing, and the vendetta against their children that's driven your existence for a decade and a half would have been a mistake. Stripped of that, you have nothing. You *are* nothing. Even if I proved to you that Edward Cho kept faith with Jerome Harbinger, you'd still murder his daughter if you could. You wouldn't know what else to do.'

If he hadn't had the knife in his hand, Hazel believed he'd have struck her. That's what she was hoping for. It would mean him leaning forward, off-balance, stretching over the recumbent Ash, and probably moving the weapon into the hand he was least confident about using it in . . .

Perhaps he saw the danger as clearly as she did. In any event, he lifted the corner of his lip in an angry sneer and left the knife where it was. 'You think I care what you think? You think it matters a tinker's damn to me? Only one thing matters to me, and that's finishing this. Finding that bitch and her brother, and scrubbing them out of history.

'And you're going to help me. And it doesn't matter if it takes all day, but it won't. Scream as much as you like – nobody'll hear you. Someone standing ten feet away wouldn't hear you.'

TWENTY-NINE

Hazel believed him. Walls that could keep the summer sun from melting ice could stop sound travelling far enough to save her. Fear put a tremor in her voice; she hoped she was the only one who heard it. 'However much you hurt me, I can't tell you what I don't know.'

Fisher glanced down then. The anger in his face mutated to a kind of savage cunning. 'Well, maybe. Maybe you wouldn't tell me where she is. Maybe some kind of stupid professional pride would stop you. There are people who can do that – swallow their own pain, face their own death, rather than compromise their principles. Not many, I don't think, but some. Maybe you're one of them.'

He leaned down and put the knife against Ash's cheek. Hazel saw a spot of blood well slowly from its tip. Ash gave a tiny moan, like a sleeping man bothered by a fly.

'But suppose it was a different choice.' Fisher was watching her closely. 'A choice between a woman you hardly know and a man who seems to care about you quite a lot. This is a pretty small knife, but it'll go through every part of a human body except bone. I can take him apart in front of you. I can give you a living anatomy lesson. This is the eye, and *this* is what happens when you cut into it. This is the heart: we'll leave it pumping for now. Now, lungs – he's got two of those . . .'

She wanted to believe it was just talk. It's a lot easier to talk about butchering someone than to actually do it. Most people, even most bad people, don't have the stomach. But this was someone who had pursued an innocent family for seventeen years, who had already killed, and Hazel had the sick certainty that John Fisher could and would carry out his threat. And Ash was unconscious – helpless. And something could happen in the next minutes or hours to keep Fisher from reaching Elizabeth Lim, but only the decision Hazel made now would keep him from blinding Ash. People would understand that it was only a betrayal if she'd had a genuine choice; wouldn't they?

What she was fighting for was time. What had Ash said? – that when he failed to find her in the Clover Hill dam, Dave Gorman would follow him to Spell. Well, he wasn't going to find her there, was he? He'd be here in half an hour.

But if she offered to take Fisher to Elizabeth Lim, they would none of them be here when he arrived. And if she *told* him where to find her, Fisher would cut both her throat and Ash's, seal the ice-house and go to deal with Lim alone.

'Well?' demanded John Fisher. 'What's it to be? Your weird but obviously devoted friend, or a woman you hardly know?'

Hazel swallowed. If it really was a straight choice, her heart had no difficulty making it. 'I'll tell you. I *will* tell you. But you have to promise me that you'll let us go. You won't hurt either of us, and you'll let us go.' The whine of hope in her voice was only just the right side of pathetic.

'You tell me where to find Felicity Cho, and I'll leave you and – what's his name? – Ash here, locked in but unharmed, and make arrangements for someone to free you in a few hours' time. How's that?' He was watching her carefully. He knew he couldn't trust her to do what he wanted just because she said she would. But he couldn't resist the siren appeal of hope.

This vendetta had occupied and overshadowed all his adult life, and finally an end was in sight. And not just an end but a victory. The man he blamed for his father's death was dead. The man who was actually responsible for his father's death was dead. Edward Cho's wife was dead, and his daughter was almost within his grasp. If he could persuade Hazel Best to give up Felicity Cho, he could persuade Felicity to give up her brother, and then it would be over. He'd have accomplished everything he'd been tasked with. He'd have eradicated the very names of those who had destroyed two families.

There had been times in the last seventeen years when he'd wondered if they must have been crazy to start this. When the chance of reaching this point had seemed vanishingly remote. When he'd been afraid he was going to waste his life in pursuit of the unattainable. But he'd been wrong. It had been attainable after all, and very soon now he'd be able to tie a ribbon round the last of it and present it as a thing complete. He knew the pleasure that gift would afford. He'd have been less than human if he hadn't wanted to believe that Hazel was telling the truth.

It was that hope, that desperate desire to believe, that blinded him to the suspicion that she'd caved in too easily.

'You have to promise,' Hazel said again. 'I want your word that you won't hurt us.'

'You have it,' swore John Fisher. 'Cross my heart and hope to die.'

'All right then. Have you got a piece of paper and a biro? There isn't an address as such, or if there is I don't know it. I'll draw you a map. There's a disused foundry behind Derby Road in Norbold. Meadowvale CID have fitted out a flat there for use as a safe house. Do you know Derby Road?'

Fisher had found an envelope in one pocket and a stub of pencil in another: he pushed them towards her. 'I'll find it. Where's the foundry?'

'You turn off Derby Road between the scout hall and the chippie – see, there.' She was sketching rapidly, Fisher peering over her moving hand. 'The foundry is the last building you come to. The door will be locked, but there's a keypad – you can let yourself in with the combination. Inside the door are some stairs, and the flat's at the top, on the right. She'll be on her own.'

Hazel started to pass him the envelope, then took it back. 'Wait, you need the combination for the door.' She started to write, then: 'Damn.'

'What?'

'The point's broken.'

He frowned. 'What?'

'The point. Of the pencil. It's broken.' She held it out for him to see. 'You've got a knife – sharpen it.'

There are few tools as versatile as a knife. You can use it to kill an animal, to prepare it for cooking, and to eat it. You can take cuttings for your garden with it, cut a piece of ribbon to tie up a birthday present, make an extra hole in your belt if you lose or gain weight. You can threaten someone's life with it, and you can sharpen a pencil.

But – and this is important – you can't do any two of these things at the same time. The moment John Fisher took the broken pencil in his left hand and applied the blade to it with his right, he surrendered, if only momentarily, that command of the situation which the knife as a weapon had given him.

The moment would have come and gone, and left nothing changed, if Hazel hadn't been waiting for it – hadn't planned for it, and nurtured it like a gardener raising a precious orchid. That moment when Fisher had both hands and brain occupied with something other than the intention to hurt her, Hazel made a determined grab for control. She slashed the envelope across his eyes, more to shock than disable him, and dived for his knife hand. Like a sprinter coming off the starting blocks, her crouch magnified her momentum, and she slammed into him, shoulder first, both hands fastening onto his right wrist with all the strength she could still generate after everything she'd been through.

For another moment, or maybe three, the outcome was in doubt. They rolled together, a tangle of arms and legs, gasping and grunting and struggling for supremacy, a wrestling match in which the rules counted for nothing because another word for Winner was going to be Survivor. Hazel Best was tall and sturdy and fit, and she'd been taught how to disarm a violent man. But John Fisher was taller, heavier and stronger, and totally unhampered by the possibility that the Independent Police Complaints Commission might accuse him of using excessive force. Hazel *could* have won against those odds, but only in the first few seconds. A battle that raged for longer than that was always going to favour Goliath over David.

In the end, it wasn't the knife which was the deciding factor, it was Fisher's left fist. Dropping the pencil, it came round like a wrecking ball, slamming into her head and hurling her against the curved wall. Stars exploded in the dim cave. Long before she'd worked out which way was up and got her face off the stones, she knew it was over.

'You bloody *bitch*!' yelled Fisher, bubbling through the gore pouring from his nose. Hazel thought she'd managed to break his front tooth as well. It wasn't a lot of consolation, but it was some. If nothing else, it might make Dave Gorman wonder how a man broke his tooth pruning rosebushes.

'You bloody, *bloody* bitch!' He came at her like a sumo wrestler, hunched under the low roof, striding over Ash's prone body. Fisher wasn't just angry, he was *affronted*: his rage filled the little stone igloo. There was nowhere to escape to, nowhere to hide, and Hazel had no energy left with which to fight. All she could do now was curl up tight against the wall, arms around her spinning head, and wait for him to take his revenge. It was, after all, his currency of choice.

He still had the knife, but now it was almost an encumbrance. He was too filled with wrath to use it surgically, to extract payment from her in precise increments of pain; if he used it now he'd kill her instantly, and that wasn't what he wanted. He still needed that number to access the flat. Fists were the answer. He could beat her to a bloody pulp and still leave her capable of telling him what he wanted to know. *Begging* to tell him what he wanted to know.

He folded the knife and stuffed it into his pocket, and fastened both big hands in her clothes and lifted her towards him, her legs dragging across the stone setts. When her face was level with his he snarled, 'I can make you wish you were never born.'

'No,' whispered Hazel. 'You can only make me wish you were never born.'

What happened then? Only with hindsight was she able to figure it out. All she was aware of in the moment made no sense. The dim light from the door dropped abruptly towards darkness; she caught a glimpse of movement over Fisher's shoulder; then the man let out a startled grunt and hurtled backwards, ending up like a beached crab, on his back on the floor where Ash had lain.

Because Ash wasn't there any more. Ash had moved. Recovering his wits at the last best moment – or possibly, lying quiet and biding his time until that moment came – he'd risen behind Fisher like an avenging angel, occulting the light, and hooking a powerful arm round Fisher's neck had swung him hard against the wall. Hazel heard the collision of his skull with the stones as a sick dull thud.

Gabriel Ash spent so much time trying not to loom over people that it was easy to forget he was a big man. Now he was eating properly and taking some exercise, he had recovered much of his strength: when he hurled someone into a wall, they stayed hurled.

But he was taking no chances with Fisher. Perhaps he was concerned that, given a second's respite, the gardener might draw his knife again. Perhaps he was aware that Fisher was a little younger, a little bigger and probably a great deal fitter than he was. Perhaps he felt that, given the stakes, it was important to render the man incapable in the shortest possible time.

In fact Hazel didn't think that any of these considerations, all of them valid, was uppermost in his mind. They were rational judgements, capable of being defended rationally, and right now Ash was not a rational being. Consumed by fury, he hauled Fisher to his knees and hit him in the face, again and again and again. The man was fifteen stone of dead weight in his hand, offering neither resistance nor defence, but Ash went on hitting him as if stopping was not an option. As if a dam had breached somewhere in his head and the turbid waters would have to drain before it would be possible to contemplate an end.

'Gabriel. *Gabriel,*' insisted Hazel. 'Stop it! You're going to kill him.'

But Ash didn't stop, until she had crawled over on her hands and knees and taken hold of the bloodied fist that was a hard knot of bones tight-packed by muscles and tendons into a convenient battering ram.

'It's all right,' she panted, moving his hand back to his side. 'He can't hurt either of us any more. Let him go.'

After a moment he did. John Fisher's unconscious body slid down the slope of the wall and lay still.

Finally Ash looked at Hazel as if he'd been away and was only now finding his way back. 'He . . . I . . .' He tried again. 'Are you all right?'

Hazel managed a feeble smile. 'More or less. You?'

'I . . . I'm not sure.' He looked at the man crumpled at his feet. 'I did that.' It was half a question.

'He was armed,' said Hazel flatly, 'and he was most certainly dangerous; and anyway, the broken tooth is down to me. Anyone who thinks we used unnecessary force can' – the ghost of her mother wagged an admonitory finger just in time – 'try to prove it.'

Ash looked again, wincing. He couldn't see a broken tooth, only blood. He looked at his own knuckles. More blood; belonging to both of them, probably. 'Do you think we should have another go at calling Dave?'

'I do. Just as soon as I've done this.'

For a bizarre moment, as she bent and rummaged through Fisher's pockets, Ash thought she was looking for money. She must have realised, because she straightened up – or half straightened – with a tired grin, waving the knife under his nose. 'In case he starts feeling better before Dave gets here.'

'Unless he's coming the scenic route via the North Yorkshire moors, I doubt that'll be an issue.'

Hazel stepped over Fisher and into the low doorway, looking for the phone. Ash had had it when he was knocked down: she'd no idea where it was now. 'If he's lying on it, you can move him. This is my best shirt. Well,' she added more realistically, 'it was.'

Ash looked round on the floor and couldn't see the phone either. He was as reluctant as Hazel to wrestle with the consequences of his handiwork; when he looked up and she'd continued on outside, he said hopefully, 'Found it?'

'No,' said Hazel. Her voice sounded odd. She came back into the ice-house, walking backwards, both hands in the air.

For a couple of seconds Ash couldn't see why. Then he could see why – the shotgun Fisher had leaned against the outside wall of the ice-house – but not who was pointing it.

And then he could.

'If you have killed my son,' said Margaret Fisher in a low, oddly level voice, 'I will blow your brains out.'

THIRTY

Hazel fought to keep her own voice clear of any trace of panic. 'Detective Inspector Gorman is on his way here right now. He'll arrive at any moment. There is no chance whatever that you could get away with it. You would go to prison, for most of the rest of your life.'

'You think I care?' There was a note almost of outrage in Mrs Fisher's tone now, as if she'd been accused of something disgusting. 'You people took my husband from me seventeen years ago. If you've taken my son as well, what possible reason could I have for *caring* how or where I spend the rest of my life? John *is* my life. If you've killed him too, nothing anyone can do to me will stop me blowing your heads off.

'Don't think I won't do it. I've been handling shotguns longer than you've been alive. One barrel each will smear your stupid, ignorant heads all over that wall.'

It had worked once before: Hazel tried again. 'If you use a shotgun in a confined area . . .'

'. . . Some of the shot will ricochet back at me,' finished Mrs Fisher. 'You think that's going to stop me? If you've left me nothing to live for, how can a bit of shot possibly matter to me? If I can face twenty years in prison, I can certainly face a trip to A&E.

'So tell me: how do we stand? Is John alive or dead? Is there anything left to talk about?'

Hazel weighed the options carefully. But in the end, all she could offer was the truth. 'I don't know.'

'I do.' It was Ash's voice, but it didn't sound like Ash. Or rather, it sounded like Ash as Hazel had heard him only a couple of times before: Ash with his back against the wall, capable of anything. She turned her head slowly to look over her shoulder. Mrs Fisher edged sideways, to look past her.

In many ways Gabriel Ash was a deeply conservative man. He wore a collar and tie in circumstances when most men of his generation would wear T-shirts; he didn't own a pair of jeans; and although he possessed trainers for quasi-sporting occasions like long walks with his dog or park football with the boys, he generally preferred a good brogue. A well-made leather shoe with a sturdy heel.

Behind Hazel, inside the ice-house, crouching under the low roof, he had the heel of his good sturdy brogue on John Fisher's throat.

'He's alive. He's got a broken nose, and a broken tooth, and tomorrow his face will be up like a melon. But he's alive now and he'll still be alive tomorrow, as long as you do the sensible thing and hand that gun to my friend Hazel.

'You're wondering,' he went on before Margaret Fisher had time to refuse, 'why, when you're the one with the weapon, I'd expect you to comply. The answer is simple. I have your son's larynx under my heel. If I shift my weight, even slightly, I'll crush it. You can't breathe through a crushed larynx. Nothing you could do will save his life if I do that. No more air will reach his lungs, no more oxygen will reach his blood, and brain death will commence in about three minutes. A surgeon could, just about, insert a breathing tube in three minutes – but then, who suffers a crushed larynx with a surgeon that handy?

'Give Hazel the gun. Then we can talk. Or you can head for the hills – whichever you prefer. Either way, we'll get help for John while his injuries are slight enough for him to benefit.'

Mrs Fisher couldn't drag her eyes away from the heel of his right foot. 'You wouldn't dare.'

'To save your own life, or someone else's, there's almost nothing that the law won't sanction,' said Hazel. 'In all the circumstances – your son has killed two people to my knowledge, Mary Cho and Lester Pickering; and he was threatening my life and Gabriel's just a few minutes ago – he'd probably get a medal.'

'John didn't kill Mary Cho!' said the housekeeper scornfully.

'He was seventeen when his father was murdered. A boy. He couldn't have done it, then.'

'But somebody did.' Hazel had the sense of creeping up to a cliff-edge, that in a moment she would peer down and all the explanations would be laid out below her.

'Who do you think?' The years had done nothing to salve Margaret Fisher's anger; perhaps they had stoked it. 'Mr Harbinger? You could say he was responsible for what happened to Cho, though he never laid a finger on him, but after that he sort of . . . ran out of steam.'

'But he *did* kill Mr Cho?' Hazel thought she could get the answers now. She wished to God she had something to record them on.

Mrs Fisher seemed to have lost all inhibition about sharing her secrets; seemed almost to want to tell someone. In a way, Hazel understood that. If she and Ash walked away from this, the woman holding them at gunpoint wasn't going to; and vice versa. So it hardly mattered what she said to them. She could afford to be honest.

'He *meant* to. He phoned him – a public phone, no records – and asked him to come to the house, said they had unfinished business. I'll give him this: Cho was a brave man to say he would. I think he was expecting an apology, some kind of reconciliation.'

'Instead of which . . .?'

'Mr Harbinger was waiting for him on the road, with a double-barrelled shotgun. *This* double-barrelled shotgun,' she noted with satisfaction. 'I have no doubt he'd have used it. But Cho was too quick for him: he saw the gun, guessed what it meant and drove off like Jehu. Mr Harbinger went after him. Cho knew the quickest way home – the quickest way to anywhere he could get help – was up the Clover Hill road. What he didn't know was how icy it gets in winter.

'He nearly made it. But he lost control close to the brow of the hill, and his car rolled over on the bank and into the reservoir. Mr Harbinger came home.'

Hazel was puzzling over the legal implications. Murder? Manslaughter? Possibly attempted murder. 'But he didn't kill Mrs Cho? Are you sure? We know he threatened her.'

Contempt twisted Mrs Fisher's lip. 'Pretty sure. I know he threatened her – he threatened all of them, the whole family. And he meant it at the time. But once Cho was dead, it became obvious he wasn't going to do it. Because she was a woman. Because it wasn't her who'd lied to us. Because . . . oh, who cares why? He wasn't going to do it.'

Hazel said softly, 'So who did?'

Mrs Fisher barked a humourless laugh. 'If you want a job doing properly, do it yourself. It really wasn't very difficult. She'd have slammed the door in Mr Harbinger's face, but I was another woman, wasn't I? And we'd both just lost our husbands. We ended up drinking tea in her kitchen. I slipped sleeping pills into hers, and when she was groggy enough I steered her into the bathroom and . . . well, you know what I did. She hardly struggled. It took almost no force to keep her head under the water, so no bruises.'

'*Why?*' demanded Ash in a horrified whisper. 'What happened was nothing to do with her or her children.'

'Why? Because she was *his* wife.' The bitterness in her voice was almost inhuman. 'Because they were *his* children. Because Edward Cho's family was still walking the earth when mine lay in ruins.

'Because he lied. He promised the police wouldn't be involved, and that was a lie, and my husband died because of it. The only possible response was to wipe everything bearing his name off the face of the earth. When the last of them is gone, then I can sleep. I haven't, you know. Not properly. Not for seventeen years.'

Which explained a fair bit, Hazel thought. Grief had turned to resentment, and resentment to a cold fury that had consumed the woman's life. And not just hers: she had passed the contagion to her son. Brought him up to it, nurtured him on it, fed him the bitter grapes of her wrath. He had had no life, no adult life, that wasn't overwhelmingly tainted by it. She had destroyed them both with her hunger for retribution.

'You found Lester Pickering. He robbed the Harbingers, he beat you when you tried to stop him, and he was responsible for the deaths of your husband and Jennifer Harbinger,' said Hazel. 'How did you find him?'

'That *wasn't* easy,' admitted Margaret Fisher. 'Which is why it took so long. But if you keep asking questions, and keep going back to remind people that you still want the information, and you're still willing to pay for it, sooner or later something bubbles to the surface. He was using Mrs Harbinger's picture to bankroll more crimes. He had no idea we knew about it. You should have seen his face when he realised who we were!'

'You were there?'

She grinned fiercely. 'You think I was going to miss that? John's stronger than me, he did the needful, but damn right I was there. I told Miss Jocelyn I needed time off to deal with some personal business. You can't argue with that. I watched that bloody man die, crawling round the lino at my feet, and I was glad to see it.' Her chin came up determinedly. 'So don't think I'll baulk at using a gun. I was born in the country: I've shot vermin all my life.'

'Where's the picture now?'

'In the butler's pantry,' Mrs Fisher answered promptly. 'I get it out and look at it sometimes. I can't return it to the Harbingers without explaining how I came by it, but at least it's back in the house.' She looked pensive for a moment. 'They say it's worth millions. I can't see it myself. It's just some girl with a cage-bird. It's called *Anime Gemelle*. That's Italian for Kindred Spirits, you know. I've never understood why a famous artist like that would paint a girl and a bird.'

'She's one of the Medici,' Hazel said softly, 'married into a rival family to seal a truce. Caravaggio was making the point that she had as much choice in the matter, as much freedom to fly away, as the bird.'

'Yes?' The older woman sniffed dismissively. 'I suppose we're all hostages to circumstance, one way or another. And he did paint the fabrics very nicely. I still can't see millions in the thing.'

'It's been hanging in the butler's pantry, and nobody noticed?' Hazel could hardly credit it. First Lester Pickering's office wall, now that of the Harbingers' housekeeper. For an internationally important painting, it didn't seem to be very recognisable.

'Who goes into the butler's pantry except the housekeeper?' asked Mrs Fisher haughtily. 'And to be fair, I don't keep it on the wall. It's packed away where no one will find it. But I get it out from time to time, to remind myself that my husband may have died for nothing but those responsible paid for what they did. The picture doesn't matter. The payment does.'

Ash was aware that time was passing. He didn't need John Fisher to start feeling better. After the hammering he'd taken, he probably couldn't have contributed much to the balance of power, but even squirming around the floor trying to get Ash's foot off his neck he'd be an unnecessary complication.

'You know this is over now, don't you?' he said. 'You're neither of you walking away from this. John's going in an ambulance, and you're going in the police car that will be here at any moment.'

'I don't hear any police car,' said the housekeeper coldly. 'So far as I can see, it's just us four. And I'm the one with the gun. Now, *get away from my son!*'

Wearily, Ash shook his head. 'Mrs Fisher, you need to believe me. I will do this. To protect my friend, to prevent *my* sons from being left fatherless, I will crush his throat and he will die of suffocation. I don't think there's anything you can do, even with a double-barrelled shotgun, as quickly as I can shift my weight onto my right foot.'

'I can shoot you dead,' she said thickly.

'Only with the second barrel,' said Hazel. She sucked in a deep breath and moved sideways, masking Ash's body with her own. 'With the first one you'll have to shoot me. By the time you can shoot again, John will be beyond help.'

'At least if we're dead, we won't have to listen,' said Ash grimly. 'You will. You'll hear him fighting for the breath that won't come. You may try CPR, but it won't make any difference. He'll no longer have an airway. In the end there'll be nothing you can do except sit here and wait for him to die. It'll be the longest three minutes of your life. Nothing you have experienced so far, nothing you have done, will prepare you for it.'

Margaret Fisher looked at Hazel and wondered if it was worth calling the bluff. Then she looked at Ash and knew it wasn't a bluff. She held onto the gun a little longer, while the sands of time ran out of her future. Then she broke it – safety is instinctive among people who shoot – and passed it to Hazel.

'Damn you,' she said, quietly and with absolute sincerity. 'Damn you both to hell. Move away from my son, you monster.'

'She called me a monster,' Ash said unhappily. 'After everything she'd done and caused to be done, she thought *I* was the monster.'

'You *were* threatening to kill an unconscious man,' DI Gorman reminded him. 'Her son. Whose blood was, right then, all over you.'

'She'd have shot us both if I hadn't.'

'I know that. That's why we're talking about it over a pub lunch instead of in Interview Room One with the tape running.'

They were. Forty-eight hours had passed, so the bruises acquired by both Ash and Hazel were now at their Technicolor best. Apart from that, both were recovering from the ordeal. It would take time to put it behind them entirely – Hazel's leave had been extended on medical grounds, Ash had put a sign in the bookshop window advising that it would be closed for a week – but the roller-coaster cycle of insomnia alternating with nightmares, of emotions unnaturally dulled or heightened to a pitch of absurd sensitivity, of uncalled-for snappishness or sudden tears, would eventually yield to normality. All they could do in the meantime was ride the peaks and troughs, and remind one another that it was only to be expected, that this too would pass.

An odd musical tone sounded in Ash's pocket. 'I want to take this,' he said, extracting his phone, 'it's the vet.' He went through the black oak door into the pub's back garden.

'How is his dog?' asked Gorman.

'She'll be fine,' said Hazel. 'The van did hit her, but Fisher was wrong when he said he'd killed her. She has a broken foreleg and three broken ribs. The vet operated yesterday. Gabriel's hoping to get her home soon.'

'Good. I don't know what he'd do without that dog.'

'First off, he'd have to get a new nickname,' she said impishly. It hadn't originally been meant kindly, but time and usage had left Ash quite sanguine about Meadowvale calling him Rambles With Dogs.

Gorman ignored that. 'I gather Miss Lim moved back into her flat this morning.'

Hazel nodded. 'I said she was welcome to stay longer, if she wanted to get her breath back, but she said there was no need. As soon as she knew she was safe, she wanted to start getting back to normal. I think she'll be back at work on Monday.'

'Tough lady,' said Gorman appreciatively. 'And she's not the only one. That was smart work, giving Fisher directions to the safe house. When you knew she wasn't there, because you'd taken her down to your house the previous morning.'

Hazel accepted the compliment complacently. She'd impressed herself with that, too. 'I hoped it would have the ring of truth, without putting Elizabeth in danger if in the end I couldn't stop him. I certainly wasn't going to tell him she was at my place. It's not long since I finished decorating – I didn't want to have to do it again.'

The DI grinned. It was easy to be flippant about danger after it's been resolved. He knew what it had taken to face up to John Fisher and find a way of protecting both Lim and Ash. 'What about her brother?'

'She can't contact him directly. But she has spoken to Martin Wade, so next time James calls, he'll pass on the news and Elizabeth's phone-number. Hopefully, they can get together again soon. They have seventeen years to catch up on.' She pushed away the last of the Black Forest gateau, still not sure why Gorman hadn't wanted any. 'So the only loose end is the men in the grey van.'

'We'll get them, sooner rather than later,' said the DI confidently. 'We know who they are – John Fisher didn't show much interest in protecting them once he realised it was over. They worked for Harbinger Transport in Leeds. Fisher identified them as potential muscle a while back when he drove Jocelyn up there to open a new depot.'

He gestured for the bill. 'I spent an hour with Jocelyn Harbinger last night, bringing her up to date. She knew her housekeeper and her gardener had been arrested, of course. She didn't know, until I told her, that her father was unlikely to face charges.'

'He *was* responsible for Edward Cho's death.'

The DI shrugged. 'He probably was. But would you want to bring the prosecution? He's not fit to stand trial. OK, Edward Cho's car probably wouldn't have left the road if no one had been chasing him – but we'd have to prove criminal culpability, and the Harbingers can afford the best defence lawyers. Jerome has nothing to be proud of. But maybe he's already paid for what he did with his own physical and mental decline.'

They sat in a reflective silence for a minute. Then Hazel said, with a kind of careful innocence, 'I'm glad Jocelyn wasn't involved.'

Gorman nodded. 'Me too.'

'Yes. That's *why* I'm glad.'

He frowned at her. 'What?'

'It's none of my business. I just got the impression that you and she were' – Hazel shrugged negligently – 'getting on quite well.'

'She was a *suspect*,' he said, outraged.

'And now she isn't. Dave, you're a single man – if you like the woman, tell her so.'

'I have a girlfriend,' mumbled Gorman.

'No, Dave,' said Hazel patiently, 'you *had* a girlfriend. You took her out, regular as clockwork, once a week, for dinner at the rugby club. More than half the time she went home alone because you got called back into work. But the last time she went home with a prop forward who works in an accountant's office and never gets paged. *And*,' she added pointedly, 'all this happened four months ago. It's time to dip your toe back in the water.'

He was staring at her, half impressed, half appalled. 'How do you *know* all that?'

'Dave!' she laughed. 'We both work in the same police station. There are *no* secrets in a police station. You want a private life, get another job.'

Gorman took a fierce bite out of a weak shandy and changed the subject. 'Gabriel's phone. He never struck me as the type to use the Bond theme as a ring-tone.'

Hazel chuckled. 'He didn't. I downloaded it one day when he wasn't looking, and he hasn't figured out yet how to get rid of it.'

Outside, Ash had finished talking to his vet. The news was all good. Patience's leg had been pinned and her ribs strapped, and she was hobbling round looking sorry for herself but would probably recover better at home now. He could pick her up this afternoon.

He was heading back inside when the stupid ring-tone went again. He thought it was the vet with more instructions, but it wasn't. It was Philip Welbeck.

'Ah, Gabriel. Everything sorted out now?'

Suddenly Ash needed to sit down. He lowered himself onto one of the picnic benches. 'Philip? How did you know?'

'Oh, one keeps a little eye open. I always like to know what you're up to. You and your little friend.'

Ash waited for him to say something more. Welbeck waited for Ash to respond. The silence was the silence of a second boot getting ready to drop.

Finally Ash said, 'What *really* brought you up to Norbold last week? Did someone ask you to warn me off?'

Welbeck managed to sound shocked and amused at the same time. Ash knew it meant nothing: the man was a born performer. 'Of course not. I just wanted to know how you were.'

'Only Hazel and I aren't particularly popular at police headquarters.'

'Really?' Now he sounded surprised, and that was every bit as disingenuous. 'Well, nobody told me.'

'You're saying it was a coincidence? That no one in the chief constable's office asked you to lean on us?'

'My dear boy,' said Welbeck expansively, 'I'm not a hired gun! I don't go round the country leaning on people just because they've annoyed some provincial chief constable. How would I ever get my day's work done?'

Ash was inclined to believe him. Not because he thought Welbeck wouldn't lie to him – he knew his old boss could and would lie like a trooper any time he thought he had anything to gain by it – but because they'd known one another long enough that he believed he could tell when Welbeck was experimenting with the truth. He mumbled, 'It felt like too much of a coincidence. About the time Hazel stumbled onto the Harbinger case, you turned up on my doorstep.'

Welbeck laughed out loud, a merry tinkling sound like a delighted pixy. 'Dear boy! The only conspiracies I take part in are those I initiate.'

'I thought you'd been asked to give me something else to worry about. To stop us wondering if we were dealing with police incompetence or actual corruption.'

'Do I?' asked Welbeck slyly. 'Worry you?'

'Always,' said Ash with feeling.

'Oh good.'

There was another of those significant pauses, when Welbeck would have ended the call if he'd had nothing else to say but in fact failed to do so. Eventually Ash said, 'Then this too is just a social call?' Though he knew that it wasn't.

'Actually,' said Welbeck, 'it's that situation we talked about. Where you might be able to help me out in return for a favour or two that I've done for you in the not-too-distant past.'

That was the second boot. Ash gave it one more try. 'This isn't my line of work any more, Philip. I'm stale and I'm out of touch. I'm not sure how much use I could be to you.'

'Let me worry about that, dear boy. I'm not trying to turn you into a field man, you know. That was never where your strengths lay – you were always a desk jockey. It's just, you were always a better one than anyone else. And right now I could use someone with your particular talents.

'Not for very long,' he added quickly. 'Don't think I want to drag you away from your second-hand bookshop and the charms of downtown Norbold for weeks at a time. Three or four days might be enough. But I'd like you here on Monday, if you could manage it.'

Ash's heart followed the legendary boot and clumped on the floor. He didn't want to do it. He knew Welbeck *knew* he didn't want to do it. And he knew Welbeck was going to make him. He was too tired to argue any more.

'All right. I'll come down, and I'll help you if I can. I owe you that much; I probably owe you more. But Philip, I want your word that you won't keep coming back. I'm retired, and I want to stay retired. And I don't want you trying to recruit Hazel Best. Your word, Philip. In your own devious way, you're an honourable man. If you give me your word, I know you'll keep it.'

There was a longer pause. Then Welbeck asked softly, 'Does she know?'

'That I used to work for you? Yes, of course she does. That you want me to work for you again? – no.'

'I meant, does she know that you love her?'

Ash blinked at his phone, genuinely astonished. 'Hazel? Philip, you've got this wrong. She's just a friend . . .'

'You mean,' Welbeck corrected him carefully, 'she *is* a friend. There's no *just* about it. And if you're telling me that you're willing to do this, that you so obviously don't want to do, to protect someone you don't love, I'll have to invite you to pull the other one, on account of it has bells on.'

Ash's brain rocked in almost the same way it had when it met John Fisher's gunstock coming the other way. Up and down lost all meaning; he felt himself spiralling towards the noonday sun. All he could manage was a stammered, 'I'm a married man . . .'

'Ah yes,' said Welbeck smoothly. 'This would be the marriage to the woman who drove you mad and then tried to kill you. Do you know, Gabriel, I think that would be grounds for a divorce in most jurisdictions. If that's what you want. Of course, lots of people these days – and I wouldn't claim to be any kind of an expert – don't consider marriage an essential part of a romantic liaison anyway.'

'Me and Hazel? Really, Philip, you're barking up the wrong tree. What could she possibly have to gain? I'm fifteen years older than she is.'

'Yes,' allowed Welbeck, 'and you're a good, kind and intelligent man. And unless you invested a lot more capital in that shop of yours than is readily apparent, also a comparatively wealthy one. She could probably do worse.'

'I don't think she thinks of me like that.'

'It might be fun finding out.' The mischief was back in Welbeck's voice.

Ash made an effort to pull himself together. 'Philip, stop meddling in things you know nothing about. I have more important things to do than listen to your nonsense. My dog is ready to come home from the vet's.'

'That *is* good news. Give her a pat from me. And, Gabriel . . .?'

'Philip?'

'I'll see you on Monday.'